A LIVING NIGHTMARE

"Sutton, this is Detective Jim Peterson for the Fairfax County Police Department," Rob continued, looking as dour as Peterson. "I'm afraid there's some bad news."

"It's about your sister, Ms. McPhee."

"Cara?" I asked, unable to get out more.

"I'm afraid she's dead, " Peterson answered glumly.

I looked at him from the silence into which his words had jolted me.

"She was shot," Peterson went on. "It looks like an ATM robbery. I'm really sorry to have to tell you this."

My own body stood up, with no conscious instruction from me. I realized I was turning in different directions, like an animal trying to find its way out of a locked cage. A cage that had no doors.

"Tell me all of it," I said, while my mind silently begged him not to say the words, not to make the nightmare real.

CORRUPTION OF FAITH
*The first in an all-new series starring
journalist Sutton McPhee*

Corruption of Faith

Brenda English

To Ellen:
Thanks for enjoying Sutton's
stories.
Brenda English

BERKLEY PRIME CRIME, NEW YORK

CORRUPTION OF FAITH

A Berkley Prime Crime Book/published by arrangement with
the author

PRINTING HISTORY
Berkley Prime Crime edition/November 1997

The Putnam Berkley World Wide Web site address is
http://www.berkley.com

ISBN: 0-425-16091-2

Berkley Prime Crime Books are published
by The Berkley Publishing Group, a member of Penguin Putnam Inc.,
200 Madison Avenue, New York, New York 10016.
The name Berkley Prime Crime and the Berkley Prime Crime
design are trademarks belonging to Berkley Publishing Corporation.

PRINTED IN THE UNITED STATES OF AMERICA

10 9 8 7 6 5 4 3 2 1

Dedicated to the memory of Beverly Wallace Curry, my lost sister, and Faye Bell, who taught me to read and gave me the universe.

Acknowledgments

I especially must thank:

Officer Kevin Brown of the Fairfax County Police Department, who did his best to keep me from making embarrassing mistakes and who is not responsible for any I managed to make anyway; the staff of the Fairfax County Police Department's Mount Vernon District Substation, particularly Officers Paul DeHaven and David Bane, and Lieutenant Ty Morrow, Deputy Station Commander; Larry Williams, Vice-President of Corporate Security, First Union Bank of Virginia; Debbie Nivens, Senior Office Technician, Virginia State Corporations Commission; Officer Onzy Elam, Public Information Officer, Fairfax County Police Department; Heather Ramser, Northern Virginia Medical Examiner's office; Joshua A. Bilmes, JABberwocky Literary Agency, my agent and adviser; Gail Fortune, my editor at Berkley; Carey and Meagan, my heart's life; and Lily, who opened my eyes to the possibilities.

Corruption of Faith

Tuesday

One

The insistent computer cursor blinked at me accusingly. It was only eleven o'clock in the morning, but my stomach, which I had given a meager breakfast, was already empty, ready for its lunch, and growling loudly. Unfortunately for my stomach, the blue computer screen stayed as blank as my mind. I had been staring at the damned screen for a good ten or fifteen minutes now, but inspiration had failed to strike. My news story for tomorrow's paper, on the Fairfax County School Board's long-term budget planning, remained stillborn in my ordinarily garrulous brain.

At this rate, I thought in frustration, the next thing I'm likely to find myself writing will be obituaries, the signal at many newspapers of a career that is on the skids.

Starting with an obit for the defunct newspaper career of Sutton McPhee?

That was from my little voice, my constant companion and chronic irritant for most of my life. I know intellectually that this voice is just another part of myself. (At least I hope to hell it is, although I do seem to hear it as a male voice, now that I think of it.) But over the years it has developed quite a personality of its own and, apparently, has taken on as its mission in life the task of never letting me indulge in self-delusion or wallow in self-pity for very long—in other words, never letting me have any fun. It has

kicked my butt regularly through ten years of newspaper
reporting jobs in three states and through one failed marriage. If it had a corporeal existence, I would have been
arrested for murder years ago.

No, starting with an obit for you if you don't can it, I
told it. Get lost.

Touchy, aren't we?

The little bastard had a point, I supposed, as much as I
hated to admit it. I *was* touchy. What else can you expect
in the middle of a career crisis? I was not a happy camper
lately. Which was, I decided, the real reason I couldn't
seem to find the words for the story that I had to finish in
the next hour, before I headed out for an Arlington hearing
on whether public-school kids there should pay to partici-
pate in school sports. I was afraid I had lost my career
bearings, and that thought was distracting in a big and wor-
risome way.

Since college, I had steadily worked my way up from a
small daily newspaper in Albany, Georgia, to a larger paper
in Tallahassee, Florida, and finally, onto the staff of the
Washington, D.C., *News*, a major metropolitan daily where
many a small-town reporter would have given her firstborn
to work. I'm thirty-two years old and in the big time, I
asked myself, so why aren't I happy? But after two years
of covering schools in northern Virginia and five years of
education reporting in Tallahassee before that, I worried
that my stories had taken on a sameness that reflected what
I feared was my own boredom with the beat. The big question that really haunted me, however, was where did the
problem truly lie? With the subject matter or with me?

Wanna know where I'm putting my money?

Don't start, I told my voice, I've got work to do. But I
worried that it was right, that the problem was with me.
And that thought terrified me. I had wanted to be a newspaper reporter since I was a fourteen-year-old ninth grader.
My high-school history teacher, who coached the debate
team on which I was an alternate that year, had asked me
to do a roundup for the local weekly paper on the results
of the school's participation in the state debate competition.

The editor ran my summary almost verbatim and gave me an unexpected byline as well. The sight of my name above a story on the paper's front page had instilled in me a drive for more, a drive that had never left me.

I became a fervent newspaper reader, noting bylines, learning to distinguish one reporter's style from another, determining the differences between hard news stories and features, and developing a sense of the power of well-crafted stories to inform, to move, to touch a reader, to evoke a time, place, person, or mood. That drive had sustained me through high school and college, had pushed me out of the nest and into an unlimited world that offered an equally unlimited number of stories waiting to be written, a world that dwarfed my small Georgia hometown.

The picture of myself as a reporter was such an integral part of my self-image that I couldn't imagine what I would do or even who I would be if that no longer was who I was. If the problem was with me and not with the beat, I was afraid I was in real trouble.

I took a couple of deep cleansing breaths to clear my head, second nature after several years of yoga classes, and focused again on the blank screen, determined to get the story done one way or the other. I was glaring down at my abortive first attempt at a lead when voices and laughter suddenly broke into the quiet of the morning newsroom. I looked up just as Ken Hale, who covered the Fairfax County Board of Supervisors, came through the door with Barbara Betts and Will Farber, who were my school-reporting colleagues. Barbara handled the schools in D.C., and Will covered those in the central Maryland counties that bordered the district. I had spent more than one after-work bar session with Barbara and Will, comparing war stories and decompressing.

All three raised their hands and said hello. Then, apparently deciding that I looked far too serious for my own good, they came in my direction.

"Hey, Sutton," Will said as they surrounded me, "how's it hangin'?"

Will was something of a multiple personality, inveterately bawdy and profane, regardless of the company—but only in the presence of other reporters. If you saw him out in public, particularly covering his school beat, you would have sworn he didn't even know any bad words. People who didn't work with him thought he was a paragon of gentlemanly manners. I long since had decided that the most effective way to deal with him in his other mode was to give as good as I got. When reporters took offense at his vocabulary, they generally brought out even more of it. And besides, I hadn't met many reporters who didn't already know all the words anyway, mostly from personal use, including myself.

I gave Will a long stare below the belt and then looked up, straight-faced, and said, "Gee, Will, I don't know. I can't tell that it's hangin' at all."

That brought guffaws from Barbara and Ken and a big grin from Will.

"You're okay, Sutton," he said, punching me on the arm. "You're okay."

Satisfied, he wandered across the newsroom to his desk, where he immediately got busy on the telephone. Barbara made some noises about needing another cup of coffee, the life's blood of many a reporter, and walked out the back of the newsroom toward the cafeteria.

Ken made himself at home in the chair that belonged to the desk behind mine, where the empty desktop signaled that it did not have a current resident.

"So what're you working on?" Ken asked. Preferring almost anything to going back to the story I was vainly trying to write, I told him. Ken and I often compared notes on our beats, since we both covered Fairfax County governmental bodies. The fact that the Fairfax County supervisors also determined the county's portion of the school system's budget meant we occasionally found ourselves at the same meeting. A few times we even had shared a by-line.

Ken was one of my favorite people at the paper. He was a first-rate reporter, whose instincts and determination to get to the bottom of a story rarely steered him wrong. And while he could enjoy the company of a flake like Will, Ken himself was a steady, stable guy with few hang-ups that I could find. He also was pretty easy on the eye. His sandy brown hair and blue eyes lived in a face that was tan most of the year from his tennis games. He was taller than I, at about six feet, and in good shape. I knew for a fact that he was thirty-six, but other people often judged him to be only in his late twenties. I had thought once or twice in my time at the *News* about asking him out, but my general reluctance to date people with whom I worked usually won out over his sex appeal. Nor had he ever issued a formal date invitation to me, I suspected because he had a similar reluctance. We both had seen one too many newsroom romances go on the rocks and derail careers to want to find ourselves in like circumstances.

I was regaling Ken with an anecdote about an argument I had witnessed between a Democrat and Republican on the ostensibly nonpartisan Fairfax County School Board when I heard my name called and looked up to see Rob Perry, the metro editor and my boss, motioning to me from his office door across the mostly empty newsroom. I'd noticed him come in about half an hour before, which would make it an early—and very long—day for him. Most editors at morning papers work afternoon and evening hours, getting the papers out in the wee hours of the morning to be waiting at dawn on the porches, steps, and driveways of readers. It wasn't unheard of for Rob to be in this early, however. With three marriages in shreds, he more or less had given up on a home life. The *News* was as much his family as were his grown children—or more—and I suspected he often put in the long hours that he did because he preferred the paper's newsroom, even quiet, to his empty Georgetown apartment.

Rob also is something of an anachronism in the increasingly corporate world of newspapers, a reporter's editor who keeps a shepherd's eagle eye on his flock of writers and produces a prizewinning metro section through a surprisingly effective and politically incorrect combination of witty sarcasm, bullying, uncompromising standards for ac-

curacy and precision in our copy, and a willingness to back
his reporters to the hilt when our stories bring someone's
wrath down on us—as long as we get those stories right.
Whether that someone is from outside the paper or from
the Sennet Newspapers corporate hierarchy. Most of us
pretty much worship at Rob's altar. Not that we'd ever tell
him that.

"Be right there," I said to Rob. Turning back to Ken, I
told him, "You'll have to excuse me now. I've been summoned."

Ken laughed. "Yeah, and I need to go and at least pretend to be working on a story myself or he'll be summoning
me next," he said, getting up from the chair and sliding it
back under the vacant desk.

He walked off in the direction of his own desk, and I
went over to where Rob stood, his pale blue oxford-cloth
shirt already looking rumpled, though he had been here less
than an hour. By the end of the day, his tie not only would
be loosened but most likely lying on the copy desk, where
he also kept a seat. Apparently the longer and harder his
brain worked editing copy, the more uncomfortable his
clothes became. I fully expect him to stand up some night
when things aren't going well and strip naked so he can
work.

As I walked toward Rob I also could see, through the
wall of windows that divides his office from the newsroom,
a man I didn't know, who was standing and watching me
approach.

"It's not nice to interrupt a meeting of great minds," I
told Rob, smiling and expecting to get a typically sarcastic
response. Instead, I got a look that I couldn't identify.

"We need to talk to you, Sutton," Rob said, no smile
in sight. Which told me right away that something was out
of kilter. He never called me—or anyone else on the staff—
by their first name. I always had been McPhee to Rob, even
during my job interview two years ago. I gave him back a
questioning look of my own and went past him into the
office where the stranger, a tall, dark-haired, big-boned man
in chocolate-brown slacks and a tweed sport coat, stood. I

had not noticed him coming into the newsroom, which he apparently had done while I was engrossed in the intellectually stimulating and highly professional conversation with the other reporters.

"Have a seat, Sutton," Rob told me, motioning to a chair facing his desk, as he stepped into the office behind me and closed the door. I sat. Rob perched himself on one of the desk's front corners, taking off the half-lensed glasses he wore when he was reading copy and laying them on the desk behind him. The big man took the chair at the far end of Rob's desk. As he sat back and his jacket fell open, I saw his belt held a gun in a holster and a leather tab on which was fastened a badge.

"Okay," I said, eyeing the gun and badge and smiling at their owner, "what did I do this time?" He didn't smile back.

"Sutton, this is Detective Jim Peterson from the Fairfax County Police Department," Rob continued, looking as dour as Peterson. "I'm afraid there's some bad news."

I glanced up at Rob, my persistent efforts at humor having been brought to a halt by his words, and then looked back at the cop, who clearly was the bearer of these bad tidings. Peterson leaned forward and rested his forearms on his thighs, clasped his fingers, looked down at the dark gray carpet on the floor, and then back up at me.

"It's about your sister, Ms. McPhee," he said.

All the air was instantly sucked out of the room and out of my lungs. A wave of fear-heat flashed through my body like electricity, and my throat and chest tightened spasmodically. It is amazing to me how the body can react so quickly, even before the brain has had time to absorb the meaning of the words.

"Cara?" I asked, unable to get out more.

"I'm afraid she's dead," Peterson answered glumly.

I looked at him from the silence into which his words had jolted me. Some part of my brain registered that Rob straightened up from his desk and was watching me closely.

"She was shot," Peterson went on. "It looks like an ATM robbery. A bank employee found her body in her car.

This morning, in a bank parking lot south of Springfield. I'm really sorry to have to tell you this."

My own body stood up, with no conscious instruction from me. I realized I was turning in different directions, like an animal trying to find its way out of a locked cage. A cage that had no doors.

"Sutton!" Rob's voice was sharp, and he grasped me by both shoulders, turning me to face him. Then he said more gently, "I think you should sit back down, Sutton."

I sat again, struggling to regain my power of speech, only to have Cara's many faces appear before my mind's eye, the years of her life flashing through my head like snippets from someone's home movies. There she was as the baby who was born just as I was going off to first grade. I remembered her as the toddler who followed in my every footstep. I saw again how she grew into the adolescent who watched her teenage sister with a mixture of awe and envy. Once more, she was the teenager whose growing up I mostly missed as I went on to college and a job. I remembered her as the grieving college sophomore who turned strongly to religion after our parents were killed in a traffic accident. The most recent Cara in my mental movie was the twenty-six-year-old woman who had moved a year ago to the Washington suburb of Springfield, Virginia, to be near her older sister and to look for work. A woman I was really getting to know for the first time and whose company I was enjoying immensely, in spite of our different personalities and views of life. Cara. My baby sister. My family. The only real family I had.

I turned my head toward Rob and now understood the uncharacteristic look he had given me at the door. My eyes filled with tears, but I regained enough control over my throat muscles to enable me to speak. I looked back at the detective.

"Tell me all of it," I said while my mind silently begged him not to say the words, not to make the nightmare real.

Two

"We don't know a lot more at this point," Detective Peterson said, watching me as closely as Rob, no doubt gauging how much to tell me, what details to censor, calculating what I could absorb, what might send me into the screaming hysteria to which I wanted to surrender but wouldn't.

"We've taken a preliminary look at the security video from the ATM," Peterson went on. "Your sister is there, and she keeps looking off to the side, from where we can hear a man's voice talking to her. We think he's the person who then took her back out to her car and shot her, but he never got within camera range. Obviously, he was holding her at gunpoint at the cash machine but was smart enough to stay out of sight himself."

He paused, still assessing how I was handling the information, giving things time to sink in.

"Go on," I said through gritted teeth. And how was I handling it? As Peterson talked I found my desire to scream, to lash out in violent protest receding behind the wall my mind threw up as it retreated into reporter's mode, that habitual dividing of brain function that can make the difference in whether or not a reporter can do the job. Most of my reporting experience had been in covering schools and local government. But my limited exposure to more grisly stories, during those times at the smaller papers when it was my turn to handle the weekend's police coverage and general assignment, had been enough to teach me the necessity of learning how to separate from my emotions long enough to cover my story. I often had paid the price at night, as the brain and those emotions reconnected in the solitude of my apartment and when what I had seen kept me awake or followed me into dreams. But on the job, the ability to step away mentally, to disconnect, enabled me to ask questions and note details, to think about story leads and structure, even in the middle of the human carnage, the accidents, shootings, and fires that I sometimes was sent to cover.

Once upon a time, this distancing ability also had gotten me through the trauma of a divorce, when Jack Brooks, the Tallahassee city planner to whom I was married for two years, decided after the fact that he hated what I did for a living. He had tried to get me to change careers, complaining that I spent too much time at the paper and that he thought the other reporters were a bunch of immature, over-sexed, budding alcoholics.

"Well, at least they're not anal-retentive, uptight ass-holes who want to completely control everything and everyone around them like some kind of dictator," I had shouted back at him. That was when he had walked out and filed for divorce, and I had retreated behind my reporter's wall to keep the pain from immobilizing me.

Now I found this ability to step outside my feelings kicking in to keep me sane and calm as I listened to Peterson's story of insanity and violence, as he told me how my sister had died.

Cara's body had been found earlier that morning, Peterson said, when an assistant manager had arrived to open the Continental Bank branch office off South Backlick Road. She had noticed Cara slumped against the driver's-side window of her blue Ford Escort, which was parked on the far side of the parking lot, also out of the ATM camera's range. The woman said she first thought Cara must have fallen asleep waiting for the bank to open, but as she got out of her own car to go inside, something about the scene just felt wrong.

"She walked over to your sister's car to tap on the window, and that was when she saw the blood," Peterson said. "She went around to the other side of the car and saw your sister had a head wound. She said she banged on the window, but your sister didn't respond, and the car doors were locked. So the woman ran inside the bank and called 911."

Still another picture of Cara flashed through my mind to join those I already had seen: Cara with a bullet in her brain, with blood running down her face, her brown eyes, so like my own, open in death and reflecting the overwhelming fear of her last moments. In my job, I had seen more than once what guns do to people, seen it up close and personal. I had no illusions to shield me from the wreckage the bullet must have caused as it entered and exited Cara's head. My stomach cramped up in aversion. The all-too-human part of my mind was continuing to shout its refusal that this could be happening, had happened. It wanted me to voice its shouts, to shatter the air with them.

No, Sutton, no, I told myself, digging my fingernails into the palms of my hands. Don't let it in, don't feel it yet. Hold on, hold on. You have to hear it all and get out of here before you give in to it. It was a reaction that was as ingrained in my psyche as an instinct. I worked in a business where you didn't let other people see your weaker moments. Many of the people reporters cover, from the politicians to police, can smell weakness, loss of nerve, fear. I had drummed it into myself until it became reflex: Don't be intimidated. Don't be afraid. And for God's sake, whatever you do, don't cry! Even now, in one of the worst personal situations I ever had faced, my reaction was to want to find a private place to feel my pain and lick my wounds, to let no one see me in a moment of what might be interpreted as weakness. It made no sense, especially in these circumstances, I knew, but there it was.

Peterson was saying Cara had been shot once in the head, apparently at point-blank range, as she sat in the car.

"We don't know where the killer hooked up with her,

whether he accosted her in the parking lot of the bank or whether she was abducted from someplace else and taken there,'' he said. ''She took two hundred and fifty dollars, the maximum withdrawal, out of her account at eleven-eighteen P.M., according to the time stamp on the ATM video. Less than a minute later the video mike picked up a sound that we're sure was the gunshot.''

I felt myself flinch at the word *gunshot,* hearing the sound of the gun's blast echoing inside my own head. Oh God, I was thinking, why Cara? Sweet, gentle Cara, who would never willingly hurt anyone. Cara, who worked as a secretary at the Bread of Life Church in West Springfield, where she had found a religious home after moving up from Georgia last year. Cara, who worried about my soul because I had no church and no desire for one. She was the sweet one, the mediator, the one who took people with a huge grain of salt, always giving them the benefit of the doubt. I was the judgmental one, impatient with stupidity, possessor of a wicked tongue that could flay skin and that took no prisoners. There was a whole list of people who might want to shoot me. But who could ever want to hurt Cara?

Cara had never been a fighter. Christ, she must have been paralyzed with fear at the sight of the gun! What must have gone through her mind? Don't go down that road, Sutton, not yet. Start to imagine that, I knew, and it would be all over for my self-control.

''There are some questions I need to ask you about your sister,'' Peterson was saying as I brought my mind back to the present once again. I nodded an okay.

Rob put a hand back on my shoulder.

''I can come back when you're done,'' he said, not wanting to intrude.

''No,'' I told him, and heard an uncharacteristic note of panic in my voice, ''please stay.'' He agreed and went around to sit in the battered leather swivel chair behind his desk. Apparently part of my mind thought Rob's presence, coupled with my horror at the idea of breaking down in front of him, would help me stay in control.

An evidence team was already at Cara's Springfield apartment, Peterson said, looking for any signs that she might have been abducted from there. He explained that the police had gotten her address from her driver's license, found among the contents of her purse that the killer had left scattered inside the car. My name and place of employment the police had learned from the application Cara had completed when she rented the apartment and had put me down as an emergency contact. But, Peterson said, he needed to know other things as well: where Cara worked, who her friends were, what she did when she wasn't at work. I told him what I knew of the current details of my sister's life. Peterson reached into an inner jacket pocket and took out a small notebook and pen, with which he started to take sporadic notes as I talked, my mind taking me back through the months since Cara had arrived in Springfield, and even to the years leading up to her move.

Cara had come to the Washington area a year ago, I explained, from Hilton, the small southeast Georgia town where we grew up. Our parents had died in a car accident when Cara was nineteen and just beginning her sophomore year in college. I was twenty-five and had moved to Tallahassee only six months before their deaths. Four months after the accident Cara left college and went back to Hilton, to the friends she had known for years. Nothing I had said was enough to change her mind. She hated college and she wanted to go home, she said, and so she had.

Back in Hilton, Cara had a couple of secretarial jobs and became very involved in the Hilton Baptist Church that we had attended as children. I was convinced that Cara's embracing of religion was a reaction to our parents' death, her mechanism for coping with their loss, but the appeal it held for her had not passed as her grief had ebbed.

Fourteen months ago Cara had called me one night to say she was considering moving to the Washington area and wanted to know what I thought of the idea. It had taken me by surprise, but Cara explained that she had been thinking about leaving Hilton for some time to move to a larger city, where the jobs and salaries would be better. And, she said, there was another reason. I remembered how she had sounded on the phone that night.

"We're the only family we have, Sutton," she had told me in a plaintive voice. "It's hard enough missing Mom and Dad. I can't do anything about that, but I'm tired of missing you, too."

So Cara came to Washington. Within a few weeks she found the independent Bread of Life Church, became a member, and soon after got a job as one of its two secretaries. She was happy and busy, and I was glad she had made the move. In spite of our schedules (mostly in spite of mine), we talked on the phone every few days, and on weekends we usually found a few hours to spend together, shopping or going out to dinner or just doing laundry, sharing the things we had in common. But there was a lot about each of our lives that was not part of the other's.

The difference in our ages meant we had grown up with different sets of friends in Hilton. The differences in our temperaments had sent us in very divergent career directions. Her church, one of the central underpinnings of Cara's adult life, held no appeal for me. Yet we felt close to each other. Our lack of siblings or other close relatives and the traumatic loss of both our parents had drawn us together as adults in ways that we had not shared as children. And we genuinely liked each other, something that common blood doesn't always guarantee. So we shared our separate bits of gossip from Hilton, and we shared our very different lives with each other in conversations that originated from our genuine interest in the other's well-being.

As far as I knew, the rest of Cara's social life revolved around church activities. She had mentioned a handful of dates with a couple of men she had met at the church, but I knew from our conversations that the men remained casual acquaintances. I didn't know the men she had dated, except by the first names that I passed along to Peterson, or anyone else from the church. I never had succumbed to Cara's requests to attend services with her, so I couldn't tell Peterson anything else about Cara's dates or colleagues from personal knowledge. But she never had been anything but positive in her descriptions of the people in that other part of her life. If there had been any serious relationship there, I told Peterson, I was certain I would have known. And I couldn't imagine anyone wanting to hurt Cara, at least not anyone who knew her. She just wasn't the kind of person against whom people held grudges or resentments. And her personality, unlike my own, was not one that tended to irritate people, certainly not to the point of murder.

"I have to ask this question, Ms. McPhee, just as a routine procedure," Peterson said, almost apologetically. "Where were you last night?"

When I realized why he was asking, I recoiled in horror and anger. "You can't possibly think that I . . . ?"

"No, Sutton," Rob interjected to keep me from jumping down Peterson's throat, "but he has to ask."

I swallowed back the hot words that boiled up in my brain. "I was covering a Fairfax County School Board budget hearing," I told Peterson. "I was there from seven P.M. until twelve-thirty this morning, when the damned thing finally ended!"

"When did you see or talk to your sister last?" Peterson wanted to know.

"Yesterday. I talked to her on the phone yesterday afternoon. The last time I saw her was about a week ago."

"Was there anything at all unusual about either conversation?"

"Nothing," I told him. "I called her yesterday to see if she wanted to get something to eat after work. We both had been busy with other things over the weekend, and so we hadn't gotten together. But Cara said she couldn't get away for dinner last night, that she had a project she was finishing up for the church and probably had several more hours to go on it. I offered to bring her a sandwich, but she said if she stopped to eat with me, she would just have to stay that much later to finish."

"That might explain why she was at the ATM so late," Peterson said, his pen pausing above the notebook as he thought through a possible order of events.

"Except that that isn't her bank, and it's nowhere near the church or her apartment," I told him, convinced Cara would not have gone so far out of her way for money when there were other bank branches much closer to her office and her apartment. "I can't imagine why she would have gone all the way out there at that time of night."

"Which probably means the person who killed her abducted her somewhere else and took her to that bank branch deliberately," Peterson said, proposing an alternate theory that made more sense. "It's an industrial-and-office-park area that's pretty deserted late at night. He probably could count on no one else being around as a witness. If she was working late, it's possible someone else from the church was around and knows what time she left. Maybe even saw whether she left with someone."

"Oh God, the church," I said, my irritation with Peterson's questioning of my whereabouts apparently having kicked my brain into some semblance of rational thought. "I have to let them know what's happened! Cara said she would make up for the late night by coming in at lunch today. The church staff won't even have missed her yet."

"I'm going over there from here," Peterson responded. "Would you like me to tell them for you?"

"Thank you," I said, relieved at having that ordeal taken off my shoulders. How could I possibly tell Cara's friends over the cold circuits of a telephone line that she was dead, murdered?

"I think you've answered my questions for now," Peterson was saying as he tore a single sheet out of his notebook, closed it, and put it back in his jacket. "The one other thing we need you to do at the moment is to let us get a set of fingerprints from you. Call this number and ask for Sergeant Costas. He'll make arrangements for you to come in." He handed me the sheet of notepaper on which he had written a telephone number.

"We'll need to be able to eliminate your fingerprints from any that we find on your sister's car or in her apartment," he explained. "And I'll give you my card so you know how to reach me if anything occurs to you that you think might be helpful to the investigation. We'll let you know if anything significant turns up, but feel free to call me anytime you want an update."

"Detective?" I asked, reaching for the piece of paper, my voice tentative with the question that I had to ask.

"Yes?"

"Where is . . . Cara now?"

"She was taken to the Northern Virginia Medical Examiner's offices out on Braddock Road," Peterson said.

"Could I see her?"

"Are you sure that's a good idea?" Peterson asked. "You understand what happened to her, what it would have done?"

I nodded.

Peterson took the business card he had promised from his outside pocket, jotted something on the back, and held it out to me.

"That's their telephone number," he explained. "If you really want to do this, give them a call. They'll also let you know what you have to do to have your sister's body released when the autopsy is completed."

My throat muscles spasmed again at the prospect. I took the card and nodded at him mutely. My sister's body, I thought, unable to get my brain around the idea that she was now a "body." Not Cara any longer.

Peterson got up to leave, and Rob, who had sat through our conversation in silence, stood and walked over to open the door. Peterson stopped in front of me.

"Again, I'm sorry about your sister, Ms. McPhee," he said.

I managed to squeeze out a "Thank you."

Rob went out the door behind Peterson and walked him out of the newsroom. I closed my eyes and leaned my head back against the window behind me. How would I survive this? I asked myself. It was too much, too much after everything else.

My mind went back again, back seven years to the afternoon in Tallahassee that I got the phone call from Mattie Patterson, our next-door neighbor in Hilton, to say my mother and father had been killed in a traffic accident. I had cried almost nonstop from the moment Mattie told me until she pulled into our driveway early that evening after having picked me up at the Savannah airport.

"Sutton," she had said, turning off the car and reaching over to grasp my hand, "I know how hard this is for you. It's a terrible, terrible thing, and the pain must feel unbearable. But you're going to have to reach down deep inside yourself and find that strong center that I know you have. Your sister Cara is in a very bad way, and she's going to need you to be strong, to get you both through the next few days. There's a lot you're going to have to deal with—decisions to make, legal details, funeral arrangements—and you're the only one to do it. And you're going to have to be the parent for your sister for a while, too. Do you think you can do all that?"

I had looked across at Mattie through the tears, at her familiar, friendly face, and I knew she was right. I had been so immersed in my own pain that I hadn't really thought about how even more devastated nineteen-year-old Cara must be. I thought about my mother and how she had always been our strength as we grew up. I knew that if she were there, she would tell me I was strong enough to survive this, just as she had always told me I would be more than a match for life, no matter what.

I had nodded at Mattie in agreement, had wiped my eyes and blown my nose, and had gotten out of the car to go find my sister. Mattie was right. There had been times over the two weeks that followed when I had worried about Cara's resilience and whether she would recover enough to function. Eventually, as some of the initial pain ebbed, she had become stronger. She went back to school, and I went home to Tallahassee and my job.

My own antidote for the pain had been to stay busy at work and to spend as much time as possible with Jack, with whom I was in love. Gradually, I was able to put the heartache of losing my parents into a separate chamber of my mind, where I was aware of its presence but where it stayed unless I decided to let it come out. But for Cara, the pain of their deaths had remained acutely present in her consciousness, interfering with her ability to focus on school, and so she eventually had retreated back to Hilton, to the friends and places she had known all her life, seeking the familiar while she healed.

Now Cara was dead, too. How can I stand it? I wondered. The pain was a physical ache around my heart, excruciating enough to stop my breath. The only answer I could find was to put the pain into that room with my parents' death, to wall it off enough that I could get through the rest of the day, or even the next hour. Someone had killed my sister, and I couldn't change that. But there was no one to deal with the details of her death except me, and I wouldn't be able to do it if I fell apart. Nor, I knew, would I be able to think straight enough to help find the person who killed her. And it was that thought that gave me the strength I needed to pull myself together. Someone had killed her. Someone would answer for it. No matter what I had to do, I would have answers about why my sister died.

As I had done that day years before, sitting in the car in my parents' driveway with Mattie, I took a deep breath and wiped my eyes. I got up from the chair and left Rob's office, to go back out to my desk, where the first paragraphs of the school-board story still glowed patiently on my computer screen. I sat down and started to type, with a clarity of thought and a grim coldness of purpose that surprised me.

"What the hell do you think you're doing?" a voice asked softly over my shoulder a couple of minutes later. It was Rob.

"Finishing this story," I told him without looking up as he walked around to stand in front of me. "Nobody else can do it but me. But do you think you can send someone else to the Arlington hearing this afternoon?"

"I'll take care of it," he agreed. Out of the corner of my eye, I could see that he looked as if he wanted to say more, but I kept typing, the reporter still in charge of my brain for the moment, still holding on to anything that would let the rest of my mind pretend my world had not just changed forever.

"When you're done," Rob said eventually, "come back to my office. If you're really going to the medical examiner's office, I'm going with you."

"Thanks, Rob, but you don't have to do that," I said, looking up, my hands finally pausing on the keyboard, where, I realized, they were shaking.

"Yes," he said, in a voice that brooked no argument. "I do."

As I typed I could feel the other eyes in the newsroom on me. Many reporters have internal barometers for when the atmosphere in a room changes, and it must have been clear to anyone paying attention that something of importance had happened with the stranger in Rob's office. And if it wasn't, the look on my face when I came out would have told them so.

As Rob reached his office after walking away from my desk, I noticed that Ken intercepted him. They had a brief, low conversation, during which they both looked at me with concerned faces. Ken asked Rob something, and I thought I heard Rob say, "Let her be for right now."

I can't believe I'm sitting here listening to them discuss me, I thought as I filled the computer screen with the words I pieced together from my school-board-meeting notes.

Ken went back to his desk, but moments later a notice of an E-mail message flashed on my screen. I saved the story and went into the E-mail system to find a brief note from Ken.

I'm sorry about your sister, he had written, apparently figuring—and correctly—that I could handle a written message better than conversation at the moment. *If I can do anything at all to help, please let me know.*

I messaged back *Thank you* without looking in his direction. I didn't think I could deal with what I would see in his eyes, the reality that Cara was dead.

• • •

Three hours later, as I stood at a restroom sink in the building that housed the Northern Virginia Medical Examiner's offices, I knew Rob had been right to come with me. I leaned on the sink with my left hand. My right hand held a cold, wet paper towel to the back of my neck. My head was down, my eyes closed, my breathing rapid and shallow. My nose was running, and my mouth was filled with the sour taste of bile because I had spent the last five minutes in one of the stalls, throwing up.

I raised my head to the mirror over the sink to see just how bad it was before going back out to where Rob patiently waited for me. My face was pale and clammy looking. My dark brown hair, which I usually wore in a loose French braid, was in disarray, the escaping tendrils around my face and on my neck now damp from my efforts with the wet paper towels. My eyes looked enormous, shell-shocked, the pupils dilated almost to the edges of the warm brown retinas, the whites now red from unshed tears and the recent ordeal over the toilet. In the color of my eyes and hair, in the planes of my face, I saw faint echoes of another face, of my sister's face, my sister whose body now lay down the hall in a room full of death.

Rob had stayed with me, quietly supportive, even at the viewing window, even as a woman on the staff had lifted a sheet from Cara's face. I moved closer to the window, resting my forehead against it in surrender to the truth that faced me on the other side. I stared at the body before me, now empty of any animating force that had ever filled it, a waxy-looking shell, utterly still, utterly without life. The ugly wound just over her left eye, which Peterson had said was inflicted at point-blank range, and the even larger exit wound that I knew must lie hidden from my eyes, on the back of her head, would become the stuff of oppressive dreams that later would wake me at night, sweating and crying, from my brain's home videos of what Cara's death must have been like.

As I looked at Cara's face I reached up to put the fingertips of my right hand against the window's glass, an unconscious gesture of reaching out to ease my sister's hurt.

As the glass broke the movement I think I must have sagged slightly toward the window. I know that Rob put a firm arm around me. His touch brought me back, reminding me that I still had questions to ask, papers to sign, details of death with which to deal.

"It is her, isn't it?" Rob asked, the tone of his voice foretelling the inevitability of my answer. Throughout the nearly silent trip out from the District, I had hoped against hope that somehow there had been a mistake, that it wasn't Cara, that it was someone else, that somehow the police had made a terrible error. Now even that tiniest, improbable hope had long since fled.

"Yes," I said tiredly, "it's her. It's Cara."

And then I had headed for the rest room.

Another hour later, when I had made it home to the solitude of my apartment, I realized I probably should call Chris Wiley and let him know what had happened. Chris was my—what? I didn't know what to call him. We had been dating for eight months, sleeping together on a semiregular basis for six. We cared for each other, but neither of us had yet used the L-word or suggested combining households. Our relationship had apparently reached some sort of equilibrium where it was. We went out three or four times a month, depending on our schedules. Afterward, we went back to one apartment or the other to spend the night. The next morning, whichever of us was the visitor would dress and leave to go back home. We talked on the phone once or twice a week. So what was that? Was that a lover? A significant other? A friend? None of the labels seemed quite right.

Chris was a thirty-four-year-old attorney, a specialist in international tax law with a prestigious law firm headquartered in Old Town Alexandria. We had met at the wedding of a mutual friend, an attorney for the National Education Association who had gone to Georgetown Law with Chris. I think we were attracted to each other because we both seemed so uncomfortable in the midst of the celebration. I was still gun-shy and licking my wounds from my divorce of a year before, so weddings touched a raw nerve for me. And when we began talking, Chris confessed that weddings made him nervous because not only the single women in the room but also the married women who wanted to change the status of their single friends always seemed to be giving him the once-over as marriage material. I had laughed at his description of his plight but had no doubt that it was true.

Chris Wiley would have been considered a catch by most women. He was tall—six-foot-two—and athletic, his body hardened by regular gym workouts and racquetball. He had black hair and green eyes, the result of some sort of wild Celtic genes, and he was very bright and very good at his job, meaning he also had a healthy income. So what was not to like?

I had sympathized with his dilemma that day at the wedding reception, explaining that I was divorced and regaling him with my own frustrations at the disastrous matchmaking efforts of my still-married friends who just couldn't believe I was happy single and who thought they knew just the guy I should meet. Chris said he had come close to marriage once, right after law school, to a woman he knew through the suburban Chicago country club to which his parents belonged. He and the woman had dated all through college and his law-school years, and the marriage was expected by both his family and hers. He had called it off two months before the wedding, however, when, after a day of picking out china with his fiancée, he had awakened in a nightmare sweat.

"I couldn't remember what the nightmare was about," Chris explained, "but I woke up absolutely terrified that the rest of my life was going to be spent worrying about things like whether I was eating off the correct china pattern."

I laughed some more, and we had struck up the camaraderie of strangers who are both scarred veterans of the romance wars. So the fact that our own relationship seemed to have plateaued well before anything like talk of marriage didn't strike me as surprising—or a problem.

Chris was out of town on one of his frequent business trips. Today was Tuesday, and he wasn't due back until Saturday. But I knew he checked his answering machine daily, so I called his apartment and left an awkward message about what had happened and saying that I wanted him to know where I was in case I already had gone to Georgia for the funeral by the time he got back to Washington.

"I really miss you," I told him, hoping my voice on the tape wouldn't sound as piteous as it did in my own ear. "I sure could use your shoulder right now. I'll let you know when I have funeral arrangements made, in case there's any way you could get away to help me get through this thing. Please call me when you have a minute."

I hung up, confident that I would hear from him as soon as he got the message. Then I went to bed, where I lay awake half the night contemplating the prospect of having to bury my sister.

Saturday

Three

A funeral in the rain would have been a cliché, but at least it would have been fitting. As it was, we buried Cara on a soft, warm south Georgia Saturday morning in May, with the sun out in a cloudless sky that arched over a cemetery lawn of emerald green. The cemetery sat at the edge of a pine forest that sloped down a hill to a small creek hidden in the trees. The sounds of the water flowing through the creek, still high at this time of year from spring rains, carried up to where I sat in the first of several rows of putty-colored metal folding chairs. As people gathered around the grave a breeze lifted around us, moving the strands of hair that had escaped onto the back of my neck and rustling through the tall pines with a uniquely susurrant whisper, a sound I could identify anywhere. As a child, I had believed that sound was the pine trees talking to each other as I walked below, small and wondering. Now the air in the cemetery was filled with the soft conversations of the trees and people, and my heart was in a hole at least as deep and dark as the one into which Cara's casket was about to be lowered.

I had spent the last four days running from one loose end that needed tying up to the next. My nights I had spent crying until, here at Cara's grave, I had no tears left to shed for the moment.

I had spoken daily with Detective Peterson on the phone, but he had little to tell me. Cara's murder had made the news, of course. I had even managed to give Rudy Black, the reporter temporarily covering the vacant Fairfax County Police beat, a quote for the story he had to write for the *News*. But without a suspect, public and press interest in Cara's murder soon waned. On the first day, it was one of the lead news stories on television and in the papers. By the third day, when no apparent progress had been made toward an arrest, it had dropped almost completely off everyone's radar screens. There were far too many other crime stories happening every single day in the District of Columbia and its suburbs for the apparently random shooting of one young woman in a robbery to remain a news priority.

The police had issued a plea for any witnesses to Cara's abduction or to the events at the bank, but none had come forth. In an unexpectedly compassionate gesture, the *News'* corporate headquarters in Chicago had offered a $10,000 reward for information leading to an arrest in the case, but so far there had been no takers. Detective Peterson had found no one else who had been at the church as late as Cara that night, no one who might have seen the man who took her. The last withdrawal from the Continental Bank ATM before Cara arrived was some half an hour earlier. No one else stopped at the ATM throughout that night or the next morning before the assistant manager had found Cara's body. Apparently the only witnesses to Cara's cash withdrawal and murder were the ATM video camera—and her killer.

Peterson had shown me the video. I had insisted on seeing it, thinking I might notice something, anything, that would provide a clue as to what had happened, to the identity of the person who had done this thing. Afterward, the videotape's images were burned into my mind. There was Cara, still dressed up from work, obviously terrified as she walked into camera range. She kept looking back and forth from the camera lens to someone or something at her left, the direction from which a muffled but distinctly male voice told her what to do. As she followed his instructions Cara would glance up at the camera, her eyes pleading for the help she knew would not come. Once she withdrew the money, the voice summoned her back out of camera range. Silence followed. Fifty-three seconds of silence, according to the videotape. A lifetime according to my brain, which knew what was coming. Long before the distinctive sound of the gunshot, my nerves were drawn out to their limit, in a silent shriek for the suspense to end.

Peterson stopped the tape after the shot. The gunman never appeared in camera range, he explained, and the only other sounds to be heard were a couple of minutes later. He said his experts thought it was the sound of Cara's car doors being closed, probably after her killer locked them for some unexplained reason of his own.

It left me devastated, watching Cara's terror, seeing the knowledge in her eyes that she very possibly was about to die. I saw nothing on the tape that gave me any insights to share with the police. All it did was add the reality of the videotape images to the fiercely painful movie that played out continually in my head.

I also had daily conversations with Rudy. He told me the same thing Peterson had, that the police had next to nothing to go on. I worried about each day that passed, fearing that it reduced their chances of finding the man who killed Cara.

At the moment I had no choice but to rely on the police to find him because my days were filled with my grieving and with the seemingly endless details of death that had to be dealt with: getting copies of the death certificate, calling my attorney about the legal requirements, making long-distance funeral arrangements, getting Cara's body to the funeral home in Hilton, notifying Cara's hometown friends that she had been murdered.

And there were the phone calls from well-meaning colleagues at the *News*. At least a dozen of them called to express their sympathy and to offer their help if I needed it. A few, such as Rob and Ken, called each day just to make sure I was still sane and functioning. But the person from whom I needed to hear the most was the one who didn't call. Each day, as I went from one errand to run, from one paper to sign to the next, I spent time wondering what was going on with Chris.

When both Rob and Ken asked if I would be okay going to Georgia alone, I had assured them that I would, that people I had known all my life would be waiting there for me and that I was hoping Chris would be able to get down there as well. But by the time I had flown out of Washington National Airport on Friday afternoon, Chris finally had called exactly once. Surprisingly, he had called my work number, even though it was 11:30 at night and he knew I most likely was at home, and he had left a message on my voice mail. The message was brief: he was sorry to hear about Cara. The two times he had met her, she had seemed like a nice person. He knew it must be hard for me. Getting to the funeral wasn't going to be possible. He would call me once he was back in town.

That's it? my voice had asked when I hung up the phone in my kitchen from where I had called the office to check my voice mail. *That's the best the guy you're sleeping with can do when your sister gets murdered?*

I'd been wondering just how much longer my little friend could stay quiet. Tactful silence was so uncharacteristic for it.

Leave Chris alone, I told it. A lot of people get tongue-tied when they have to talk about someone dying. He isn't the only person who hasn't known what to say to me.

You'd think he could force himself to be a little more supportive, considering what he's getting in return.

"Screw you," I said aloud.

No, you, my voice retorted, *which is exactly my point.*

And I had to admit later, as I lay alone and in tears in bed that night, that maybe my voice did have a small point.

I hadn't expected Chris to feel Cara's death the way I had. He and my sister probably had spent all of three hours together since I had known Chris, the sum total of two dinners out early in our relationship when I had invited Cara to join us because I knew she didn't have Saturday-night plans of her own.

They had gotten along well enough, talking and laughing comfortably with each other. But Cara remarked to me several days after the second get-together that while she liked Chris, she hoped he wasn't going to disappoint me eventually.

"What does that mean?" I had asked her.

"You know what it means, Sutton," she had answered. "It means I don't think he's the type to ever get really serious about your relationship, to want to get married and tie himself down."

"You could be right," I had told her, "but did it ever occur to you that the feeling might be mutual, that I might not want it to be any more serious than it is either?"

"After growing up around Mom and Dad, how could you not want what they had?" Cara had asked, cocking her head to look at me as if she really had been surprised by my disavowal of a more serious interest in Chris.

"After my little error in judgment with Jack, how could I want to go through that again?" I had countered.

"Well, all men aren't like Jack," she had responded defensively.

"Thank you, Ann Landers," I had told her, laughing, "but enough of them are that I don't much like the odds."

"That's not my point anyway," Cara had complained, but smiling, too. "My point was that I just don't like to see Chris using you when he . . . when he . . ."

"When he has no intention of making an honest woman out of me?" I had finished for her. "Don't you think that concept is a little dated?"

Cara had looked sheepish, but I also noticed that her mouth had set along stubborn lines that Mom had called her Sutton look.

"Make fun of me if you want," she had said, "but you know I'm right about him."

I relented from my teasing and hugged her. "Even if you are," I had told her, "it's okay because it's a relationship of consensual adult usage."

But Cara hadn't been placated quite so easily.

"That sounds really cold, Sutton," she had concluded, shaking her head.

Her words had come back to me, in light of Chris's puzzling absence.

Chris never had been terribly demonstrative in public, a fact that I thought probably was the result of what he described as a very propriety-conscious family in the suburban Chicago social set. It hadn't bothered me, however, because he was as demonstrative as I could have wished in private. And that was why his unexpected remoteness now did bother me. I wasn't hoping for some public display of affection, but I had thought he would reach out to comfort me as I struggled with my pain. I didn't understand his behavior, why he hadn't called me at home and spoken with me directly.

But a long list of things I had to take care of had been waiting for my attention in the morning, a list that hadn't seemed to be getting any shorter. Now, as I stood here in the Georgia morning, I had put my concerns about Chris on hold because I had a sister to bury.

There had been no question but that I would take Cara's body home to Hilton to lie next to our parents, here in the cemetery that belonged to the Hilton Baptist Church. I knew it was what Cara would have wanted, even though she had moved to Virginia and a new church. And it was what my parents would have wanted.

Because Cara no longer was a member of the Hilton church, having transferred her membership to the Bread of Life Church, I had decided to hold only graveside services and to keep them as simple as possible. I had declined to hold receiving hours at the funeral home the night before or to subject Cara's body to a "viewing," a practice I thought was somewhat morbid under the best of circumstances and that would have been gruesome in these. But even when the graveside services here in Hilton were over and done with, the ceremonies of mourning wouldn't be over for me. I also had agreed to a memorial service at the Bread of Life Church.

The evening after Cara's body was found, I had begun

receiving phone calls and messages from members of the congregation at the Virginia church, all telling me how sorry they were about Cara's death and how much they had liked her. As one of the church secretaries, Cara apparently had interacted with, and impressed, quite a few people there. The Reverend Daniel Brant, the church's minister and Cara's boss, had called to tell me that they would like to hold a memorial service for Cara once I returned from Georgia. His call was followed by one from Marlee Evans, the other church secretary and Cara's coworker, whose voice I knew from my calls to Cara at work. We set the memorial service for the following Saturday, one week after the funeral in Hilton, and agreed to meet on Monday morning after I returned from Georgia to make the arrangements. I didn't know how I was going to get through one service in Georgia, much less a second one back in Springfield. But those people were Cara's friends, too, and they deserved a chance to say good-bye.

I looked across the newly dug soil of Cara's grave to those of my parents. Did they blame me? I wondered as the Reverend Lumley Mann, minister of the Hilton Baptist Church, began his graveside remarks. Could they see me from wherever they were now? Did they hold me responsible for Cara's murder because I had encouraged her in her plan to move to the Washington area? Some big sister I had turned out to be, I thought. I never should have told her to come. I should have told her to stay in Hilton, where she knew who people really were because she had known them all her life, knew whom to trust, whom to avoid. I'm sorry, Mom and Dad, I thought, so sorry. But there was only silence from where they lay, encased in concrete and granite.

Around the three graves were gathered so many of the other people who had loved Cara all her life. School friends, teachers, neighbors, a handful of distant cousins who were my only remaining relatives but who I barely remembered. Many of these people also had stood in this spot seven years before to say good-bye to Wheeler and Mary Sue McPhee, killed when the driver of a tractor-trailer

suffered a heart attack and lost control of his rig one afternoon on I-16 between Savannah and Statesboro, leaving
their two daughters orphaned. Now those faces watched me
again, with concern and pity. Poor Sutton. First her parents;
now her sister. First an orphan; now completely alone. Beside me on my right was Mattie Patterson, our lifelong
next-door neighbor in Hilton, who held my hand tightly all
through the service and who probably knew better than almost anyone here what this day was costing me. On my
left was Amy Reed, Cara's best girlhood friend. They, too,
looked at me in grief and concern and pity.

But I don't do pity. Since learning of Cara's death, my
chief emotion, when I could let myself lower the barriers
to it, had been grief. As I saw the pity in the faces around
me at the grave, I was overcome with a new feeling, a
growing rage, not at these people, but at the man who had
killed my sister and put the looks of pity on those faces. I
had been far too numb and far too busy to think clearly
about him yet. But the fury that now blasted me had, I
realized, been building inside me for all this time. No
longer masked by all the other things with which I had to
contend, the anger now poured out like a dark, thick, foul
smoke and threatened to suffocate me.

"It can be so difficult in times such as this for us to
understand how God could allow such a tragedy," Reverend Mann was saying, "to understand what His plan for us
could possibly be, to see how we must learn to trust in God
and to forgive, just as God forgives us."

Forgiveness would be a long time coming to my heart,
if ever, I thought angrily. Now I understood the furious
impulse that drove people to take revenge when their loved
ones were harmed. At that moment there was nothing I
wouldn't have done to have just a few minutes alone with
Cara's murderer and with the gun he had used to kill her.

At the sound of Ellen Byerly's lovely voice, lifting above
the group of mourners in an a capella rendition of one of
the hymns Cara loved, I managed to bring my anger under
tenuous control. Ellen, who was a few years older than I,
was the town's first choice for any occasion that required

a song, from weddings to funerals, and her true alto voice made musical accompaniment a complement to her singing, not a requirement. I heard a great deal of sniffing and some soft sobs as Ellen sang, but I sat dry-eyed and stone-faced, listening to lyrics that talked about the joy of knowing Jesus. Those words, I knew, explained a part of the reason why Cara attended church and I didn't. I had found religion, as taught by my Baptist church, to be a thing of repression and control, of censure and condemnation, of fear and the threats of hellfire. Cara, on the other hand, had seen it as a thing of love and joy, of promise and salvation. What repelled me comforted her.

Ellen's voice lifted again in the second verse, and I closed my eyes and offered an awkward prayer to whatever was, a prayer that Cara had not been disappointed, that somewhere Cara still existed, basking in the joy she had believed waited for her. There was none here for me.

Ellen's voice faded from the hymn's final notes, and Reverend Mann began to lead the mourners in the Lord's Prayer. When he finished, I stood at the graveside, shaking the hands of the people who filed slowly by, and promised myself, promised Cara and my parents, that one way or another I would find out who killed her. There could never be justice. Only giving Cara back her life, untainted by the violence done to her, would be justice. But there could be retribution. I intended to see to it.

Four

I no longer had a home in Hilton, so after the graveside services, everyone went to Amy Reed's house for a reception. When our parents were killed, Cara and I had agreed to sell the big white 1920s house in which we had grown up, playing in the enormous green backyard of its half-acre lot, putting in hundreds of hours in the wooden swing that hung in one corner of the wraparound porch. Selling that house broke both our hearts all over again, but it seemed to be the only choice we had. I was in Tallahassee building my reporting career far away from Hilton, and Cara had three more years of college ahead of her and no income. While there was a small estate from our parents' death, the house still had a sizable mortgage on it, and there was no way we could maintain the house or live in it. So we had cried bitter tears together and put it on the market. Now, as I had no suitable place to hold the expected funeral reception, Amy had volunteered her own home for it.

"I really appreciate your generosity," I told Amy in her sunny yellow kitchen, where she had gone to replenish a tray of sandwiches, and I had gone to escape for a few minutes from all the condolences. The house, which Amy and her husband, Ray, an accountant, had bought and renovated, was from the same era as my childhood home and only six blocks away. Walking through its high-ceilinged rooms and its lush yard, where Amy had planted roses and camellias and rambling beds of annuals and perennials, filled me with a sharp longing for my parents and sister.

Amy, who was six months' pregnant with her first baby, stopped her sandwich making and hugged me, tears welling in her hazel eyes.

"Cara was like my sister, too," she said. "I'd have done anything for her, but I never thought I'd be doing this."

I hugged her back in silence, my throat too tight to speak.

"Have the police turned up anything more?" Amy asked as she released me, tucked her short, honey-colored hair behind her ears, and went back to the bowl of chicken salad and the loaf of whole-wheat bread spread out on a large section of butcher block set into the white laminated countertop.

"They say not," I answered thickly, still recovering control of my voice. I sat down on one of the square-topped oak kitchen stools to watch her work for a few minutes and to ease off my black high-heeled dress shoes. "I've talked with the lead detective every day, but there's nothing new. It's like she was invisible between the church and the bank. They haven't turned up a single witness. They haven't been able to connect it to any other ATM robberies in the area, and the guy was smart enough not to be photographed on the ATM camera. If he picked her at random, I don't know how they'll ever find him. And I have to think that's what he did, because I don't know how anyone who knew Cara could want to kill her."

Amy spread the chicken salad on the bread and sliced it into triangular sandwiches in quick, efficient motions, but her face was thoughtful. Then she paused with her knife in the bowl of chicken.

"Was everything okay with Cara?" she asked.

"What do you mean?"

"It's just . . ." Amy hesitated, as if deciding how to word her answer.

"I had a letter from her," she said finally, putting the knife down on the cutting board and picking up a dish towel to wipe her hands. "It came the day before she died.

She didn't really say anything specific in it, but the whole tone of the letter left me thinking that something was wrong."

"Wrong how?" I asked.

Amy frowned, trying to articulate her reaction to the letter. She put her left hand on her growing stomach in a protective gesture and leaned her right hip against the counter.

"Well, she talked about missing all of us here in Hilton," she said finally, "and that sometimes she got homesick for it. It just sounded sort of unhappy in general. But I remember one thing she said. She said she had had some disappointments recently, that people weren't always what they seemed, and she wasn't sure what to do about it."

"Did she explain what she meant by that?" I asked, wondering, of course, if Cara had somehow been disappointed in me. Had I disappointed her by being too busy with work to spend more time with her than I did? Was she sorry she had moved all the way to Washington to be where I was?

"No," Amy answered, "but I remember thinking that she was even more upset by whatever it was than she was saying."

"Do you still have the letter? Could I see it?"

"Oh, sure." Amy nodded, smiling gently at me, and went back to making sandwiches. "I'll get it for you before you leave."

Later, when the formalities were finished, when the last of the guests had gone, when the dishes were washed and Amy's house was restored to its usual order, I was preparing to leave to catch my flight back to Washington. Amy looked briefly for the letter but couldn't find it.

"It's here somewhere," she said apologetically, looking up from a stack of bills and papers she had just thumbed through on the desk in her family room. "I know I'll find it as soon as you drive away. Do you want me to put a copy in the mail?"

I told her that would be fine. I gathered up my things and walked with Ray and Amy out to my rental car, where they hugged me fiercely and I thanked them for all they had done. Later, as I drove east along I-16 toward the Savannah airport, I wondered what exactly Cara had said in the letter and what had made her so unhappy—but that she hadn't mentioned to me. How could she have been unhappy without my knowing? I wondered. How long had she been unhappy, and what had caused it? And how could I have missed it? Was I so self-involved, so caught up in my own things that I had completely missed something serious enough to make her think about moving back to Hilton? Apparently, if Amy remembered the letter's contents accurately, the answer was yes.

It was after eleven P.M. when I finally pulled my white 1976 VW Beetle convertible into the parking lot at my apartment building in Alexandria. The sixteen-story building rises out of what is known in the area as Condo Canyon, an extensive tract of tall condominiums and apartment buildings, shopping malls and commercial strips that cluster along western Duke Street at its intersection with I-395 and make up Alexandria's West End. The area, built up mostly in the sixties and seventies, is the antithesis of historic Old Town Alexandria, whose eighteenth- and nineteenth-century architecture sits at the other end of Duke Street, on the banks of the Potomac River. From my fourteenth-floor nonhistorical apartment, I have a stunning view of northern Virginia, its heavily treed hills disguising much of the incredible urban sprawl that stretches for at least thirty miles south and west of the nation's capital.

I lugged my garment bag in from the far corner of the parking lot and through the chrome-and-glass sparkle of the building's lobby. As I waited tiredly for an elevator to descend from the upper floors, I wondered what tomorrow would be like. Getting up, having a leisurely breakfast, reading the Sunday papers, doing all my usual things, a normal day—except that my sister was dead. Rather than teary, the thought left me feeling numb and exhausted.

And where was Chris? All through the trip to Georgia, the funeral, and the reception, I felt his absence, his silence.

But he hadn't called again. I had checked both my office voice mail and the answering machine in my apartment daily, and there had been nothing. I had even called his answering machine and left Amy's name and telephone number where I could be reached. I was surprised and disappointed at his lack of contact during my ordeal. I couldn't expect him to shorten his business trip to come back and be with me, I supposed. Cara wasn't his relative, after all. But he was supposed to have finished his meetings on Friday, the day before Cara's funeral. And I didn't think hoping for a phone call was asking too much. The more I thought about it, the more my head ached with fatigue. If I can just make it upstairs to the bed, I thought, I'll figure it all out tomorrow.

My apartment, once I reached it, had the lifeless stillness that rooms take on when they haven't been occupied in several days. There was no dog or cat to greet me, my schedule being far too erratic to provide predictably for the needs of living creatures. There was only the quiet, the unmoving air, the inertness of a room where no consciousness dwells. Like a body from which the soul has gone, I thought morosely, then gave myself a mental kick.

Don't start thinking that way now, my little voice said. *I've been gentle under the circumstances, but you've got to keep it together.*

My voice was right, I thought (although I really hated it anytime I had to admit that). Don't think. Sleep. Be a real Southern belle. Deal with it all tomorrow.

I passed by the doorway to my small galley kitchen and barely noted the other rooms on my way through them to my bedroom. Ordinarily when I come home to my apartment, I let myself in with anticipation of the recurring pleasure I take in the way it looks. The three-quarter-length windows that extend without interruption along the entire western wall of the living room, dining area, and guest bedroom, the neutral oatmeal-colored carpeting, and the clean lines, bold colors, and uncluttered surfaces of my eclectic mix of contemporary and traditional furniture always help soothe my jangled nerves and slow down the wheels of my brain. This time, however, all of that barely registered in my need to get to the bedroom, to put down my baggage—both literal and emotional—and to lie down and give myself up to sleep.

Once there, I hung the garment bag in the closet and pulled a set of lightweight navy-blue sweats, which I use for pajamas, out of the dresser. Habit took me through my nightly routine of washing my face and brushing my teeth, after which I turned out the lights and sank down on the bed without even pulling back the covers. In the dark, I realized the red message light on my answering machine was blinking, so I fumbled around until I managed to press the play button, hoping to hear Chris's voice.

There were three messages, but none was from him.

"Sutton, it's Marlee Evans," I heard when the first message began. "I was just calling to confirm our meeting Monday at nine A.M. to plan Cara's memorial service. I hope everything went okay in Georgia. I'll see you on Monday morning."

The machine beeped several times.

"It's Rob. Just checking in to see how things went at the funeral. When you're back in town, give me a call. We can talk about work, but take as much time as you need to get everything taken care of."

The last call was from Detective Peterson.

"Sutton, it's Jim Peterson." I had become Sutton somewhere during our daily telephone conversations about the investigation. "We're all done processing your sister's apartment for evidence. I figured you probably needed to get her things packed up and moved out, so I just wanted to let you know that it's okay to do that now. And just so you'll know, we didn't find anything to indicate that she was abducted from there. I still think someone took her from the church parking lot."

I sat up and pressed the erase button on the answering machine and then fell back against the pillows once more, a tremendous sigh escaping my lungs, followed by a long indrawal of air, as if I was breathing for the first time in days. And when I thought about it, that was exactly how it

felt. As my eyes adjusted to the darkened room I stared at
the ceiling and thought again of my sister and how she had
died. But the hypnotically plain, off-white surface above
me remained blessedly free of images, and I never even
knew when my eyes closed and I slept.

Monday

Five

After a Sunday of sleeping late, doing my laundry, napping, reading, and going to bed early, my first stop on Monday morning was going to be at the U-Haul store just down Duke Street from my apartment. I had decided to go over to Cara's apartment as soon as I finished my meeting at the Bread of Life Church, and I needed packing boxes for Cara's things.

Over a breakfast of toast and an apple, I scanned the *News* and found a brief story under Rudy Black's byline inside the metro section. The Fairfax County Police, he said, were not happy about their lack of progress or leads in Cara's murder.

"We know there's someone out there with information that could help us solve this case," Rudy quoted Jim Peterson as saying. "We urge them to come forward with anything they might have seen or heard."

I read that to mean the police were still facing the brick wall they seemed to have run up against at the beginning and that, without some new development, and soon, I would be the only other person still interested in the case. It was a grim realization.

Rudy also mentioned Cara's burial in Georgia over the weekend and reminded readers of Sennet's reward offer because I was a *News* employee. Dispiritedly, I put the paper aside and got up to go to the U-Haul store.

Just before nine A.M., I pulled off Old Keene Mill Road and into the parking lot of the Bread of Life Church. The sign in front gave the church's name, followed by the biblical quote from which it had been taken: I AM THE BREAD OF LIFE: HE THAT COMETH TO ME SHALL NEVER HUNGER, AND HE THAT BELIEVETH ON ME SHALL NEVER THIRST. JOHN 6:35. Underneath were listed the minister's name and the times of Sunday and Wednesday-night services.

The church was an expansive edifice of modern architecture that looked as if its brick-and-glass wings would take flight at any moment. It was a long way from the small, white, wooden-sided Hilton Baptist Church to which Cara and I had been taken on endless Sundays as children. I didn't much care for the newer model.

But Cara had loved it, and all the people connected with it.

"I do wish you would come with me just once," she had said again for the umpteenth time early on a Sunday afternoon some seven or eight weeks ago. We had met for lunch at Mick's, a restaurant in the Springfield Mall, after her obligatory Sunday-morning church attendance, and Cara was still on an emotional high from the services.

"The people there are all so nice," she went on enthusiastically over our soup and sandwiches, hoping to convince me. "And Reverend Brant is one of the best speakers I've ever heard. I love to listen to his sermons. He has this terrific deep voice, and when he's preaching, it just sends shivers through you."

"No thanks," I had told her. "That's what I have Chris for—to send shivers through me."

"That isn't what I mean, Sutton, and you're terrible," Cara had said, partly in jest because she knew I was teasing her.

"I know," I conceded. Teasing Cara was too easy to be fun for long. "But I've told you a hundred times, honey, that I'm just not interested in going to any church at the moment, no matter how good the minister is."

"I worry about your soul," Cara replied, her expression

looking as if she sincerely did worry about me, which was touching. "What if something happened to you, and you still felt this way? Don't you think about what happens when we die? Don't you want to be in heaven with Mom and Dad?"

"Well sure, as long as it's more than boring harps and clouds, and there's something else to eat and drink besides milk and honey. I don't like milk, and honey gives me hives," I replied, teasing again. It just wasn't a topic on which I felt in the mood for a serious conversation with her. Especially given the number of times we had had this same conversation, or its first cousin, before.

"If I could only get you to come, I just know Reverend Brant could change your mind about so much," Cara had concluded wistfully, knowing it was the subject I was ready to change.

Now, ironically, here I was. At the Bread of Life Church, right where she had wanted me. And it had only taken her murder to bring me here.

The double glass doors to the main foyer closed behind me, leaving me in a cool, quiet space of brick interior walls and tall, green ficus trees in brick-red tubs. On the wall to my right hung a display case with a black grooved backboard and those little white, removable letters. The board repeated the information on the days and times of services, gave Reverend Daniel Brant's name just ahead of a list of seven deacons, and provided the additional information that the church had been founded by Reverend Brant. Ahead of me were a set of wide wooden doors standing open into a large, darkened space that I was sure was the main sanctuary. On the wall next to the doors were signs that directed me down a hallway on the left, to the church offices. When I reached the end of the hallway, I looked through a smaller open door to my right and saw a young redheaded woman of about twenty-two typing on a computer and sitting at a desk that faced me. She looked up as I stood in the doorway, her blue eyes and full mouth smiling at me.

"Are you Sutton?" she asked.

"Yes. Are you Marlee?"

"I sure am," Marlee Evans answered as she stood up from the desk and crossed the carpeted floor to meet me. We shook hands. She was a tiny thing, probably only about five-foot-three without the heels she was wearing. She had an open, smiling face, a delicate build, and a somewhat high, childlike voice.

"Come have a seat," Marlee said, delicately touching my upper arm and motioning me over to a small sitting area along the wall next to the office door. I sat down on the black leather sofa, and Marlee took the gray upholstered chair at the sofa's end, sitting down gracefully and crossing her ankles below the full skirt of the pastel-blue shirtwaist dress that she wore.

"I just can't tell you how sad we all are about Cara," Marlee said, leaning in my direction across the cushioned arm of the chair. "It just isn't going to be the same without her. Everyone liked her, and she was a terrific secretary. I learned a lot from her."

She reached out a hand to pat my right arm. "How are you holding up through all this?"

"I'm all right," I answered. Her mother-hen manner in a woman even younger than Cara made me smile. Marlee apparently knew no strangers, and I could see why Cara had liked her friendly, easy manner. It was, I knew, part of the reason she and Cara had become friends as well as colleagues, and Cara had mentioned her to me more than once. "It has been difficult," I told Marlee, "but what choice do I have but to get through it?"

"Do the police have any idea yet who . . . did it?" Marlee hesitated, stumbling over her words in an effort to avoid the harsh reality of murder.

"I don't think so," I told her. "It could have been anyone from anywhere. They haven't found any witnesses, and they don't have much in the way of physical evidence to go on."

"Yes," Marlee said, shaking her head in a sympathetic negative. "That Detective Peterson was here two different times talking to us about whether anyone would have wanted to hurt Cara and if anyone was here when she left.''

''No luck on finding anyone who saw anything, I take it?'' I asked dispiritedly.

''No. The night she died was one of the few nights when there wasn't some sort of activity going on here. And Cara was working late by herself. I left about six-thirty, and she said she still had at least two or three more hours of work to do.''

It was basically what Peterson had told me the last time we had talked: no witnesses, no motives, nothing to indicate anything other than a random robbery and killing. He hadn't sounded very optimistic. I didn't know how I could accept the prospect of never knowing exactly what happened that night or why Cara had been killed.

Voices came toward us down the hall, and seconds later two men walked into the office, stopping as they saw us. Marlee jumped up from the chair, smiling in greeting at them.

''Good morning,'' she said to the newcomers.

''Morning, Marlee,'' responded the first man. He was tall, well built, with brown eyes and a full head of dark hair graying slightly at the temples. Both he and the second man, who stood slightly behind him, looked to be somewhere in their late forties. The second man merely nodded at Marlee.

''Reverend Brant,'' Marlee continued, walking over to take the first man by the arm and move him in my direction, ''this is Sutton McPhee, Cara's sister. She's here to arrange the memorial service.''

I stood and shook the hand Reverend Brant extended toward me.

''I'm sorry we have to meet for the first time under such tragic circumstances,'' he said, smiling solicitously. ''I just don't know how we'll manage without Cara here to keep us in line. She's in all our thoughts and prayers.''

Brant carried himself well. His physical appearance, the custom-tailored look of his glen-plaid suit, his strong, accent-free voice and facility with language all said substance, strength, directness. No question that he would stand out in any gathering, and I was certain it all was a real asset in his career as a minister. But I noticed that his handshake was tentative, brief. He doesn't like to touch people, I realized, and thought it odd for someone in his job. I looked at him more closely, wondering where my thought had come from. Was it the result of the sort of intuitive knowing I sometimes had about people, or was it a product of my general indifference—if not outright aversion—to organized religion and those who tried to sell it to the rest of us?

As a child, I had realized I had an ability to sense things about people, things that appeared to escape the awareness of most others around me. My mother said it was my legacy from my Gaelic ancestors—all that Irish, Scottish, and Welsh blood. They were a race of people who had been famous for two thousand years or more for their fey abilities, abilities that had resulted in more than one of them being tried as a witch. Whatever it was, it seldom was pronounced enough for me to articulate what I sensed, just that something was wrong, off-key, or not what it seemed to be. I also had learned to pay attention to this special sense of mine, and now it was telling me that the surface here did not match what was underneath.

To be fair, however, I didn't have much use for ministers as a group. It wasn't that I was an atheist; I felt there must be some organizing force or intelligence in the universe. I just thought it was pretty presumptuous of humans to be so certain they knew the thoughts of this intelligence that they could insist on everyone else adhering to their particular beliefs. My own farewell to organized religion had stemmed jointly from my dislike of anyone else setting rules for me and from a conversation with a Baptist minister who told me that those who died without baptism, including babies, went to hell. So it was highly possible that I was put off by Reverend Brant for reasons that had more to do with myself than with him.

When Brant turned back to his left and introduced his companion, however, I had no trouble identifying the source of my negative reaction to the man who stood behind Brant. "Sutton, this is my assistant, Al Barlow,"

Brant said. Barlow made no move toward me, kept his hands in his pockets. As he had with Marlee, he merely nodded silently in my direction.

Al Barlow looked completely out of place, both in the church and in the company of Daniel Brant. Barlow was rail-thin, with a sallow complexion. He had jet-black eyes that looked around him with the same lack of emotion as a cat's—or a snake's. In contrast to Brant's expensive suit, Barlow wore an ill-fitting, dark brown jacket on which the collar stood awkwardly away from his neck, and tan knit slacks. While Brant worked to project sophisticated ease and bonhomie, Al Barlow was dark, coiled energy, hard-bitten and taciturn. What a mismatched pair, I thought. What could Barlow possibly do to assist Brant?

"Well, if you will excuse us," Brant was saying apologetically, "we have work to get to. You're in good hands with Marlee. She'll help you set everything up, and we'll all do our best to make sure the service for Cara is something special."

"Thank you," I told him. "I know it would make Cara happy to think people here will remember her."

"Of course, of course," Brant responded. "So we'll see you on . . . Saturday?" he said as a question, looking at Marlee for confirmation of the day. She nodded yes. "Saturday," he concluded, looking back at me, his hale-fellow-well-met smile still in place. With that, he and Barlow turned and went into the first of two inner offices, the one that had Brant's name engraved on a tastefully small brass plaque on the door. Through it all, Barlow had remained as silent as the grave.

"Is Barlow always that talkative?" I asked, a little sarcastically but also curious, turning back to Marlee once Brant's office door had closed.

"Don't mind him," Marlee said, smiling reassuringly. "He's like that around everyone."

"He's not much of a people person, is he?" I observed understatedly. "What does he do as Brant's assistant?"

"Whatever Reverend Brant needs," Marlee explained. "He runs errands, drives Reverend Brant around. Mostly he makes himself available for whatever comes up.''

''I guess he just didn't strike me as Reverend Brant's type.''

I'd say that's putting it mildly, my personal Greek chorus chimed in. *He looks like an escapee from the carnival. I wouldn't trust him with my quarter.* He was right, but I wasn't in a place that I could discuss it with him at the moment.

''I think they go back a long way,'' Marlee was saying in explanation for the odd match. ''I don't know any details, but Reverend Brant said once that he helped Al out with some trouble several years ago and gave him a job. Al is very loyal to him, sticks to him like glue.

''So,'' she went on brightly, in a complete non sequitur, ''would you like to see the chapel where we'll hold the memorial service? And then we can come back here and go over the details.''

''Sure,'' I told her, wondering if the abrupt change of subject meant she wasn't terribly comfortable discussing Al Barlow or just that she found him a less than interesting topic of conversation.

''Let me just turn on the answering machine to catch the phones,'' she said, walking over to her desk and pressing a sequence of buttons on her telephone. As she straightened up, a third man came through the office door. He looked to be in his mid-twenties and was carrying a garment bag. He gave me an assessing look as he walked past me toward Marlee.

''Oh, John,'' Marlee said, ''this is Cara's sister, Sutton. We're setting up Cara's memorial service.''

John whoever-he-was stopped at that bit of information and turned back to look at me more thoroughly. He started at my feet and slowly brought his gaze up my body to my face. The boldness of his once-over surprised me; we were in church, after all, not some cheesy singles' bar.

''Oh, yeah?'' he asked. ''Her sister, huh? You don't look much like her.'' Although Cara and I had shared a slight resemblance physically, people who had met both of us were more likely to notice the differences in our personalities and demeanors than any similarities in our looks.

I silently gave this John-person the once-over in return, though mine was of a completely nonsexual nature.

"Behave now, John," Marlee said hastily. She tried to affect a light tone, as if chiding an innocently mischievous child, but I could hear the anxious embarrassment beneath the tone that told me she thought John's behavior was something other than innocent mischief. She looked at me apologetically. "This is John Brant, Sutton, Reverend Brant's son."

"Oh, yeah?" I responded, still facing the younger Brant. I took in his blond hair and blue eyes, which apparently had been inherited from his mother. "You don't look much like him."

John Brant laughed. Marlee turned red. John shifted the garment bag to his other arm.

"Nice to meet you. Sorry about your sister." He turned and went into the other inner office, next to the one occupied by his father and Al Barlow.

"Oh," Marlee said in a whisper, clearly mortified at John's behavior, "he can be so shameless, sometimes."

John Brant came back out of his office and walked over to me. He handed me a business card.

"If you ever want to go out sometime, call me," he said, smiling unctuously at me. Marlee was speechless. He turned away and, this time, went to his father's office, where he knocked, entered, and closed the door behind him.

"Let's go see the chapel," Marlee said, grabbing me by the arm and hustling me out into the hallway.

So these are the people Cara trusted with her immortal soul, I thought. What I had seen so far didn't instill in me any desire for baptism, however wonderful a minister Daniel Brant might be. I was far too put off by his son and his assistant.

"I am so sorry, Sutton," Marlee apologized as we walked down the hallway. "Sometimes John just doesn't know when to quit."

"Does he always come on that strongly to complete strangers?" I asked. "I wouldn't think most people would appreciate it in a church setting. And surely his mother must have taught him better."

"His mother died when he was a boy," Marlee said. "He was mostly raised by his father, and he does behave much better when Reverend Brant's in sight," Marlee said. "He's just one of those men who thinks he's irresistible to women. He can't understand why any woman would turn him down."

We had reached the chapel door.

"Here we are," Marlee said. "Let's go in and let you look around."

I had glimpsed the church's cavernous main sanctuary from the entry foyer when I first arrived and again as we walked past it on our way to the chapel. But the chapel was much more to my taste. It was small, and without the warehouse atmosphere that today's larger sanctuaries often have. There were beautiful red oak pews stained a burnished gold, with wine-red cushions, enough to seat a hundred and fifty to two hundred people. The oak floor was carpeted in a wine color that matched the cushions and that brought out the glow of the wood under our feet as well. The walls and ceiling were a warm off-white. Behind the pulpit, which faced us from the far end, was a beautiful stained-glass window, probably eighteen or twenty feet tall, showing the biblical scene of Jesus gathering the children around him.

"It's lovely," I told Marlee, walking halfway up the aisle and sitting down in a pew to my left. My problems with organized religion never had prevented me from appreciating the beauty of many churches or from loving the music of the Southern hymns. I didn't have any problem believing that God, whatever God was, was present in some of the churches I had seen. My problems had much more to do with what got said in those churches in God's name, while He maintained His silence.

"It was Cara's favorite place in the whole church," Marlee said, joining me on the pew. "She often came in here during her lunch hour, to just sit and enjoy it. She said she could hear God in the quiet."

My eyes burned, and it took me a moment to regain control. And did she hear Him at the ATM? I wondered bitterly. Did He hear the silent prayers she must have been sending up in her terror? I looked for a way to change the subject. I felt the business card still in my hand.

"So how did you escape John Brant's clutches?" I asked, turning to look at Marlee.

She laughed at the memory.

"He came on to me pretty heavy when I first started working here about a year and a half ago," she said. "I finally had my boyfriend, Matt, come by to take me out for lunch one day when I knew John would be in the office. Matt is at least four inches taller, and probably outweighs John by fifty pounds. One look at Matt, and John apparently lost all interest in me." She smiled again.

I smiled, too, more at the image of tiny Marlee with the Incredible Hulk than at the picture of the two males checking each other out, but I didn't tell Marlee that. As I imagined the scene that she described, however, another picture occurred to me, one that wiped my smile away.

"Did he come on to Cara, too?"

Marlee didn't answer for a moment, clearly thinking how to word her response.

"I'm afraid so," she said finally.

"Just how obnoxious was he?" I asked, confident that Cara would not have welcomed his brash, brazen approach.

"A lot sometimes," Marlee admitted. "He really had a bad case for Cara, and she wasn't interested in John at all, which just made him that much more interested. She told me she finally had to threaten to go to his father after John tried to kiss her in the office one day."

"Did that work?" I asked much more calmly than I felt, not wanting Marlee to see the anger that the picture of John Brant mauling my sister conjured up.

"I think so," Marlee said.

"He doesn't strike me as someone who would handle such rejection well," I commented. "Was he nasty to her after that?"

"Not really. Mostly he just ignored her from then on,"

Marlee said. "Except for when he got mad at her about his computer."

"What was he mad about?"

"He thought she had been messing around with the computer in his office."

I looked confused.

"You have to understand about John," Marlee explained patiently. "He's very good with computers and very particular about anyone but him touching his computer here."

I looked down at the business card. It said *John Brant, Brantlow, Inc.,* and included a local telephone number that was only one number away from the one I had written down days before for the church office.

"If he works for this Brantlow, Inc.," I asked Marlee, "why does he have an office here at the church?"

"Oh, that's a company his father and Al started," Marlee continued. "But John really does most of the work. He does computer-system consulting for businesses, so he travels a lot. But he also spends time keeping the church records computerized, at no charge, so he just uses the office here at the church for everything when he's in town. As I said, he's real good with computers. It's what he was studying in college, before he got sent home."

"Sent home? For what?"

"I don't know for sure. I heard some talk that it had to do with a girl, which I guess would be no surprise. It was before I came to work here, but the secretary I replaced told me about it. She said Reverend Brant was pretty mad, but that John just said a college degree wasn't that important anyway for what he wanted to do."

I pondered the developing picture of John Brant, would-be Casanova of the churchy set.

"So what did Cara do to his computer?" I asked.

"Nothing as far as I know." Marlee frowned, remembering. "John and I had been in the main sanctuary checking on a couple of things, and when we walked back into the office, Cara was coming out of John's office. He flew off the handle at her, asked what she was doing in there. She told him she wasn't doing anything, just looking for a dictionary. John wanted to know if she had been fooling around with his computer, but Cara said she hadn't touched it. He acted like he didn't believe her. He was pretty mad."

"What did he say then?"

"He told her the next time she wanted something from his office to ask him, and to stay out the rest of the time. Then he went in and slammed the door. He sat looking at the computer for a few minutes, did a couple of things on it, and then made some phone calls."

"What did Cara say about it? Was she okay?" I asked. Cara never had handled being yelled at very well. As a girl, it always sent her out of the room in tears.

"She said that if whatever he had on it was all that important, then he should remember to turn the computer off when he went out of the office. But I think it bothered her a lot more than she let on. She didn't seem herself the rest of the day. She and John really didn't speak to each other after that."

"And Reverend Brant didn't intervene?" I asked, wondering why he would let his son be abusive to such a good secretary.

"He wasn't here at the time," Marlee explained. "And I don't think Cara ever said anything to him about it. She admired Reverend Brant so much, and in spite of her threat to go to him when John was so . . . ah, attentive, I don't think she really wanted Reverend Brant to know that she was having problems with John."

I was surprised that I hadn't heard a word from Cara about her argument with John Brant about the computer. But then she hadn't mentioned his coming on to her either.

"When did this big argument happen?" I asked, still trying to put the whole story together in my mind. Marlee had to think about it for a minute.

"Actually, it was on the Thursday before she . . . died," she said finally. "I remember thinking I wished John had apologized for yelling at her. I hated to think that Cara died with anger still between them."

To myself, I thought that John Brant probably didn't have enough of a conscience to feel bad about it. To Marlee, I said, "It *is* too bad. Cara hated being upset with anybody. She just couldn't rest after an argument until it was settled and everybody's feelings were smoothed over."

Our conversation seemed to run down at that point. After a moment we both stood up, knowing it was time to get back to the office and take care of the details of Cara's memorial service. When we arrived, the Reverend Brant's office door was open. There was no sign of him, his son, or his assistant.

Six

In my car twenty minutes later I indulged my irritation with John Brant for yelling at Cara. It was either that or think about what I was on my way to do. I needed to pack up Cara's things so the apartment manager at the Easton Arms Apartments could rerent her unit. I knew that the packing was going to be like dissecting her life and then burying her all over again. I wasn't looking forward to it.

John Brant did sound paranoid about his computer, I mused. Granted he probably was much more proficient with it than either Marlee or Cara, but wasn't he overreacting just because Cara had walked into his office while the computer was on and he was someplace else? It wasn't like the church operations were a big secret to her; she was one of the secretaries, after all. He certainly seemed to have an unreasonable side to his personality that also extended to his ideas about his effect on women. What a conceited asshole, I thought, and then put him out of my mind as I pulled into the parking lot at Cara's apartment.

The Easton Arms is a 1960s-era apartment complex just north of the commercial area of Springfield. Its apartments cluster in two-story buildings of eight units each, with an open-air stair/hallway onto which the apartments open and that divides each building in half. While the architecture of the complex is less than memorable, its age means the apartments offer more spacious rooms than much of anything built since the mid-seventies. The size of the rooms, the reasonableness of the rent, by Washington standards, and the complex's proximity to shopping and to my own apartment two miles away had been selling points for Cara.

At the Easton Arms rental office, located in the first building of the complex, I introduced myself to the secretary, a plump woman in her late twenties, with brassy blond hair and a little too much makeup for my taste. I wasn't crazy about her floral challis dress either, which featured a ruffled V-neckline that was much fussier than anything I would wear. But she had kind, intelligent eyes. I noted the desk nameplate that said GINA APPLEGATE and introduced myself. I told her why I had come, and she got up and stuck her head around the door of the office behind her.

"Charlie, can you come out?" Gina asked into the back office, and then returned to sit down at her desk. A moment later a man of about my age came out into the reception area. He was an inch shorter than I and one of those small men with more energy than his frame could quite contain. He wore khaki slacks and a navy-blue knit shirt with the Britches of Georgetown's tongue-in-cheek warthog emblem on the left breast. The blue-and-white Nikes on his feet told me that either he did a lot of running around the complex responding to problems or that his feet just hurt.

"May I help you?" Charlie asked from the doorway of his office.

"This is Cara McPhee's sister, Charlie," Gina explained on my behalf. "She's come to pack up Cara's apartment."

"We were so sorry to hear about what happened," Charlie the Manager said, coming from the doorway to reach out and shake my hand. "Let me get you the spare key, and we'll walk over."

He took a ring of keys from his pants pocket and walked behind Gina's chair to open a shallow cabinet that hung on the wall next to her. From it, he chose a key and then relocked the cabinet door. He handed the key to me. The small round paper tag tied to it with white string said "D-7," Cara's apartment number.

"If Gina can get a photocopy of your driver's license, you can just keep the key and return it when you've got everything out," he said. "Take a couple of days if you need it."

I thanked him and reached into my purse for the wallet where I kept my license. Gina took the laminated card and went over to a small photocopy machine on the right-hand wall, where she made a quick copy of the license and brought it back to me.

I stuck it back in my wallet and followed Charlie out the door.

"Terrible thing, what happened to your sister," Charlie said solicitously as we walked over to Cara's apartment. It was a one-bedroom on the second floor, three buildings down from the one that housed the rental office. "Have the police turned up anything?"

"I'm afraid not," I said, really not feeling up to discussing it with him.

"One of them was by the office Friday, to say they were finished with the apartment. But they've been pretty close-mouthed. Except when they questioned everybody around here about it. Me, Gina, our maintenance staff, all her neighbors. They sure weren't leaving any stones unturned."

"I don't think they have much to go on," I replied, "but I'm glad to hear they're being thorough."

"That's for sure," Charlie said.

Our brief attempt at conversation was followed by silence until we reached the top of the stair at Cara's door.

"Here we are," Charlie said, putting the key into the lock and opening the door for me. Then we both stood rooted in the doorway.

"What the hell . . . ?" Charlie exclaimed.

"Jesus," I said, my voice coming out in a whisper.

Inside, the apartment had been turned upside down. In the living room, lamps and books were on the floor, clearly flung there at random. The foam cushions from Cara's sofa and matching chair were tossed in a careless pile. The cushions' dusky blue covers had been pulled off the cushions and thrown around. We stepped into the apartment.

To our left, through the kitchen doorway, I could see that all the cabinet doors and the drawers were open, with their contents spilled out across the countertop and floor.

My anger rising, I walked through the living room and into the short hall. On the left, the open bathroom door showed me all Cara's cosmetics and other items from the medicine cabinet had been pulled down into and around the sink that sat underneath. Ahead of me was Cara's bedroom, in which I found a similar scene. All her clothes were tossed into the middle of the room or scattered over gaping drawers. Even the linens had been stripped from her bed and left in a pile, and the mattress sat at an angle, half off the box spring underneath. Everywhere pictures and posters had been taken off the wall and left on the floor or the furniture.

I turned around in a fury, almost tripping over Charlie, who had walked into the bedroom behind me.

"I can't believe this," I said heatedly. "Why would the police possibly have needed to do this to her things?" Charlie looked at me and shook his head.

"I had no idea this was how they left it," he said apologetically.

"Excuse me," I told him, going around him and out to the living room. I snatched up the telephone extension off the floor and plugged it back into the wall outlet from which the cord had been pulled. At the dial tone, I angrily punched in Detective Peterson's pager number, which I had memorized by now, followed by Cara's phone number. I slammed the receiver back down and waited in anger for Peterson's call.

"I'm going to give those cops a piece of my mind over this," I told Charlie, who had drifted back into the living room, where he still looked around him in amazement. Within no more than a minute, the phone rang in my hand. I answered.

"Detective Peterson here," he said.

"This is Sutton McPhee," I told him heatedly. "I'm here at Cara's apartment, and I am just furious about what your people did to it!"

"What are you talking about?" Peterson asked.

"It looks like it's been ransacked," I exclaimed. "Everything is thrown around all over the place. Was it really necessary to do this to look for evidence?"

Peterson was silent for a moment.

"Are you in the apartment now?" he asked.

"Yes, and I'm telling you—"

"Leave," he ordered. "Hang up the phone and leave right now!"

"What do you—"

"My men didn't trash the place," he said forcefully. "Someone else has been through it. And for all you know, they could still be in there. Now hang up the phone and go wait outside. I'll have a marked car there in a few minutes, and I'll be there myself as quick as I can."

I admit I was slow on the uptake, but eventually I did the calculations.

"Right," I said abruptly, and hung up the phone. Charlie the Manager was standing at my elbow. I grabbed him by the arm.

"Come with me," I told him. "We need to talk outside."

He looked at me like he thought I was crazy, but he followed me out, closing the door behind him. On the sidewalk in front of the building, I explained to him what Peterson had said on the phone.

"Oh my God," he was saying, "do you think it's safe for us to stand here? Maybe we should go to the office."

Before I could answer, a dark-blue-and-putty-colored Fairfax County Police unit pulled in front of the building, its siren silent but its colored lights flashing furiously, and two uniformed cops got out.

"You Sutton McPhee?" the driver, a burly man in his late thirties, with an almost military haircut and florid cheeks, asked.

"Yes," I told him. "It's apartment seven, on the second floor." I handed him the key Charlie had given me.

The policeman and his younger partner, a slimmer, less ruddy version of the driver, eyed the building behind us.

"Check the back," the older partner said, motioning his arm in a circle to the right. The younger cop did as he was told, unsnapping the cover over the gun on his belt and going around the building, his right hand firmly on the gun's grip. In a moment he came back out front through the open-air hallway that separated the apartments on one side from those on the other.

"Nothing," he said.

"No sign of anyone in there since you came out?" the first cop asked me.

"No," I told him.

"Let's check it out," he said to his partner, his hand going back to his own gun. They went up the stairs to Cara's door, where they finally drew their guns before unlocking the door cautiously, taking a quick look inside and then stepping in rapidly and moving to either side of the door.

Charlie was almost beside himself at the excitement. A few curious souls had wandered over from neighboring buildings, wanting to know what was going on. Charlie was explaining manically; I fully expected him to start jumping up and down at any moment. I wondered how he ever coped with any real emergency at the complex and suspected that Gina must have her feet more firmly on the ground than her boss did.

"This is too wild," Charlie was saying. "What if the guy was in there while we were there?"

If only he had been, I thought. Then, perhaps, I could have done a few of the things I'd been planning for him.

Yeah, right, my little voice spoke up. *Like you could have done much with a gun staring you in the face!*

True, I told it, but a girl can dream, can't she?

The younger cop walked out into the breezeway of the apartment building's upper floor.

"It's all clear," he called. "You can come up."

Before Charlie and I could respond, Peterson pulled up in his gray unmarked police sedan.

• • •

It was pretty evident, once I had time to think about it, that it was Cara's killer who had ransacked her apartment. There was no sign of the door having been forced, and the windows were intact. Cara's keys had not been found with her body, so chances were the person who killed her had taken them. Just as clearly, whoever it was had been canny enough to wait until after the police had finished with the apartment before going through it. That way, they'd had all the time they needed, without worrying about a cop walking in on them. What, if anything, had been taken was anyone's guess at the moment.

Peterson took me on a cursory walk-through to see if I noticed anything missing. The only thing that obviously was gone was some jewelry that had belonged to our mother, a sapphire-and-diamond necklace and matching earrings. Checking a sheet of paper on a clipboard he had taken from his car, he told me that the police had not taken the jewelry into evidence, having found no usable fingerprints on it. The jewelry should have been in Cara's top dresser drawer, but I couldn't find it anywhere in the apartment. I had told her more than once that she ought to keep the jewelry in a bank vault, but she had refused.

"They help me remember Mom," she had said defensively. "I can take them out and see her so clearly, wearing them with that royal-blue dress." The dress to which she had referred was the one Mom had worn the night Dad had taken her out for their wedding anniversary, the last one they celebrated. He had given Mom her gift—the necklace and earrings—before they left the house that evening. As Cara had talked I could see Mom again, too, as clear in my mind's eye as when she was alive. I had understood Cara's need to keep the jewelry easily accessible, even though I thought it was foolhardy. But now it meant that one more precious memory had been stolen from me, tainted by Cara's killer.

"Chances are he'll try to fence the stuff pretty quickly," Peterson said, when I had finished describing the jewelry for him. "We'll get the word out on the street that it's part of a murder investigation. Most of the fences won't want to touch it.''

Other than the jewelry, there was nothing whose absence caught my attention. Until I could go through everything, I wouldn't know for sure what else might have been taken, and that would have to wait at least another day while the police processed the place a second time for fingerprints and any other evidence.

The shock of finding the chaos in Cara's apartment was wearing off. As I stood in the deliberate wreckage of the artifacts of Cara's life, the shock was replaced by the same anger that had overcome me at her grave, making me clench my fists in an effort not to strike something or someone. Detective Peterson was talking to me, but I turned and walked out of the apartment, onto the covered front walkway, where I tried to focus my runaway thoughts and emotions enough to talk sensibly.

I realized Peterson had followed me out.

"Just be grateful he wasn't still in there when you walked in," he said practically. I glared at him. I knew he was right, but it didn't help much. The destruction in Cara's apartment felt like the killer had attacked her all over again.

"You'd think killing her would have been enough," I told him.

"The world is full of scumbags, who will do pretty much anything," Peterson responded, wearily rubbing his forehead with the fingertips of his left hand. "Several times a year we get called by people whose houses were robbed while they were at the funeral of a family member. The funeral announcements in the newspaper tell anybody who's interested the exact time the family won't be home."

Peterson told me to go on home. There was nothing more I could do at the moment, he said.

"Come back tomorrow and pack up," he continued. "If you notice anything else missing, call me."

I nodded, now dreading closing up Cara's apartment even more than before. Anticipating it the first time had been hard enough. Now it would be doubly difficult, knowing that everything I picked up had been touched, handled, defiled by her killer.

Peterson went back inside the apartment. I went downstairs to my car, where I reassured an anxious Charlie that I didn't hold him responsible for what had been done to Cara's apartment. On the drive home, I called Rob Perry from my cellular phone and told him what had happened and that I would need one more day away from work.

"Take whatever you need," he said. "I'll have Rudy check with the cops for an official comment. Will you be around so he can get a quote from you?"

"Just have him call me at the apartment. I'll be there in a few minutes."

"Good enough. We'll make sure to mention the reward money again. And Sutton?"

"Yes?" I answered tiredly, the anger and disgust that had consumed me now ebbing and leaving me drained.

"I'm just glad you're okay."

Was I? I wondered. I sure didn't feel okay. I wasn't looking forward to the long night ahead.

Which promised to be even longer after the phone conversation I finally had late that afternoon with Chris.

I had not heard from him on Sunday either, and when I had called his apartment, all I got was his answering machine. I hadn't bothered to leave another message. Perhaps, I thought, he was late getting back into town and was still on his way home, or he was out catching up on errands that had piled up while he was gone all week.

At any rate, I fully expected him to call me from his office on Monday. But my answering machine at home had taken no messages while I was out all day, and he wasn't on my voice mail at work either. I sat down on my bed and called his office.

"Chris Wiley," he answered in his baritone voice.

"Hi," I said, feeling no need to identify myself.

"Oh, Sutton, hello."

"I didn't hear from you yesterday, so I thought I should check in."

"Yeah, uh, right," he said. "Well, I was pretty tired from the long trip, so I turned off the phone and slept most of the day. How are you?"

I gave him a brief account of the funeral and reception and talked about my surprise—and gratitude—that so many people had shown up.

"But yesterday was really tough," I added. "It was the first time I've been able to slow down since Cara was killed. There were just so many things to take care of. But sitting in my apartment alone, all I could do was think about her and what she must have gone through."

"That sounds hard," Chris agreed, an uncharacteristic awkward note in his voice. "Ah, look, Sutton, I really need to get back to work here. I've got a lot of catching up on paperwork to do. Can I call you later?"

I bit back the sarcastic reply that my mind automatically voiced, something along the lines of "Don't knock yourself out." Instead, I asked, "Would you like to come over after work?" I was lonely and depressed, and I thought that a night with Chris's arms around me might go a long way toward turning off the violent kaleidoscope that kept going through my head.

"No, I don't think I can tonight," he responded after a second's hesitation. I waited silently for him to continue. "Maybe we can get together this weekend and do something," he added eventually as my silence dragged on. "Why don't I give you a call later in the week?"

"Oh, okay," I said. Even I could take a hint eventually. Chris was not comfortable with this conversation. "I'll wait to hear from you."

I hung up, completely perplexed. Something was going on with Chris, but I had no idea what. It wasn't the sort of reaction I had come to expect from him. Belatedly, I realized that I had been so taken aback at his anxious desire to cut the conversation short that I had forgotten to tell him about the break-in at Cara's apartment. I was still sitting in confusion, phone in my lap, when it rang under my hand. It was Ken Hale.

"I was checking to see if you could use a dinner out,"

he explained when I answered. "I know it's been a rough week. I thought you probably needed a break and a sympathetic ear."

Those were exactly the things that I needed, I thought to myself, but I had expected the offer to come from Chris, and I couldn't figure out why it hadn't. Still, Ken was always good company, and the fact that he wasn't my love interest didn't change the reality that I did need precisely the sort of evening he was offering.

"You're a mind reader," I told him with a relieved sigh. "Where should I meet you and what time?"

"How about the Westend Raw Bar? Seven o'clock?" Ken asked. "It's down the street from you, and it'll be on my way home since I'm coming out from D.C."

"Good choice," I told him. The Westend Raw Bar was a popular local seafood restaurant on Duke Street that did tasty things with every kind of fish and shellfish. "I'll see you there. And Ken?"

"Yeah?"

"Thanks for the thought."

"Whatever I can do," he replied.

Ken was relaxing on the restaurant's front porch when I turned off Duke Street and pulled into a parking space that a dark green Camaro convertible had just vacated. He waved and stood up when he saw my car, which was known on sight by most of the *News* reporters and was looked upon fondly in the newsroom as some sort of retro-pet from the seventies. As I climbed out, Ken came down the steps to meet me and gave me a big hug.

"How're you doing?" he asked, and held me out at arm's length for an inspection.

"I've had better months," I told him, smiling tiredly at his friendly concern. "They say it gets easier eventually, but all the things I still have to wrap up keep bringing it all back to me."

"I know what you mean," he said, still holding my arms. "My best friend in high school was killed in a car wreck the summer before our senior year, and it was like every time I walked down the hall at school that whole year, or drove past someplace we used to hang out, it hurt all over again.''

He dropped my right arm, but slipped his own through the crook of my left arm and steered me toward the restaurant's front door.

''Now let's go have something powerful to drink and a decent meal, and you can tell Uncle Ken all about it,'' he said. I decided I was in good hands.

Too bad they're the wrong guy's hands.

I was too tired for an internal argument, especially one I would lose. I didn't bother even to think a response.

It wasn't until Ken and I were inside at our table, inhaling the aromas of fresh seafood being fried, baked, grilled, and blackened, that I realized how hungry I really was. Ravenous just about came close to describing it. And it was no wonder, I suppose. I had been able to eat next to nothing since Cara had been killed. I had been going nonstop for days, and the thought of my sister's ordeal had wiped out any appetite I might have had when I had time to eat. But my body was a pretty healthy one, and self-preservation eventually kicks in. Suddenly I felt as if I could have eaten an entire boatload of fish.

''Oh my God,'' I said, looking up at Ken from the menu, ''I think I'm starving. Just bring me one of everything.''

Ken laughed.

''It's my treat tonight,'' he said. ''Have whatever you want!''

I asked the waitress for iced tea, an appetizer of crab-stuffed mushrooms, and the grilled red snapper, with a salad and steamed vegetables.

Ken raised an amused eyebrow at me. ''Make that two of everything,'' he told our blond, college-aged waitress, grinning, ''and I think we need the basket of hush puppies and corn bread on an emergency basis.''

''I'll be right back with your bread and tea,'' she promised, nodding an understanding smile. She was as good as her word, and I attacked the basket of bread as if I hadn't even seen food in days.

I told Ken, much later after everything was over and I could think straight again, how much his dinner invitation that night meant to me, that it had been a lifeline of sanity and normalcy to grab onto for a short time in the middle of the madness of what had happened to Cara. At the time, however, I was too busy stuffing my face and talking to analyze it; all I knew then was that it was the first time I had felt at all relaxed and halfway normal in a week.

"I want to hear anything you want to talk about," Ken said, after the waitress brought our mushrooms. "If you'd like to talk about everything with your sister, you can. And if you'd rather not, we can talk about something else."

How on earth, I wondered, looking at him in gratitude and amazement, had Ken managed to stay single until now? I had heard him comment once that he just hadn't found the right woman yet. But he had a busy social life, I knew, unlike some of the rest of us, and it was hard to imagine, when they understood the kind of man he was, that all sorts of women hadn't done their level best to snag him. Or maybe they had and he really was waiting for some sort of romantic lightning to strike.

"I would like to talk about Cara, actually," I replied. And that was what we did.

I told him about what I had been through since her body was found—the trip to the morgue, the details, the funeral. We talked about the police investigation and the ransacking of Cara's apartment, a story Ken had missed even though he had been at the paper earlier.

"Thank God whoever it was was gone when you came in," he said, his voice echoing my own outrage and sounding an even larger note of concern. "That may have been a much closer call than you know."

"That's what Peterson said, too," I agreed, around a mouthful of coleslaw. "I was too mad about what I saw to think straight at the time, but later it was pretty unnerving to realize what might have happened."

Ken talked about Cara, too, whom he had met once when she came to the office to join me for a lunch in D.C., and then listened as I reminisced about our lives growing up as sisters. When I laughed about a funny memory, he laughed with me. When I teared up, he waited patiently. It was the best therapy I could have gotten. Until he brought up a sore subject.

"So did Chris make it down for the funeral?" he asked finally, over coffee. Ken had met Chris once at the paper's annual softball game, in which the news staff took on the business side, usually resulting in lopsided victories that alternated back and forth in yearly grudge matches and that always seem to result in as many injuries—sprained ankles, pulled muscles, and scraped knees and elbows—as points on the scoreboard.

"No," I said simply, not really wanting to go into it, "he didn't get down."

Ken looked appalled.

"Do you mean to tell me," he asked incredulously, "that he let you go down there for your sister's funeral all alone?"

"He was out of town on business and didn't get back in time," I offered lamely. Ken's reaction had just reinforced my own mystification with Chris's behavior.

"Not good enough," Ken pronounced. "If I had known he wasn't going to show, I'd have gone with you myself. Under the circumstances, you had absolutely no business being down there alone."

"Could we talk about something else?" I asked.

Ken looked at me closely, then changed the subject and asked about the upcoming memorial service.

He had never voiced any opinion of Chris based on their limited exposure to each other, and I had never asked for one. It was just as well, because I suspected that whatever opinion of him Ken had held formerly, it had just gone down several large notches.

In the parking lot after dinner, I returned the hug he had given me in greeting.

"I really owe you one for this," I told him. "I'll figure out how to repay you later, but right now I think I have to go have my stomach pumped. That chocolate-mousse cake and coffee, on top of everything else I scarfed down, just about did me in.''

Ken laughed. ''I wanted to do it, Sutton,'' he said. ''And if you need to talk again, we will. About your sister or anything else you want to discuss.'' I knew that last comment was a pointed reference to Chris and his apparent lack of attention, but I let it pass without a response.

Instead, I thanked Ken again, and we said our good nights. Ken pulled out of the parking lot ahead of me to go home to the house off Rolling Road in Springfield in which he lived alone. I puttered more leisurely back up Duke Street to my apartment building, relaxed from the good food and a few hours with a friend. Yet my doubts about Chris nagged, even through my mellow mood, and Ken's comments had not reassured me about whether things between Chris and me were okay.

A little while later I went to bed alone, still grateful to Ken for reaching out to me and wondering what was wrong with Chris. His vagueness on the telephone earlier, the awkwardness of that conversation still puzzled me. Though I knew we each had our own hang-ups about relationships, he had never made me feel uncomfortable before. Telephones aren't good for reading between the lines of a conversation because you lack all the other nonverbal cues that can say so much—body language, a facial expression, the truth in the eyes, the more subtle tones of voice that the telephone's electronic mechanism can't reproduce. There was something Chris wasn't saying, and I wasn't getting it.

How about ''Don't call us; we'll call you''?

I didn't bother to dignify the question with a response. But eventually I fell asleep, wondering if the little pimple on my soul might be right again.

Tuesday

Seven

The break-in at Cara's apartment was on the *News'* metro front the next morning. A police spokesman who was not Peterson had refused to speculate on whether the burglar was also Cara's killer or on what the motive for the break-in might have been.

"As far as we can determine, the only thing taken was some jewelry," the spokesman said. "Other than the timing, we have no evidence yet to connect the break-in to Miss McPhee's murder, but we haven't stopped looking."

Once I finished the paper and breakfast, I drove down to the post office on Pickett Street to pick up all the mail that had been held while I was out of town. In my car, I sorted through the stack. There wasn't a lot: a magazine, several bills, a couple of credit-card offers, and an envelope with Amy Reed's return address in Hilton.

It must be the copy of Cara's letter, I thought, remembering Amy's promise to send it. I tore the envelope open, glanced quickly at Amy's brief note, and hurriedly read the photocopied page:

Dear Amy,

I'm really missing you and Hilton these days. The Washington area is still an exciting place to live—so much to see and do—but I'm learning that the people aren't always what they seem to be. Not a very Cara-like comment, huh?

If I sound down, I suppose I am. I've just had some disappointments recently, in someone I thought I knew. But clearly I didn't know them nearly as well as I thought. And I'm arguing with myself over what to do about what I've learned. I've thought about talking it over with Sutton, but she probably would wonder how I could have been so blind. Her opinion of me means too much for me to want to prove how stupid I was. It's been pretty hard for me, realizing just how wrong I was about this person, and has made me wonder if moving here was really such a good idea. I've even wondered if I should consider coming back to Hilton, especially now. I'd miss Sutton if I left, I know. But the idea of going home has crossed my mind more than once in the last few days. Still, is it a good idea to run away from your problems?

Enough doom and gloom, however. . . .

The letter went on from there, for two more paragraphs of questions about Amy and how her pregnancy was progressing, and about people she and Cara knew.

In spite of the first part of this letter, don't worry about me, Cara had concluded. *I'll figure it out somehow. Take care of yourself. All my love. Cara*

I sat in the post-office parking lot and pondered the message from my sister. What on earth had been going on with her? I wondered.

She was right; it was a very un-Cara-like letter. She had been one of the most nauseatingly cheerful people I knew. She could always find the good side of almost any situation or person. In all the letters she had written me over the years, before her move to the Washington area, I never had received anything like the letter in my hand. Though I knew she must have had disappointments and heartaches along the way, she almost never let anyone else see them, not even me. Apparently, especially not me.

What kind of problem would it have taken for her to

have written a letter like this? Amy was right: something had been bothering Cara, and bothering her a lot. I reread the letter and read it still again, trying to get a sense of what was hidden behind her words.

She spoke of being disappointed in someone. My first thought was that it was me. But that didn't make sense, if she had thought about coming to me to talk about it. Obviously, it was someone else. But who? Cara didn't have a busy social life, at least not outside the Bread of Life Church and at least not to my knowledge. Although my knowledge where Cara was concerned was appearing to be far more limited than I had realized. Was it someone at the church? I wondered. Had something happened at work that had disturbed her?

Well, of course something did, Sutton. Where's your brain? What about that John Brant character?

I must be in a mental fog, I thought, if it had taken my voice to remind me of that. But the voice was right. It was clear from what Marlee Evans had told me that Cara had not welcomed John Brant's advances. Having the minister's son angry with her after she turned him down must not have been very pleasant, especially when she thought so highly of the father.

Still, I told my voice, I can't believe that Cara would have considered moving back to Hilton just because of one grabby womanizer. She was pretty and likable; it couldn't have been the first time she had to fend off an amorous or horny man. If she were uncomfortable enough to quit, she could have gotten another job in the area easily enough; she was an excellent secretary. I just didn't believe John Brant's testosterone fits would have been enough to make Cara question her own judgment and run back to Hilton.

There was something else here, I thought, something more upsetting for Cara than that. Why on earth hadn't she just told Amy what it was? How bad could it have been?

Bad enough to get her killed?

It was the thought that had been lurking in the back of my mind ever since my first reading of the letter. At some level, Cara's words had set off alarm bells, and my little voice finally had brought the alarm to the surface in words too blunt to ignore. Could Cara's murder have been something more than a random killing? Was it connected somehow to the disappointment to which her letter so obliquely referred?

The idea that Cara had been targeted deliberately was not one I had considered seriously until now. The police, after all, seemed convinced that she had been in the wrong place at the wrong time. It happened to people in and around Washington on a daily basis. But now the question had occurred to me, and now it seemed very important to know the answer.

What the hell could have happened that would have been threatening enough to someone to cost Cara her life but that she would have kept secret from me?

If there was something, whatever it was, you know perfectly well why she wouldn't have told you.

Yes, I thought, I probably do. I was Cara's big sister, the one who went out into the world first. And never looked back. Cara had said to me more than once that she wished sometimes she were more like me.

"You never doubt yourself," she had explained. "It would never occur to you that there's anything in the world that you can't handle. You're so capable. Nothing scares you."

She was wrong, of course, as I had explained to her then. I had doubts, just like anyone else. But as a reporter, I had learned to look confident on the outside, no matter what might be going around inside my head.

And she had been wrong that nothing scared me, I thought as I went back inside the post office and used the lobby photocopier to make a copy of the letter for Detective Peterson. This letter scared me, and I didn't know why.

On the drive to Cara's apartment, I paged Peterson. As I pulled into the apartment parking lot my cellular phone rang.

"I have something I think you need to see," I told Peterson after he identified himself.

"Something from your sister's apartment?"

"No, a letter. From Cara, to her best friend in Georgia. The friend mentioned it to me at the funeral, because she thought something was wrong, but I just got a copy in the mail this morning."

"What does it say?" Peterson wanted to know.

"Nothing real specific. It's more the whole tone. You need to read it to see what I mean, but I think something happened with somebody she knew, something that she was worried about."

"Where are you now?"

"I just got to her apartment."

"I should be able to get over that way before lunch. I'll want to pick up a copy of the letter from you."

"I'll be here. And I've already made a copy for you." We hung up.

I got out of the car and walked back up to the rental office to get the key to Cara's apartment. Charlie the Manager was in and immediately volunteered to go back to the apartment with me to make sure it was safe. I couldn't imagine that Cara's killer was there this morning; he had tossed the place pretty thoroughly the first time. But I acquiesced because I thought it probably would be quicker than arguing with Charlie over whether I needed an escort.

"I think you'll be okay," Charlie said as we walked down the sidewalk toward Cara's building. "I had the lock changed last night after the police finished, just to be sure whoever it was couldn't get back in, at least not without a lot more trouble this time." He handed me a new key.

"I'm sure I'll be fine," I told him. Not because the lock was changed, I thought, but because the killer already had whatever he had wanted from the apartment.

Or he knows by now that whatever he was looking for wasn't there.

That comment almost brought me to a halt, not only because of the implications, but also because I couldn't believe that my mind had been so out to lunch that I hadn't thought of the possibility until now. But it was a perfectly logical question, especially if one entertained the idea that

Cara had not been a random victim. Could the person who wrecked the apartment have been looking for something specific rather than just anything of value? What could Cara possibly have had that was worth killing her over?

A logical question, perhaps, but I couldn't find answers that made any sense.

Once Charlie assured himself that the apartment was empty, he helped me carry the packing boxes up from the car.

"Now you lock the door behind me," he said from the doorway, "and if you need anything at all, you just call or come to the office."

"Thanks, Charlie," I said, meaning it. "You've been a big help."

"Your sister was a nice person," he said and closed the door. Explanation enough, I thought, especially where Cara was concerned. All her life, her sweetness had motivated people to want to keep her happy, to go out of their way to do things for her. At least until someone had gone out of his way to kill her.

I walked over and threw the dead bolt on the door to put Charlie's mind at ease, and then I gathered my wits and my self-control to tackle the jumbled remains of the short life of Cara McPhee.

A couple of hours later a knock on the door brought me back from a teary memory prompted by the stack of *Hilton High Lights*, the high school yearbooks Cara had collected. I went to the door and saw through the eyepiece that it was Detective Peterson. Figuring he could pass Charlie's litmus test if anyone could, I let him in.

Peterson eyed the boxes I had packed and stacked in the living room. By the time he arrived, I had finished with the sorting and packing in the front room, the kitchen, and the bathroom, and finally was working my way through the bedroom.

"Anything else missing?" he asked, also taking in my red eyes and nose.

"Not that I've noticed," I told him, "but of course I might not."

"Right. So let's see the letter you called me about."

I went to my purse on the sofa, whose cushions I had restuffed into the covers, and took out the copy I had made for him. I handed it to Peterson and collapsed onto the sofa, suddenly tired from all the bending and packing. Peterson sat down in the side chair, his arms propped on his thighs, and read the letter through once, then again.

"Not much in the way of details, is there?" he asked when he finally looked up at me.

"None," I agreed. "But the whole tone of the letter bothers me a lot. There was something wrong. And now, after thinking about it, I have to wonder why Cara wouldn't have told Amy, who was her best friend, what it was, even if she had been reluctant to tell me. Could she have been afraid to say more?"

"Mmm," Peterson said noncommittally, and studied the letter some more, his forehead wrinkled into a frown of concentration. After a few minutes he folded the letter up.

"All right if I take this with me?" he asked.

"Sure, if you think it will help."

"I'll be frank with you, Sutton," he said, putting the letter into the inner pocket of his jacket. "I really don't see anything here that gives us a single new thing to go on. Obviously, your sister wasn't happy, but that happens to a lot of people who move to the area from small towns."

"But surely it tells you more than that. Can't you tell from reading it that she was more than just homesick? Something happened. I know it did."

"You may be right, but where's the evidence? Where are the specifics? We're following up on every little lead we get, but there's nothing there to tell us where to look. We've talked to the people at the church and here at the apartments more than once. We haven't found a thing to give us a direction."

I gritted my teeth. How do I get through to him? I wondered. How do I make him see what I see there? How do we ever find who killed my sister? I was frustrated, and I don't handle frustration well. I lost my temper.

"I'll tell you where to look for starters," I said angrily, standing up and starting to pace back and forth. "Why don't you check out John Brant, the minister's son at the church where Cara worked. Apparently he couldn't keep his hands off Cara and wasn't real happy when she threatened to complain to his father. Maybe he couldn't take no for an answer. Maybe you should find out just how mad at her he was for turning him down. You're the police. Isn't that your job?"

I regretted the words and the anger as soon as they were out, but it was too late. Peterson's face already had hardened into lines that told me he was working to control his own temper. He stood up as well, but his demeanor was a lot calmer than mine.

"I think I should get back to work now," he said, moving toward the door.

I realized how stupidly I had behaved and followed him. "Hey, look, I'm sorry," I said, holding my hands out to either side in a gesture of culpability when Peterson stopped at the door and turned back to face me. "I don't mean to take it out on you. I know you're working hard on this. I just can't accept that we might not ever find out who killed her."

Peterson looked down at me. "Just a couple of things," he said finally, his face and voice expressionless. "Just so you can put your mind at rest, we have checked out John Brant. The Evans woman told us he had the hots for your sister, which made him worth looking at as a possible suspect. But he was at a Fairfax restaurant the night Cara was killed, and the people with him as well as the restaurant staff all back up his story. He may have had a thing for your sister, but he didn't kill her."

"Oh," I said with the brevity of chagrin and embarrassment.

"We also checked out the other people at the church who worked with her, right down to the maintenance staff. Even turned up a record for that Barlow guy. He's done time for bank robbery and some other things. But Brant vouches for

Barlow and says Barlow was at his house for dinner that night. So Barlow's got an alibi, too. And with the exception of one poor schmuck who worked on the grounds and who turned out to be an illegal alien from Mexico, to which he's being sent back as we speak, everyone else at the church comes up clean. Right up to Brant himself.''

I just nodded. What could I say?

''And finally,'' Peterson went on, ''you ought to be careful how you play detective. If you are right and your sister was killed deliberately, if something happened that got her into trouble like you think, you could find yourself in the same sort of trouble if you say the wrong thing in front of the wrong people. It's a bad habit for amateurs to pick up.''

He walked out the door and down the steps. I watched him through the open door until he reached his car, and then I closed the door and locked it.

''Shit! Shit! Shit! Shit!'' I said, standing in front of the door and softly banging my head on it.

Way to go, McPhee! It was my little nemesis. *You not only look like a hysterical female, but you managed to piss off the lead detective on your sister's murder!*

''Thanks for the news bulletin,'' I told it. ''Now shut up!''

I turned and walked tiredly back to Cara's bedroom to finish the packing. My voice was right, of course, if a little late. The damage was already done. I'd have to try to patch things up with Peterson. But I also knew I had no intention of stopping my search. Not now, not when I was convinced that there was meaning in Cara's letter, meaning that related somehow to her murder. Somebody killed her for a reason. Okay, so maybe it wasn't John Brant with his narcissistic ego. Or Al Barlow with his prison record and his lousy taste in clothes. But the person was out there. I hoped the police would find him, but I wasn't going to stop until someone found out who killed her and why, even if I had to do it myself.

Eight

It took two trips in my VW Beetle to the Salvation Army store on Little River Turnpike in order to haul over all the boxes of Cara's things that I decided to give away. While I was there I also made arrangements to donate all her furniture, which the Salvation Army would send a truck to pick up. I gave the clerk I spoke with the phone number at the apartment rental office in order to make the arrangements. I told Charlie, when I made my last stop at the Easton Arms to return the apartment key, that someone from the Salvation Army would call him to arrange a pickup time and that they would be taking everything left in the apartment. Finally, I was on my way back to my own apartment with the three remaining boxes, each filled with things that had been special to Cara. The afternoon had warmed up considerably. My car had no air-conditioning. I was hot and tired and angry and frustrated. It had been an exhausting day, and tomorrow I expected to have to go back to work.

I decided that what I needed more than anything at the moment was a yoga class. I kept my five-foot, eight-inch frame in some sort of shape through regular sessions on my NordicTrack and through yoga classes whenever I could squeeze them in, preferably two or three times a week. It had been almost two weeks since I had gotten to a class, and I was needing one badly. I fully expected to find that every muscle in my body had tightened up during the time I had taken off.

I had begun practicing yoga in Tallahassee, primarily as a way to keep myself flexible. Long hours of sitting at a desk in front of a computer or in interminable school-board meetings had taken a toll on my body in terms of back problems and headaches, and a chiropractor friend had suggested that yoga might help. So I had signed up for a class and soon became a convert. Initially, there was nothing philosophical or mystical about my enthusiasm for the discipline. It was simply that it worked. My back problems and headaches went away, and my body seemed to function better than it ever had. Eventually, I realized that the yoga also had other effects, not the least of which was its ability to energize me when I was tired and to soothe and relax me when I was too wrought up to sleep. And I found it seemed to fine-tune my mental processes as well. More than once, as I lay in the total relaxation of Corpse Pose or sat in the meditative silence of Lotus, I had felt my thoughts effortlessly fall into place involving some question I faced—whether about a story I was covering, some important personal decision, or a necessary insight into myself. All the good things I got from yoga were habit-forming, in the best possible sense, and I felt the lack when I was too busy to get to a class every few days.

I looked at my watch and saw that I probably could just make Teresa's four o'clock class. I swung in at my apartment in Landmark just long enough to change into a leotard and tights, over which I threw a T-shirt and jeans shorts, before heading into Alexandria.

Teresa, my yoga teacher, lived in Alexandria's Rosemont section, just off Commonwealth Avenue. She had converted the entire upper floor of her 1930s-something house into a yoga studio, where she taught a variety of daytime and evening classes. Teresa had left her job as a registered nurse about ten years ago, after the back injuries from a car accident had almost crippled her. It was the discovery of yoga that had rehabilitated her back and provided her with a whole new career. Her own centeredness, which she attributed to her years of regular yoga practice, made her a popular teacher and, I suspect, amplified the positive mental effects that her students experienced in her classes.

Too bad you can't keep her with you all the time, my little friend piped up as I turned into Teresa's driveway and pulled into the parking area she had created in back. *If we could keep you calm on a regular basis, you might not do dumb things like fly off the handle at that detective.*

I know it was dumb, I thought back at my voice, but I was annoyed and frustrated.

Chronic conditions where you're concerned.

I gave a mental snarl and grabbed my gym bag from the passenger's seat.

The little jerk wasn't saying anything I didn't already know, of course, but it didn't make me feel any better to hear it again. I did regret going off at Peterson, and I was unhappy that none of my excuses fully explained why I had lost control. As I climbed the exterior stairs that led directly to Teresa's yoga studio, I relegated my confusion to the back of my mind, a place that sometimes gets pretty crowded, for later consideration.

Some ninety minutes later, however, as all my muscles sank into the floor in the mental and physical cleansing of Corpse Pose, or Savasana, I had a sudden understanding of the real source of the frustration that I had taken out on Peterson. I was angry at everything and everyone—at Cara's killer, at fate, if there was such a thing, at the universe—angry that I hadn't had a chance to say good-bye. Most of all, I was angry at myself.

Corpse is a position of total relaxation, usually done at the very beginning or end of a yoga session. As you lie on your mat with your arms at your side, palms up, eyes closed, you consciously relax each set of muscles in the body from head to toe, muscles that have been stretched back and forth and are happy just to lie there. As I worked to empty my mind of all thoughts, I remembered that my last conversation with Cara had been about mundane, meaningless things. Work, dinner, the need to wash my car.

But I hadn't told her how much she meant to me, how much I loved her. In fact, I couldn't even remember the last time I had said it. And now she was dead, and I never would have the chance to say it again, to explain what a gaping hole had been ripped in my life by her absence. All the things I could have said, should have said, and hadn't. And now never could.

You're just like that guy you're sleeping with.

The fact that my voice could intrude even as I was supposed to be emptying my mind of thoughts showed how much I had needed the yoga class. I didn't encourage it by answering back, but the observation made me feel even worse than before.

Had I been as negligent of Cara as Chris suddenly had become of my own feelings? Was I as locked inside myself as he seemed to be, withdrawing when someone else reached toward me? I certainly hoped not, but the fact that there might be any grounds for comparison just made me angrier at myself.

I was so filled with regret for the time that I never could get back that I could hardly bear it. Although my mind could stand outside my anger in the objectivity of Corpse, I saw that I was furious with myself for having been so careless of the person I loved most in the world. My only salvation, my only hope of living with my anger—and my anguish—was to find Cara's killer. I had lashed out at Peterson in my frustration that something or someone might keep me from finding the answer, which would condemn me to a lifelong hell of regrets.

Finally, I could see the shape and power of what drove me. I wanted answers, in part to ease my own conscience. I didn't expect the need for those answers to disappear with my new understanding of what was wrong with me, but at least I now knew what it was I was feeling. The anger wouldn't leave me, I knew, until Cara's murder was solved and someone was held to account. But at least now I could try to focus the anger at Cara's killer, where it belonged, instead of letting it scorch everyone around me—including me.

• • •

By the time I got home to sit out on my small balcony, catching the breeze that wafted by at fourteen floors up and eating the salad that I had picked up from the salad bar at the Giant supermarket off Van Dorn Street, my brain was working full-time again. Ironically, my insight into my anger at the end of the yoga class had helped calm the turmoil I had carried around since the day I learned Cara was dead. I was thinking a little straighter now, feeling a little better, but I still wanted answers as much as ever. I was more determined than ever to have them.

I read Cara's letter to Amy again, trying to find a place to start in figuring out what connection her cryptic comments had, if any, to her death. If there was a connection, where would I even begin to look to find it?

Eventually, I decided the logical starting point was where Cara spent most of her time: the Bread of Life Church. Okay, so John Brant and Al Barlow were off the list. But the church staff were people who knew Cara pretty well, who spent a lot of time with her. Maybe someone there knew something that would point me in the right direction. Marlee Evans, for example. Considering how much time the two of them had spent together, perhaps Cara talked more to Marlee than she had to me. Marlee was quite a chatterbox. I decided to start with her.

I took my empty plate and glass into the kitchen, refilled the glass with fresh lemon and more iced tea, and took it and the cordless kitchen telephone out into the dining area, where I could look out the windows and enjoy the fading afternoon light that came through. I dialed the church office, expecting to get the answering machine. Instead, Marlee answered on the third ring.

"Bread of Life Church. This is Marlee. How may I help you?"

"Marlee, it's Sutton McPhee. I didn't expect to find anyone there at this time of day."

"Oh, hi, Sutton. It's good to hear from you again. I was just finishing up some things here that Cara had been working on."

"Look, I don't want to keep you, but do you have ten minutes to talk? I need to ask you some questions about Cara."

"Sure," Marlee said. "You know I'll help in any way I can."

"I've learned recently that Cara was upset about something," I went on, "that there was someone she was having a problem with. Whatever it was, it bothered her enough that she had even thought about going back home to Georgia. So I'm trying to figure out whether or not it might be related to what happened to her. If I could find out what she was unhappy about, maybe I could at least rule it out as having any connection to her murder."

"That makes sense," Marlee said agreeably.

"You told me about her problems with John Brant," I went on. "The police already have eliminated him as a suspect in her death because he was with friends the night Cara was killed. But I thought you might know whether there was anything else unusual that had happened in the last few months, anything you might have seen or that Cara might have mentioned to you. Anything that seemed to be bothering her more than usual."

"Nooo," Marlee said, thinking as she answered. "I can't think of anything like . . ." She paused. "No, wait, there was one thing I just remembered, but I don't see how it could have anything to do with Cara being killed."

"It probably doesn't," I told her, "but fill me in anyway, just so I can rule it out."

"Well, this was about three or four weeks ago. It involved Nash Marshall."

Nash Marshall. The name rang a bell, but it took me a few seconds to track down the information in my brain.

"You mean the ElectroTech guy?"

"That's right. The one who died in the car wreck."

Nash Marshall, I remembered, was the CEO of a Fairfax-based company that specialized in the research and development of high-tech medical diagnostic equipment. Some three weeks before Cara was murdered, Marshall had been on his way home from the office late at night and had died in a fiery one-car accident on the Fairfax County Parkway. Police never could determine exactly what caused the accident, but speculated that he might have lost control of his car while swerving to avoid a deer. Deer are one of the very real hazards of driving in the rapidly growing but still heavily forested northern Virginia suburbs and are especially numerous along the less developed stretches of highways such as the new cross-county parkway.

"Mr. Marshall was a member of our church," Marlee went on, "so of course people here were upset when he died. But Cara seemed to be as upset as anyone about it, and I remember it surprised me because I didn't think she knew him very well. He hadn't come to church much in the last year."

"Why not?"

"I don't really know, but these things happen. Sometimes people get real interested in a church at first, and then after a while they lose interest and go someplace else. But in all the time Cara worked here, I don't think she could have seen him more than two or three times."

"So why would she have reacted so strongly to his death?"

"I think it must have been because of the argument."

"What argument?"

"The one she overheard between Mr. Marshall and Reverend Brant. You know how Cara was. She wanted everyone to get along. And she always thought so much of Reverend Brant that I just figured maybe it bothered her to think that he and Mr. Marshall had had an argument just before Mr. Marshall died."

"Did you overhear the argument, too?" I asked hopefully.

"No, not really. I was on the way out the door to go down to one of the Sunday-school rooms when Mr. Marshall came into the office. He looked real unhappy about something. I spoke to him and he just ignored me, walked right into Reverend Brant's office without asking if it was okay or even knocking. Thank heaven Reverend Brant was alone. Mr. Marshall closed the door, and I went on out."

"But Cara was in the office?"

"Yes, she was," Marlee said.

"So then what happened?"

"Well, I was coming back up the hallway a few minutes later when I saw Mr. Marshall go storming across the foyer and out of the church. I hurried back up to the office to explain to Reverend Brant that I hadn't been able to stop Mr. Marshall from barging in the way he had. And when I walked in, I saw Reverend Brant over at Cara's desk. I couldn't hear what he was saying to her. He was sort of leaning over her and speaking softly, but she looked—well, not right. She was pale and tense looking."

"So what did Reverend Brant say when you came in?"

"I started trying to apologize, but he just said to forget it and went back into his office and closed the door."

"And what about Cara?"

"She got her purse out of her desk and left. She didn't say a word, just left."

"Had she ever left like that before?" I asked.

"No, never. It wasn't like her at all. I even asked Reverend Brant about it when he came back out of his office."

"And what did he say?"

"He said that he and Mr. Marshall had had a disagreement that had gotten a little heated, and that it had really upset Cara to hear them arguing. So he had told her to take the rest of the day off. I asked Cara about it the next day, and she wouldn't talk about it at all. So when Mr. Marshall died and it seemed to bother her so much, I figured it was the argument thing again."

As I listened to Marlee's story there were a hundred different questions going through my head. If Marlee was right, and Cara barely knew Nash Marshall to speak to, why had his death been so upsetting for her? Did she know him a lot better than Marlee realized? It was doubtful. I thought I remembered from the news stories when he died that Marshall had a wife and some kids. And that he was a middle-aged guy, probably at least twenty years older than Cara. He didn't sound like her type, and I would have bet everything I had that there was no way Cara would knowingly have been involved with a married man. So if it was the argument that had disturbed her originally, what had the two men argued about? Was it the fact of their arguing that had bothered her, or something she had heard them say?

Perhaps, I thought, it would be worth my time to go back and reread the stories about Nash Marshall. And while I was at it I might as well find out what I could about Reverend Brant. He had told the police that he was at home having dinner with Barlow when Cara died, and I couldn't think how any of this could be connected to Cara's murder. But, reporter that I am, I figure it's always best to turn over all the rocks.

"Well, you've been very helpful, Marlee," I said. "I think you're right that it doesn't seem to have anything to do with what happened to Cara. But I appreciate you telling me about it. There is one thing, though."

"What's that?" Marlee asked.

"I know that everyone there is very interested in what's happening with finding the person who killed Cara, but I really need for you to keep this conversation to yourself for the time being. I don't think it has any bearing on her death, but I wouldn't want anyone getting the wrong ideas about where the police are looking. For the church's sake and all."

"Oh, yes, I see what you mean," Marlee agreed. "Well, don't worry, Sutton. I won't talk about it."

"Not even with Reverend Brant, please. If it looks like there is some connection, I'll speak with him about it then. But there's no point in worrying him for no reason."

"Okay."

Keeping things to herself might be easier for Marlee to say than do, I thought, but I could only hope that she would try to squelch her natural chatty inclinations.

I thanked Marlee again and promised to see her on Saturday at the memorial service. Then I went to the kitchen to hang up the phone and refill my glass. It was time to sit down and think hard about where to go from here.

Wednesday

Nine

The first place I had to go was back to work the next day. As I walked into the newsroom I realized how glad I was to be there. My ennui over the school beat notwithstanding, I realized I had missed the office and the only slightly controlled chaos that a newsroom can be—although it was relatively calm at the moment. The first local copy deadline at 6:45 P.M. was still more than eight hours away. That meant a handful of editors and reporters were in, but things wouldn't really heat up until late in the afternoon, when the rest of the editing staff arrived and the other reporters began wandering back in from their coverage of daytime events.

There was no sign at the moment of Rob Perry or of Mary Blaine, the general-assignment reporter Rob had pulled in to cover the suburban Virginia schools while I was away. Rudy Black, the temporary reporter on the Fairfax County cops, was at his desk, however, so I stopped by to check in with him.

"Hey, Sutton, you're back," Rudy said, smiling, when he looked up and saw me crossing the newsroom toward him.

"Hi, Rudy," I replied. "Yeah, I'm back. I finally got Cara's stuff packed up yesterday and out of the apartment. I figured work would help me keep my mind off things.

And speaking of things, any more developments with the cops?''

"About your sister? No, nothing. I checked with Peterson this morning about the apartment, but the evidence guys haven't come up with anything helpful.''

"I didn't expect they would,'' I told him. "Whoever did this knows enough not to leave fingerprints all over the place.''

"Yeah, the cops are pretty frustrated over it,'' Rudy agreed.

"They're not the only ones. So would you keep me posted if you hear anything?''

"Sure thing, Sutton.''

"Thanks, Rudy. I appreciate it,'' I told him, and I did. It gave me another ear to the ground where the police were concerned. And now that Peterson was put out with me, I figured I might need all the friendly ears I could get.

During my long afternoon thinkfest the day before, one of the people I had decided to go to for help was Cooper Diggs, the *News'* head research librarian and a computer-phile and hacker. Cooper had been told in no uncertain terms to confine his hacking to his own time, I knew. But that didn't mean there wasn't plenty of useful information that he could get for me through legitimate channels. And if I needed more clandestine help, I suspected he would be up for whatever electronic snooping I needed done outside the office.

When I arrived at Cooper's corner of the second-floor library, where he had laid claim to extra space that once had housed research interns, he was wearing his usual path from the two computers he used to a printer/fax-modem/copier. He had a chair, of course, but I rarely saw him sitting in it. Most of the time he walked, back and forth across his area. Cooper said it kept his blood circulating and his brain working up to speed, but it drove the other two library staffers crazy. That little idiosyncrasy, coupled with the fact that he could extract more information from the electronic ether in two hours than most people could in two days, explained how he had managed to convince the powers that be to create his own personal fiefdom within the library. A set of tall office dividers gave him a modicum of privacy and kept his constant movement from distracting the rest of the staff.

I stuck my head around the end of a divider and knocked. Cooper stopped in mid-stride and turned in my direction, a concerned smile on his face.

"Hey, Sutton," he said, walking over with the surprisingly graceful and always appealing amble that I've noticed on many tall, lanky men who are not self-conscious about their height.

"I need your help, Cooper," I told him.

"Name it," he said, pulling out his desk chair and offering it to me. He, however, chose to prop his lean frame against the desk on which stacks of files and computer printouts competed for space.

Cooper Diggs gave the lie to just about every stereotype ever promulgated about computer jockeys. There was nothing nerdish about him. No glasses with tape around the frames. No pocket protector full of pens. No pizza gut from too many junk-food meals at the computer terminal. Instead, Cooper looked like what he was: the tastefully dressed eldest son of an upper-class family whose antecedents went back more than two hundred years in a small South Carolina town near Charleston. He wore immaculately clean and perfectly pressed white shirts whose roominess spoke of Brooks Brothers or J. Press, tucked neatly into gray pin-striped suit pants and set off by maroon-and-navy-striped suspenders and a similarly colored silk tie. On an oak coat tree in the corner hung the jacket that went with the pants. He spoke with the lilting accent of his roots, with the perfect grammar and diction of an educated man delivered in the slow, sweet vowels of the deep South. His longish blond hair, which he constantly raked back with his fingers, and his blue eyes could have belonged to a California surfer. If you saw Cooper on the streets of D.C. at lunchtime, you would assume he worked at some high-powered law firm in one of the many marble-foyered buildings scattered throughout the power districts of the capital.

In fact, although he had studied both library science and computers in college, he had dropped out before completing his degree. That helped explain why his relationship with his family, which boasted several attorneys and physicians, was rather strained and why he was in the newspaper's library and not with some up-and-coming computer company. But here again, appearances were deceptive. His title at the *News* belied not only his expertise, but also, I suspected, his salary. For the truth was that Cooper's slow-spoken manner was less an indicator of what went on beneath the hair than was his inability to sit down. Behind those blue eyes was one of the fastest, sharpest minds I had ever met. A lot of reporters at the paper owed significant portions of the information in their best stories to Cooper Diggs's abilities.

"I need background on some people," I told him. "It may or may not have something to do with my sister's murder. I won't know until I see what comes up."

Unlike Marlee, there was no need to ask Cooper to keep it to himself. It went without saying with Cooper that whatever he was working on for any particular person, no one else on the staff would hear about it.

"I spent my first eighteen years in a family and a place where some of the biggest influences in your life are the family secrets that you don't talk about," Cooper told me once. "Secretive is my middle name." It was another reason reporters liked him, and in a perverse way probably helped explain his desire to travel the electronic highway to places he wasn't supposed to go.

I handed him the typewritten list I had put together at home the night before. On it were the names of Daniel Brant, John Brant, Al Barlow, Brantlow, Inc., and Nash Marshall. Cooper scanned the list and whistled softly. Given his job, I was sure he knew immediately who Marshall was, if not the others.

"Are you serious?" he asked incredulously. "I can't wait to read the story that goes with this," he said. "Nash Marshall and your sister's murder?"

"Actually, I doubt if there's any connection at all," I

said. "But his name came up in a conversation involving something my sister was worried about, and I thought I should find out more about him. Daniel Brant is the minister at the church where she worked. The other Brant is his son, and Barlow is his assistant of some kind or other. And as you can see from the company's name, Brant and Barlow own it."

"I'll do my best," Cooper said, folding the sheet of paper in half and putting it on the desk behind him. "I might have something before you leave today."

"I'll take whatever you can find," I told him. "I think it's probably a wild-goose chase or a needle in a haystack or one of those metaphors, but I figured it's smart to check it out and make certain there's nothing there. Oh, and I understand from the police that Barlow has a record. Bank robbery. Although he apparently has an alibi for the night Cara was killed."

"I'll call you as soon as I have something," Cooper assured me. "And by the way, Sutton, I was really sorry to hear about your sister. It must be pretty hard for you, losing her like that."

"I can't begin to tell you how hard. The only way I can stand it is to tell myself that I can help make sure they find the person who did it."

Cooper nodded in understanding.

"Thanks, Cooper," I told him as I got up to go back to the newsroom.

"Anytime."

Back in the newsroom, I saw that Mary Blaine had come in, so I spent the next hour getting a fill-in from her on what had been happening with the schools. There wasn't much. It was May, and over the next three weeks all of the school systems in the area would be getting out for the summer. There were a couple of controversial speakers scheduled at high-school graduations, but most of the arguments from the winter and spring, over the next year's school calendars, budgets, and teacher salaries, had been settled, at least until the fall.

Mary had ten years' experience on general assignment, which was what she wanted to cover. She was good and fast and knew a lot about a lot of things. Every time some editor tried to get her to consider one of the specialized beats, she declined, explaining that covering the same thing day after day would soon drive her to consider a career change. But there wasn't much in the way of beats that she couldn't handle with little advance notice, as long as no one expected her to do it permanently. I thanked her for filling in for me with no advance warning. Like everyone else, she offered her condolences and asked about the investigation. I gave her my now well-practiced answers. Then I went back to my desk and began a series of phone calls to follow up on a fight between the Fairfax County Parent-Teacher-Student Association and the school board over the school system's sex-ed curriculum.

At one P.M., Rob Perry came in, saw me at my desk, and pulled me into his office for an update on everything—Cara's case, my beat, my emotional state. I told him there was nothing new on the investigation, that I had talked to Mary Blaine and would have a story on the parent/school-board fight for tomorrow's paper, and that my emotional state was pretty frustrated at the cops' lack of suspects, at the idea that Cara's killer might get away.

Rob looked at me sagely. "And you feel some responsibility for finding the person who did it?"

"Well, yes," I answered. "She was my sister. The last real family I had. I loved her. How does she have peace, how do I have any peace if no one finds out why?"

"I know you, McPhee," Rob went on. "No matter what I say, you're not going to rest until either the police find the answer to that question or you do. I know you're probably out there right now, trying to conduct your own investigation. Just remember two things, okay?"

"And those are?"

"One, don't let whatever you're doing interfere with your job, which I know you won't."

"And two?"

"Not every murder is solved. You have to be prepared

for the possibility that in spite of the best efforts of the police and yourself, you may not ever know why or who."

"No," I said, shaking my head and standing up. "I'm not ready to accept that. If I can't find out who killed her, if I can't make sure that person pays for it, how good a reporter can I be?"

"I'll admit that's about the answer I expected," Rob said, shaking his head back at me, but a smile played around the edges of his mouth. "Go back to work."

At four P.M., Cooper called to say he had some articles for me to pick up. I told him I'd be right down.

"Well," Cooper asked, "do you want the bad news or the good news first?"

"Okay, I can talk in clichés just like the next person," I responded. "Give me the bad news first."

"Actually, it's not so much bad news as it is non-news," Cooper explained, handing me photocopies of several articles.

I scanned through them quickly. They were from a variety of area papers, including ours. Most were about Nash Marshall. He had had a fairly high profile in the business community over the last six or seven years, including appointed stints on a couple of regional boards, some chamber-of-commerce activities, and participation in a special advisory group on technology that the Fairfax County Board of Supervisors had set up at one point. All pretty much what one would expect from the guiding light of a large and successful local company. In fact, about the only thing that seemed at all odd about what I saw was that there was nothing very recent. The last article that mentioned him was from some eighteen months ago—until, of course, the stories about his accident and death in April. It was as if sometime in the last two years he suddenly had burned out on civic responsibility.

That final article from the time before he disappeared from the news was one about a ribbon cutting for the new building at the Bread of Life Church, the first in a series of expansion projects the church had been planning. Along with the article was a boring group shot of a whole host of folks holding scissors and standing behind a big ribbon draped across the doorway of the church. Cooper had highlighted two names, which appeared in both the article and the caption with the photo. The first name was that of Daniel Brant, who was to be expected, considering the article was about his church. The second was Nash Marshall, who, according to the article, had helped in a major way with the fund-raising for the building. So, I mused silently, in spite of both the argument that Cara had overheard and Marshall's loss of interest in the church recently, at one time he had been a strong supporter of Brant's. I filed that thought away in my mental folder and looked back up at Cooper.

"And the good news is?"

He gave me a big grin and picked up another set of articles from his desk, but held them tantalizingly out of my reach while he set the stage.

"That piece about the ground breaking was all I could find locally about Brant," he explained, enjoying the moment. "But it mentioned that Brant had his divinity degree from the"—Cooper reached over with his free hand and turned my arm so he could see the article about the church—"Holy Word Divinity College in Ypsilanti, Michigan. So, just on a whim, I called up the librarian at the *Ann Arbor News*, which is the closest daily paper for Ypsilanti. I decided to just give her your whole list, since it was short, and asked her to fax me copies of anything she found. Here's what came through just a little while ago." He ceremoniously handed me the articles, obviously quite proud of himself.

There were four of them, beginning with an article about the holdup, by two men in ski masks, of an Ypsilanti bank in 1980 and the subsequent arrest, trial, and conviction of one Alfred Reuss Barlow for the robbery. The article on Barlow detailed the fact that, at the time of his arrest for the bank robbery, he already had a record for burglary, assault, and receiving stolen property. He received a sentence of another five to ten years and was sent off to the state prison in Jackson to serve it. His partner in the robbery was never found, and Barlow adamantly denied his guilt or any knowledge of an accomplice.

With the article about Barlow's trial was a photo of the defendant being escorted into the Washtenaw County Courthouse by police. Even in the grainy reproduction from the fax machine, it was clear that it was a slightly younger-looking version of the Reverend Daniel Brant's current "assistant." Once more I looked up at Cooper, this time the surprise clearly written on my face. His grin was even bigger.

"You were right about his record," Cooper said. "But I'll bet you didn't know that he and Brant apparently are from the same area. And isn't he kind of an odd bird to be in business with a man of God?"

"I thought so when I met him," I said, looking at the articles again. "Now I know it wasn't my imagination."

"More like ESP," Cooper agreed.

"Thanks, Cooper. This is good stuff. I don't know what it means yet, but at least it gives me someplace to really start digging."

"Well, I wouldn't want to be in their shoes if you're looking into them, Sutton," he said, "but it sure is fun watching from the sidelines. If you need me to find anything else for you, just let me know."

"Oh, you can count on it," I said, feeling a little less helpless for the first time in days. I thanked Cooper and left, taking the articles with me to read in detail when I got home.

As I read and reread the articles Cooper had unearthed, at my dining-room table that night, it became obvious that while Detective Peterson had forewarned me about Barlow's record, he had not hinted at how extensive that record really was. Still, I felt that the real cipher in the picture was not Barlow but the Reverend Daniel Brant, and I had found nothing that would help me unlock the code to him. Doing a good turn for another was one thing, but to take on a man as unsavory as Al Barlow as a personal assistant and to go into business with him? That seemed to me to be taking Christian charity to the extreme, not to mention possibly tarnishing the reputations of both Brant and his church.

So the next logical question to answer seemed to be the question of who was Daniel Brant. I knew next to nothing about him. Based on the church groundbreaking article, I knew he was the head of a clearly wealthy and prosperous organization, one that had managed to attract at least one parishioner of the caliber of Nash Marshall and probably others. I knew the name of the divinity college where he had trained to be a minister. And that was about the extent of it.

The most important question, of course, was what any of this, as fascinating as it might be, had to do with Cara's murder. Probably nothing, I knew, but I didn't have anyplace else to look at this point. I figured I might as well keep tugging on the string in my hand.

Thursday

Ten

One of the first lessons a reporter learns, usually the hard way, is to question everything, to assume nothing, to take nothing for granted. I know of more than one reporter who suddenly acquired a new anal orifice, courtesy of some angry editor, for screwing up a story by making an unjustified assumption. And I also know of more than one major story that has been broken open by a reporter who went back to square one and started checking into the basics such as the credentials on a résumé, thereby unraveling a tissue of half-truths and outright lies invented by a public figure with things to hide. So that was where I decided to start when I got to work the next morning, in an effort to answer my questions about Daniel Brant and his relationship with the questionable Al Barlow.

A few seconds' effort on the telephone got me the phone number of the Holy Word Divinity College in Ypsilanti, Michigan. In another minute I was talking with a pleasant female voice that answered, "Admissions and records. This is Lacy Settle."

"Good morning," I told her. "This is Sutton McPhee. I'm a newspaper reporter in Washington, D.C., and I'm doing a profile of one of your graduates. I was hoping you could help me double-check the year he got his degree."

"Certainly," Lacy Settle responded. "What was his name?"

"Daniel Brant, B-R-A-N-T." Print reporters become compulsive about the spelling of names, since it can help avoid sometimes embarrassing—and potentially actionable—mix-ups.

"Just a moment," Lacy said, and I could hear the click of computer keys as she called up information.

"Are you sure he went here?" she asked a few seconds later.

"Why yes, at least according to his résumé."

"Well, that's very strange, then," she continued, "because I don't show any record of anyone by that name."

"Maybe Daniel is a middle name," I suggested. "What do you have under Brant?"

"Nothing. I do show a Brantley," she said, and then immediately added, "Oh my, that's interesting."

"What's that?" I asked, my ears pricking up at the tone of her voice.

"Well, his name is Daniel, too. David Daniel Brantley. Isn't that a coincidence?"

"Oh, how stupid of me," I said quickly, not wanting to make her suspicious of my motives. "I just looked back at my notes and the last name is Brantley. That must be him. What year did he graduate?"

"Just one second," she said, and more keyboard clicking went on at the other end of the telephone line.

"Apparently he didn't," Lacy Settle said finally.

"He didn't?"

"No. According to the records here, he was terminated as a student in his first year."

"Terminated? You mean he dropped out?"

"No," she explained patiently, "he was expelled."

My jaw dropped.

"For what?" I asked.

"If I had the information here, it would be confidential, but I don't see any reason listed. That was in 1969, you understand, and sometimes information from our earlier records got mixed up or left out when everything was computerized.''

"Is there a way to go back to the original records?" I asked hopefully.

"Sorry, no, they were destroyed a couple of years ago in a fire at the warehouse where they were stored."

My heart was pounding like a John Philip Sousa score.

"Well, thanks anyway, Lacy," I told her. "You've been very helpful."

"You're welcome," she answered. "Good-bye." I heard the connection break.

Slowly, I put the telephone back in its cradle. Not only was my heart racing, so was my brain. Reporters will tell you—and I've heard the same thing about cops—that many of us develop some sort of extra sense about stories, some kind of radar, if you will. The result is that sometimes we find ourselves in the position of knowing without any doubt that we have stumbled onto something significant, something that says there's more there, that one and one aren't adding up to two. Even when we can't articulate how we know, this sense is what keeps us digging and pushing until the picture comes clear, until we discover what the real story is. Right now my radar screen was going nuts. I didn't know yet what the conversation I'd just had meant, but my radar knew there was something out there. There was something wrong with the picture at the Bread of Life Church, and I knew I was going to have to find out what, even if for no other reason than to put my mind at ease that it had nothing to do with who killed Cara.

The next question, I decided, was who was this David Daniel Brantley who had attended the Holy Word Divinity College, at least for a short time, and was he the same person as Daniel Brant? I called down to the library.

"Cooper," I said, when he answered, "it's Sutton. Listen, I need you to make another call to your helpful newspaper librarian in Ann Arbor."

"Sure," Cooper said. "What's up?"

"I've got a new name for her to run through her archives. David Daniel Brantley."

There was silence on the other end for a beat of five.

"He changed his name, didn't he?" Cooper asked, sounding delighted. Cooper probably could have been a hell of a reporter in his own right, had he been interested. He met the requirements: curiosity, a wide streak of cynicism, and dog-with-a-bone tenacity when he was after some bit of information. I'd said as much to him on more than one occasion, but he always just gave me his easy grin and said he'd never survive the boredom of covering things like city-council meetings.

"That's what it looks like to me, too," I answered, smiling grimly to myself. "And Brant—or Brantley or whatever his name is—not only didn't graduate from the Holy Word Divinity College, but he also managed to get himself expelled the first year, for unknown reasons."

"So how did he get to be in charge of this church?"

"He started it himself and lied about his degree."

"Whoa!" Cooper exclaimed. "A sinister minister!"

I broke up. It felt good to laugh, to laugh out loud. I couldn't remember the last time I had found anything funny in the last two weeks. Somehow the laughter provided almost as much catharsis as all my recent tears had.

"Stop it, Cooper!" I said, once I could talk again. "The pulpit police are going to come and get you—if the lightning doesn't get you first."

"They can try," Cooper said. "Call you back as soon as I can."

I had nothing I needed to work on for tomorrow's paper until the evening, when I had to go out to Mount Vernon High School, just up the road from George Washington's former digs in the southern part of Fairfax County, and cover a graduation speech by one of the more controversial Supreme Court justices, who also happened to live in that school's district.

While I waited to hear back from Cooper I spread the copies of the articles he had given me out on my desk. There was something more here somewhere, I felt. My eyes went back and forth across the pages of small print. I found that my attention kept being drawn back to the articles about Nash Marshall—the articles about his accident and death, and his involvement with the Bread of Life Church.

As I wondered again why his death had upset Cara so much, I reread the accident stories and his obituary, which explained that he was survived by his wife, Phoebe, and two children, Samuel and Elizabeth. Perhaps, I thought, it might be worthwhile to talk to Phoebe Marshall. Although the police had a theory about Marshall's car accident, it was only a theory. Could it have been anything other than what the police thought? I decided to leave a little early for the graduation and make a stop out in Fairfax Station, one of the favorite nesting grounds of successful CEOs, where Phoebe Marshall lived.

Before heading out, I called Cooper back to let him know I'd be gone for several hours and gave him my cellular-phone number in case he came up with something in the meantime.

Finally, I made another phone call to redeem a favor I'd had outstanding for a year. I paged David Edwards, a Fairfax County police officer who works with the school system on crime prevention in the schools. The year before, I had done a very positive profile of Edwards and the program he spearheaded, and he had told me to call if I ever needed a favor. I suspected what I needed was a miracle, but a favor was a start. So I was calling.

"Sutton, it's David Edwards," he said when I answered my phone a few minutes later. "It's good to hear from you."

"Hi, David," I answered. "How are things with you?"

"Busy as all hell," he said. "If I had a kid these days, I swear I think I'd keep him home and teach him myself just to make sure he survived until his eighteenth birthday. And by the way, Sutton, I was really sorry to hear about your sister."

I guess word travels through the police grapevine just like any other.

"Thanks," I said. "It hasn't been easy, especially when we don't know who killed her."

"Yeah, that has to be rough," he sympathized.

"Listen, David," I said, wanting to change the subject, "I finally need to take advantage of that favor you promised me."

"I'll do my best," he said.

"I need criminal background checks on some people. And I need them soon and confidential."

For a moment there was no response.

"That's quite a favor," David said finally. "You do realize what you're asking is illegal and could get me fired?"

I hadn't.

"No, and I don't want to get you into trouble," I told him, "but I really need this information, and you're the only person I know to ask for help."

"Does this have something to do with your sister's murder?" he asked.

"It might."

Another brief silence while he thought over what I was asking.

"Okay," he said finally. "I'll get them for you, but you have to promise to keep them to yourself or you might have to support me while I find another job."

"No one will see them but me," I assured him.

"How many people are we talking about?"

"Five names."

"I should be able to manage that. Let's have the names."

I gave them to him: both the Brant and Brantley names, as well as John Brant, Barlow, and Marshall.

"Nash Marshall," David said. "Isn't that the high-tech guy who bought it in the car wreck a few weeks ago?"

"That's him. I don't expect you to find anything more serious than traffic tickets on him, but I have to be sure."

"And these others?"

"Barlow, I know, has a record. But I need details. I think Brant and Brantley are the same person, but I don't know whether there's a record under either name. His son I don't know about at all, but he's worth checking."

"Okay, Sutton, it may take me a couple of days, but I'll get this over to you as soon as I can."

"I can't thank you enough, David, especially now that I know what a risk you're taking to get this for me. The favor ball is definitely back in my court, so let me know if I can return it."

"Oh, I will," he said, laughing. "Take care, Sutton. You'll hear from me."

I hung up, gathered up the scattered articles from my desk, grabbed my purse, and left the paper to drive out to Fairfax Station.

Eleven

There was a "For Sale" sign on the lawn in front of Nash Marshall's impressive brick Colonial house, and that struck me as odd. Pretty fast work, I thought, considering the man had been dead less than a month. I assumed the memories must be so painful that Marshall's widow couldn't bear to live there any longer. Which just goes to show why I should make a point of remembering what Rob Perry always loves to say the first time a new reporter screws up a story and then says, "But I just assumed . . ." He gives them that old saw about assume making an ass of you and me. In fact, the "For Sale" sign in the Marshalls' front yard turned out to be a signal flag for a whole new set of questions.

I parked my car in the semicircular driveway and noticed that the yard looked a little ragged, that, in fact, it was overdue for a mowing and shrubbery trim. I pondered this incongruity as I walked up the brick-patterned sidewalk to the double stained-oak front doors, where I rang the bell. In a minute or so the door was answered by a thin, blond woman who looked to be in the process of coming apart at the seams. In spite of her slim build, her face was puffy, and as soon as she spoke, I picked up the sour smell of alcohol. That, combined with the bloodshot eyes, told me she already had spent a good part of the day crying or drinking—or both.

Under better circumstances, I probably would have been intimidated by her. Ordinarily, I suspected, she looked like the women you see all over the northwestern sections of Fairfax County, wives of successful businessmen, perfectly groomed and made up, their clothes from Talbot's and Saks, their days spent in volunteering for good causes, exercising at their health clubs, picking their children up from their private schools, and generally exuding absolute conviction of their superiority. But there was nothing intimidating about Phoebe Marshall now. She looked like she had found the short road to hell, and it was proving to be a very rough trip.

"Yes?" she said, stepping forward to stand in the doorway, the sort of defensive move women in urban areas learn to make when a stranger appears at their door, a move designed to make it more difficult, physically and psychologically, to get inside.

"Mrs. Marshall?"

"Yes?"

"My name is Sutton McPhee. I'm a reporter with the Washington *News*. I wondered if I might talk with you for a few minutes."

"I thought all you people already had said everything there was to say," she responded in irritation. I gathered that her experience with reporters thus far had not been entirely positive.

"I'm not here about your husband's accident, Mrs. Marshall," I told her. "At least not directly. I thought you might be able to help me with some information about my sister, Cara McPhee."

The woman looked at me blankly.

"She was a secretary at the Bread of Life Church, the one who was killed in the ATM robbery about ten days ago."

"Oh. Oh, yes, I remember hearing about it on TV." That seemed to sink in and clear her head a little. Her gaze focused on me more closely, as if only really seeing me for the first time. She looked me up and down. "She was your sister?"

"Yes."

She stepped back into the foyer. "Come in," she said, and opened the door wider to let me inside.

I stepped in after her. The house was what one would expect of a man in Nash Marshall's position. Large, elegant, tastefully furnished in expensive reproduction furniture in a traditional style. But as I followed Mrs. Marshall into her living room, I also noticed there was a layer of dust on the mahogany hall table, and scuff marks on the Italian marble foyer floor. The flowers in the Waterford vase on the table had long since lost their bloom, and I wondered what was happening in this house. I couldn't imagine that Phoebe Marshall didn't have a maid at least once a week, if not daily. Yet the whole house and the yard outside spoke of recent neglect, as if the people in it no longer had the heart to make even the minimum effort.

"Please have a seat," Phoebe Marshall said, dropping tiredly onto one of a pair of off-white sofas that flanked the fireplace on the wall opposite the living-room door. I crossed the dusky blue carpet and sat down opposite her.

"Now, what is it you think I can tell you?" she asked, her recent trauma apparently having worn the finer points of subtlety off her conversational skills. "I was sorry to hear your sister was killed, but frankly, I can't remember if I've ever even met her."

"I understand Mr. Marshall was very involved in the church. Perhaps he knew Cara better."

"What are you implying? Are you saying you think there was something between my husband and your sister?" she flared up at me.

"No, no," I told her quickly, not wanting to alienate her right off the bat. But it did occur to me that she seemed surprisingly touchy about her husband. "I just thought that he might have known Cara well enough to have mentioned it if he noticed anything out of the ordinary recently."

"Ms. McPhee . . ." she began.

"Please, call me Sutton."

"Sutton, my husband had not had much to do with the Bread of Life Church for months and months before he died. Even if there was something to notice, he wasn't there to see it."

"Well, that's the thing, Mrs. Marshall," I said. She didn't interrupt to ask me to call her Phoebe. "I had heard he didn't attend the church anymore, but I understand he was there at least once just before his accident."

"Oh? He never mentioned it to me."

"No? I guess I'm surprised, because I was told that he was very angry about something when he came to the church and that he barged into the office and got into an argument with Daniel Brant. Apparently something about that argument unsettled Cara a great deal, to the point that she left the office for the rest of the day. I was hoping you might have some idea why Reverend Brant and your husband were arguing."

"No," she said, shaking her head, which dropped an expensively highlighted clump of hair with noticeably brown roots into her eyes. "No idea. Maybe Daniel was trying to talk Nash into going back to church."

"It's none of my business, but can you tell me why you stopped attending?" I asked, hoping the reason might hold some clue to Brant and Marshall's argument.

"Nash just said he had decided it wasn't the church for him," she explained. "I didn't go very often anyway. I was raised Episcopalian, and I found the mind-set and the sermons to be a little too fundamentalist for my tastes. The children and I usually go to the Episcopal church in Falls Church. That's why we had his"—she hesitated, as if the words were difficult to say—"his service at the funeral home. I didn't think either church really was appropriate."

I suspected that in spite of the house's current neglect, appropriate probably had been quite important to Phoebe Marshall when her husband was alive.

"Did the police ever come up with a firm explanation for your husband's accident?" I asked, changing tacks. "Was there ever any reason to think it was something other than an accident?"

She looked at me hard again and gave me a bitter smile.

"For all I know, he killed himself," she said bluntly.

Well, that sure came out of left field, I thought as I quickly tried to pick my jaw up off the floor and to reorder my thinking.

"I never saw any suggestion to that effect in the stories," I told her after a moment. "Why would a man as successful and respected as your husband kill himself?"

She laughed. A laugh tinged with acid and anger.

"Because," she explained, her full mouth twisting around the words as if tasting something unexpectedly sour, "if he didn't kill himself, he damned well should have!"

"I'm sorry," I said, trying not to sputter. "I don't understand." That was an understatement.

"Neither do I," she responded. "You wouldn't think, looking around at this house and knowing who my husband was, that you're looking at a pauper, would you?"

I just silently nodded my head from side to side. This was definitely an unexpected turn in the conversation.

"He left us with nothing . . . nothing!" I saw angry tears pooling in the corners of her eyes. "The attorney called me in, a couple of days after the funeral. He was working on processing Nash's will and estate, and had a surprise for me. There was no estate left to process!"

"Nothing?"

"His life-insurance policy. It was a benefit through ElectroTech, so it wasn't the type of policy he could sell. For two hundred and fifty thousand dollars. That's all. All the rest was gone. The property. The stocks. The other life insurance. The children's college funds. Every goddamned thing we had. Probably close to two million dollars. He even took out a second mortgage on this house. And he never said a word to me about any of it. Not a word!"

I was finally beginning to collect my wits again. "May I ask you what he did with all that money?"

She laughed that bitter laugh again as tears finally overran the edges of her eyes and tracked down her cheeks, which were bare of the expensive and expertly applied makeup that I knew must once have been a requirement before anyone saw her.

"We have no idea," she said angrily, wiping the tears

away so hard that her hands left red finger marks on her fine-pored skin. "John, the attorney, hasn't been able to find a trace of it anywhere. It all just vanished!"

"Did your husband sell everything all at once? When did he do this?" I asked, wondering if perhaps he had been making plans to run away from home for some reason. No wonder she had jumped down my throat when she thought I was implying that Cara and Marshall might be having an affair. An affair with someone was certainly a possibility that must have crossed her own mind.

"John said Nash started selling things off just over a year ago. He apparently forged my name to all the paperwork to avoid telling me what he was doing."

"And your attorney didn't know about any of this?"

"He said not. He was pretty upset about it, too. I guess he was afraid I would think he knew what Nash had done or that he had been a party to it."

"Do you seriously think your husband might have committed suicide?"

"Well, look around you, Sutton," she answered sarcastically, waving her arms to take in the house and, apparently, all that it represented. "I have two hundred and fifty thousand dollars and two kids to support, and I don't know how to do the first thing except be a good corporate wife. I have to sell my house, which isn't worth much more than the two mortgages on it. I don't know where or how we'll live. I'll have to pull my kids out of their private schools. And somehow I have to provide for them, put them through college, and support myself for the next thirty-five or forty years off that money. Pretty soon Nash was going to be forced to tell me what he had done, because it was all gone. Suicide probably looked easier than facing his family!"

I was beginning to understand why the house looked neglected and why Mrs. Marshall might have resorted to heavy drinking in the wake of her husband's death. There was no longer any money for the maid—or, apparently, for anything else. And it was clear that Phoebe Marshall felt her life with her husband had been a lie, that the man she was married to was not the man she thought he was. She not only was dealing with the bleakness of a future of drastically reduced circumstances, but one of forever wondering why her husband had deceived her and left her and their children in such financial and emotional straits. Perhaps he really had killed himself rather than face her with the truth.

"Did you tell the police you thought Mr. Marshall's death might be suicide?" I asked her.

"And screw myself out of the life insurance, too? The policy had an exclusion for suicide. Besides, the police had already decided it was an accident and closed the investigation when we found out everything was gone. So what would be the point of reopening it? At least this way, my kids don't have to live with the stigma of suicide on top of knowing their father left them with nothing. I've explained our financial problems by telling them that their father's business was having difficulties and that everything was just turning around when he had the car wreck. I don't have the heart to let them know what he really did to us."

She had a point, I supposed. Knowing your father squandered away your future for unknown reasons and then took the coward's way out was not a particularly positive legacy for the children. Just then, my pager beeped, deep in the recesses of my purse. When I pulled it out, the screen showed Cooper Diggs's library extension. I stood up to take my leave of the widow Marshall.

"I have to get going now, Mrs. Marshall," I told her, "but I appreciate your taking the time to talk to me. I'm so very sorry about your husband and your situation."

She looked up at me bleakly from the sofa, where she continued to sit, her body language one of hopelessness and pain.

"Sorry I couldn't be of any help about your sister," she told me. "I have no idea what Nash was arguing with Daniel about, or why he was even there at the church, but then I don't know anymore why he did anything."

I thanked her again and said good-bye, then showed myself to the door and out to my car. As I pulled out of the driveway I took out my phone and called Cooper.

"It's Sutton," I said when he answered.

"I've found something I think you'll want to see."

"Are we going to play twenty questions?"

"Let's just say it probably would be wiser to discuss it in person rather than over a phone."

Shit, I thought, he's right. Even cellular phones could be tapped, nor was it uncommon for people to inadvertently get their cellular airwaves crossed and hear someone else's conversation.

"How late are you there?" I asked. "I've got a graduation to cover, so I won't be back until nine or ten."

"I've got nothing better to do tonight," Cooper said. "How about if I just hang around until you get here."

"Whatever you have must be good, but your lack of better things to do isn't saying much for your social life."

"What social life? It's too scary these days to have one!"

I laughed, but my laughter had an edge to it. I hadn't heard a word from Chris all week, not since I had called him on Monday night. I had to wonder whether I was doing so well in the social-life department either.

"I know what you mean," I said. "Okay, I'll stop by as soon as I get back to the paper."

"See you then."

I pressed the off button and tossed the phone on the passenger's seat. A few blocks from the Marshall home, I picked up Route 123 and took it south to the Lorton area, where I could jog across to Route 1 and over to Mount Vernon. And then I took a look at the questions that had been nagging at me since leaving Phoebe Marshall.

What the hell had Nash Marshall been up to? Had he really killed himself rather than come clean to his wife? And what had he done with all that money? Even if he'd had a gambling habit, that was a lot to lose in a year's time. And surely his wife would have had an inkling of that sort of problem. But she seemed genuinely surprised—and devastated—by what she had learned.

And there were still the questions about his argument with Daniel Brant. Had he confided in Brant about his money problems? Could they have argued because Brant urged Marshall to come clean with his wife about whatever it was he had done with the money? But that made no sense. Phoebe Marshall said her husband had stopped going to Brant's church months ago. Why would he have decided after all this time to confide in its minister? And why would any of that have bothered Cara so much? Nobody seemed to think there was any relationship between her and Marshall. So why would she care?

The same questions were still asking themselves several hours later when I pulled into the parking garage a block from the *News*, in which the paper rented parking spaces for its employees. And I still had no answers for any of them.

Twelve

It was actually pretty surprising, I thought as I walked into his cubicle, that Cooper Diggs could say he had no social life. It certainly wasn't because he couldn't have one if he wanted it. He was a good-looking guy with brains and a family with money. And he had one of the world's great grins, which currently was aimed at me.

Without a word, he handed me a sheet of paper from his desk. I read the brief verbiage:

> *Brantlow, Inc.*
> *c/o Harlan Bancorp*
> *Box 4009*
> *Grand Cayman Island*
>
> *P.O. Box 92045*
> *Springfield, VA 22152*
>
> *President: Daniel Brant*
> *Vice President: Alfred Barlow*
> *Secretary/Treasurer: John M. Brant*
>
> *Brantlow, Inc., is a privately held company chartered in the Cayman Islands and specializing in computer-system consulting.*

A fuzzy line of type at the top of the sheet, which was clearly a fax, said, *Corporations Office.*

I looked back up at Cooper.

"Can you think of one good reason," Cooper asked, obviously relishing my reaction, "why a man of the cloth would be an officer in an offshore corporation in the Cayman Islands?"

"Not a one," I told him. "Rich men and camels through needle eyes and all that. Where did you find this?"

"I talked to the folks in the state corporations office down in Richmond," he explained. "Companies doing business in Virginia have to register their names and their officers with the department. That"—he pointed to the fax—"is what they had on file."

"But what does the company actually do?" I wanted to know.

"Computer-system consulting, whatever that means. Apparently they don't have to give much more than a minimal explanation of what they do. The corporations office is a registry agency. Its primary job is to keep a list of companies that do business in Virginia, regardless of where their headquarters are. But it doesn't regulate the businesses, so they only have to file basic information. Officers, annual reports, articles of incorporation, the names of registered agents, stuff like that. With a privately held company like this one, there isn't even an annual report."

"Does it strike you as odd that they would be chartered in the Cayman Islands, instead of Virginia?" I asked.

"Depends on your point of view," Cooper replied. "If you had something to hide, it would make a lot of sense. Offshore corporations are favorites of people who have money they want to launder or that they don't want someone else—usually the IRS or a divorce-court judge—to know about. Of course, they're more often people like the Mafia and drug kingpins, not ministers."

"Jesus, Cooper," I said, leaning against the wall next to his desk and looking again at the fax, "who is this guy? And what is he really up to?"

"Sounds like a story to me."

"Yeah, whether there's a connection to Cara or not." I stood away from the wall and folded the sheet of paper in half. "I've got to get to my desk and write this graduation piece for the last couple of editions of tomorrow's paper," I told him. "But thanks for following up on this. Although, if I'm not careful, you'll be doing my job."

"No danger of that," Cooper said, standing up and taking his suit jacket off the coatrack. "I'd much rather be the power behind the throne."

I said my farewells and headed off to tell our readers about the advice for surviving out in the world that Justice Theron Polk had imparted to the graduating class of Mount Vernon High School. And to mull over the meaning of Cooper's latest find. The Reverend Daniel Brant, possibly aka David Daniel Brantley, definitely was assuming the proportions of a story of some sort. But did it involve Cara? I still didn't see how.

The phone on my desk rang just as I walked up and put my purse in the bottom drawer. It was Detective Jim Peterson.

"Long day?" I asked, noting the time on my watch and calculating just how fast I was going to have to write to make the deadlines.

"Criminals don't keep office hours," Peterson said, sounding as if he might have gotten over most of his earlier annoyance with me. "Although actually, I'm at home. I called your apartment earlier and got your machine, so I thought I'd try you at the office again. It's about your sister's car."

Cara's car, which she had bought used in Hilton several years ago, had been impounded by the police as part of the investigation of her murder.

"What about it?" I asked.

"Well, we're pretty much done with it, so I wanted to let you know we can release it back to her family."

"Oh," I said, feeling my heart tighten at the sudden mental image of Cara dead in that car. "Thanks for letting me know. Where do I go to get it?"

"Uh, that's the other thing." He hesitated. "I think you

might want to consider maybe selling it and letting the buyer pick it up.''

"Why?" I asked, stupidly.

Again Peterson hesitated before answering. "It's not in real good shape, if you know what I mean," he said. "We've processed it for evidence, but that didn't clean it up."

Only then did I get what he was telling me, that Cara's blood was still on the upholstery and wherever else it had fallen or spattered. It would be a graphic, appalling reminder of her death.

"Oh, God," I said, sighing. "What should I do about it?"

"I'd sell it to a car-auction company if I were you. There are several in the area. All you'll need to do on our end is let me know who you're selling it to, and I'll notify the impound about who'll be coming to pick the car up. The police impound is over on Woodburn Road in Annandale. This way you wouldn't have to go out there or see the car."

Would this nightmare never end? I wondered.

"Oh, and you'll need to give them keys if you have an extra set, since we never found the ones your sister was using. I'm sure the killer took them. It's why there was no sign of a break-in at the apartment."

I sat down in my chair, propped my head on one hand, and closed my eyes. No, it would never be over. I was certain that the pain and horror of Cara's murder would continue to ambush me forever. I opened my eyes again and reached for a pen.

"I think I'd better take your advice," I said to Peterson. "Can you give me a name?" I jotted down the three he rattled off and made a note to myself to make the calls first thing tomorrow. I thanked Peterson for the suggestion and hung up, weary and even more heartsick at the mental image I now had of what Cara's car must look like. I tried to lose myself in the banalities of Justice Polk's speech and to make the story at least somewhat interesting by putting it into the context of his controversial opinions. At one point I looked up to find Rob Perry standing in his office door and watching me with concern writ large on his face.

"Five minutes," I told him, giving him a thumbs-up and a feeble smile. Then I went back to my keyboard.

Once I finished the graduation story and sent it to the editing queue in the computer system, I sat back and argued with myself over whether to call Chris.

He did say maybe we would get together over the weekend, I thought, so I probably should call and find out if we were still on and for when.

Can you say "grovel"? It was my little buddy, never content to let one of my internal arguments go by without chiming in with another two cents' worth.

Can you say "butt out"? I asked back.

But was I groveling? Had I become desperate enough for human companionship that I had sunk to begging for it?

I'm not begging, I answered myself. I'm just wondering if we're going to see each other. We do have a relationship, after all. It's not like my calling him to check on Saturday-night plans is out of the ordinary.

So then why are you hesitating?

I was loath to concede it, but it was a good question. The answer, I knew, was that I thought I sensed misgivings on Chris's part. His reaction to the news of Cara's death, his lack of visible, tangible support when I really needed someone there had surprised me—and it had hurt. It was as if I had asked him for a marriage proposal, for God's sake, when I just wanted someone to hold me and tell me it would get better. But he had made himself noticeably scarce.

And now, I knew, the perverse part of me was taking over, wanting to force him into acknowledging his misgivings, to admit that he had fallen short. It was the same part of me that inevitably had come to the fore when Jack and I had argued. Jack would always clam up when he was upset, and I would be determined to make him say what was wrong. I would pick at him (okay, nag) until he finally would lose his temper completely and say what he thought in the harshest possible terms. I would glare at him in triumph, having forced him to admit that what he had been thinking was just as bad as I had suspected, and then we would have a screaming match that would leave us both sullen and silent for days.

It was just about the last thing on earth that I wanted to do with Chris Wiley. Yet I couldn't let it go when I knew that something was wrong between us.

I called.

"Hello?" he said, picking up on the third ring.

"It's Sutton."

"Oh, hi, Sutton. I was just thinking I should give you a call."

"Oh really?" I didn't know whether to believe him or not.

"Yeah, do you want to do dinner Saturday night?"

I sighed in relief. Once again, I thought, my imagination had been working overtime.

"That would be great," I answered.

"If it's okay, do you want to meet me at Copeland's at seven? I need to spend the afternoon at the office, but after dinner you could invite me out to your place for coffee."

I smiled. This sounded like the Chris I knew.

"I'll be there," I told him. We chatted for just a minute longer before hanging up. Feeling better, I gathered up my things and went home.

Friday

Thirteen

First thing the next morning, I looked up the number for Greenbelt Auto Auctions, one of the auction companies Detective Peterson had mentioned to me. The woman who answered the phone when I called told me what the company required in the way of paperwork—a title signed over to them and a copy of Cara's death certificate—and said she could have the driver stop by the paper to pick it all up, along with the keys, on his way out to the impound lot.

That reminded me that I didn't have a set of keys for Cara's car. I remembered Cara telling me, however, not long after she moved into the Easton Arms, that she had given a set of car keys to Gina in the rental office. It seemed Cara once had managed to lock herself out of her car, with her purse and her spare set of keys inside, one morning before she left for work. After that, she had given Gina the extra set of keys so she could get to them if she ever made the mistake of locking herself out again. In the shock of Cara's death and the trashing of her apartment, I had forgotten to ask for the keys back. I felt certain Gina had forgotten about them too, which meant she should still have them. So I drove out to the Easton Arms before heading into D.C.

"Oh my goodness," Gina said when I told her what I needed. Looking flustered, she opened a desk drawer and started sorting through its contents. "You're right," she said a minute later, looking at me and smiling in triumph, "I do still have them."

She pulled out a small manila envelope and laid it on the desk. I saw that it had Cara's name and apartment number on it in my sister's handwriting. My heart turned over at the sight of that familiar script.

"I'm so sorry I forgot about those," Gina said as I picked up the envelope, feeling the keys slide around inside with a clinking noise. "You had to make an extra trip back out here to get them. And I should have remembered them because Cara just used them last week."

"Did she lock herself out of her car again?" I asked.

"I guess," Gina replied. "It was one night the week before last. Friday, I think. She came in just as I was leaving and said she needed the envelope for a couple of minutes. I got them for her and left, so I guess she returned them to Charlie. That's probably why I didn't think about needing to return them to you."

"That's okay," I told her. "I'd forgotten them, too. I only remembered last night when the police called about her car. They're done with it, and I'm selling it. It's not something I want to have around reminding me of what happened to her."

I put the envelope in my purse, which already held the title to the car and a copy of Cara's death certificate, and thanked Gina. Hoping that I was closing at least one chapter in the seemingly endless saga of the aftermath of Cara's death, I went back to my car to drive through the tail end of rush-hour traffic going into the District up I-395.

Half an hour after I made it to the newsroom, a tall, thin black guy, who looked to be about nineteen, with a shaved head and wearing a Washington Redskins jacket over his jeans, found his way to my desk.

"You Sutton McPhee?" he asked, towering over me and removing the tiny headphones that had been in his ears. I nodded.

"I'm from Greenbelt Auto Auctions. My dad sent me for the stuff on the car you want picked up from the cops."

"Oh good," I said, getting my purse out of the desk drawer. "Thanks for doing this. It saves me a really unpleasant trip." I took out the things he needed and handed them to him. "Here's the title, which I've signed as the executor of her estate, and a copy of the death certificate. And here are the keys."

He put the paperwork down on the desk and tore open the envelope to check the keys, which he shook out into his left hand.

"This don't look like a car key," he said, picking up a small green cardboard square and holding it up for my inspection. I took it from him and saw that it was actually a tiny envelope. On the front were the words *Century Bank*. On the back, the flap was closed with a small metal snap. I opened the snap and reached inside, pulling out a long key, completely unlike Cara's car keys, and which had a number engraved on it.

"It's a good thing you're thinking straighter than I am this morning," I said to the driver. "This must go to something else of hers. I didn't even think to look in the envelope."

"No prob," he said, picking up the papers again and walking away.

It went to something else all right, I thought as I looked back at the key in my hand. Clearly it was a key to a safe-deposit box at Cara's bank. But I hadn't known Cara had a safe-deposit box. I remembered my insistence that she ought to put our mother's jewelry in one and Cara's equally stubborn insistence on keeping the jewelry with her in the apartment. Perhaps the jewelry had not been stolen after all. Had Cara finally relented and taken the jewelry to the bank? I wondered. She probably hadn't mentioned it because she didn't want me to think she had decided I was right. Although I had notified the bank of Cara's death so they would stop all activity on her account, I had not yet had a chance to go there in person to take care of closing the account. Which meant I hadn't learned about the safe-deposit box she also had rented. Clearly, it was time to take care of it now, and to find out what Cara had kept there besides her money. At lunchtime, I made the drive back out to Springfield, to the bank branch where Cara did business, just down the street from the Easton Arms Apartments.

John Kingman, a handsome man in his late thirties whose closely cropped hair was just beginning to show some threads of early gray that went well against his coffee-hued skin, was the Century Bank officer who showed me over to his desk off the bank lobby and took the small green envelope when I held it out and asked about it.

"Yes," he said, "it clearly is from Century. Let me check and see if your sister rented a box at this branch." He put the key envelope on his desk and turned to his computer screen, where he typed a number of words and commands.

"The computer shows your sister did have a safe-deposit box here, so the key must be ours," he said finally, looking up from the computer. "In fact, she rented the box only two weeks ago, so we will refund most of the annual rental fee to you." He picked up the envelope. "Would you like to clean the box out first and then we'll take care of closing her account?"

I told him I would, and we rose and crossed the blue-carpeted lobby, where a handful of people stood in line for the next available teller. We went through the door of a glass dividing wall and stopped at the open outer steel door of the bank vault, which revealed safe-deposit boxes in stainless-steel rows along the wall, visible through the metal bars of the vault's locked inner door. Kingman took a signature card out of a file drawer next to the vault, asked for my mother's maiden name, and had me sign the card in Cara's stead. Then he unlocked the inner vault door and went into the vault ahead of me. From his ring of keys, he chose another to insert into the first of the two locks on box 177 and then took Cara's key from the envelope to unlock the second lock. From behind the small door that opened, he pulled out a long metal drawer with a covered top and handed the drawer to me.

"You can use one of the rooms right out here," he said, leading me back out of the vault and locking the barred door behind him. Next to the vault were two wooden doors. Kingman unlocked the first one, reached inside to flip a light switch, and gestured into the tiny room that was illuminated by the flickering of the fluorescent overhead lights.

"Just let me know when you're done," Kingman told me, "and we'll get her account closed out."

I thanked him, stepped into the room, which held a desk-high shelf along the right-hand wall and one chair, and closed the door behind me. I put the metal drawer on the shelf and sat down to find out what Cara had valued enough to put in a bank vault. I raised the lid gingerly, expecting to find my mother's jewelry.

Inside, there was only a single sheet of paper, folded lengthwise to fit in the narrow drawer and showing signs of additional creasing as if it once had been folded down to pocket size. I took the paper out and opened it. On it was a list of three names, which looked to have been printed on a laser or ink-jet printer. The first two were names I didn't know: Neal Pursell and James Kelton. The third name was Nash Marshall.

I'm not certain just how long I sat there, staring at the short list of names. Several minutes. But I know it was during those minutes that I became convinced I could feel something of the fear that I suddenly knew Cara had felt in the days before she was killed. She had been afraid of something, I knew without a doubt. It was as if the paper itself still held some powerful residue of her fear, which now was flowing off the sheet and up my arms to my heart and brain. I realized the hairs on my arms had raised in response to the sensation. I felt nauseated. I dropped the sheet on the counter and rubbed my forearms briskly, then wiped my palms on my skirt before picking the list up again.

I had no idea what the list was. But clearly it had been very important to Cara. Important enough that she had felt the need to protect it in a bank vault to which only she had access. And there was no longer any question in my mind that whatever Cara was upset about, whatever was worrying her, whatever it was she had feared, it had something to do with Nash Marshall and his death. The subject matter of the argument between Marshall and Daniel Brant took on a new importance.

And who were the other two men on the list? Had Cara put this list together herself, or had she gotten it from someplace or someone else? And if she really had been afraid— if I wasn't slipping into hallucination—why in hell hadn't she talked to me about it? How could I not have known?

I picked up the list again, folded it, and put it in my purse. I took the empty safe-deposit box outside to Kingman and spent the next few minutes going over Cara's checking and savings accounts and signing the necessary forms to close them. But I don't remember much of our conversation, which was perfunctory on my side, and I made the drive back to the paper on automatic pilot. My mind was still seeing Nash Marshall's name on the list Cara had secreted away.

Fourteen

The bright white light of the photocopy machine flashed out from under the edges of the cover, and then half a dozen copies of Cara's list shuffled into the tray. I handed one to Cooper Diggs, who was standing next to me at the library photocopier.

"I need to know about these other two men," I told him. "Anything you can find. Especially anything they have in common with Marshall."

Cooper looked the list over, blinking twice when he got to Nash Marshall's name.

"What is this?" he asked, looking back up at me from the page.

I lifted the copier's cover to retrieve the original list, then turned and walked back into his cubicle and sat down in his extra chair at the end of the desk. Cooper followed me and, for a change, sat down, too.

"I got it this morning from a safe-deposit box at Cara's bank," I explained. "A box she rented only two weeks ago. Three days before she was killed. That list was the only thing in the box, so she clearly rented it just for that. I need to know why it required a bank vault for safekeeping. And I need to know who these other two men are and how they're connected to Nash Marshall."

"If I'm not crossing the bounds of propriety to ask, what

was your sister to Nash Marshall?'' Cooper wanted to know.

"That's just it," I told him. "As far as I can find out, she was just barely an acquaintance, if even that. She started working at the Bread of Life Church just about the time he quit going. But she apparently was very bothered by his death." I gave Cooper the brief version of Marlee's story about Cara overhearing the Marshall–Brant argument, about her going home that day, and about her reaction when Marshall was killed in the car crash.

"But everybody," I explained, "including Marlee and Phoebe Marshall, say Marshall and Cara barely knew each other."

"Yet your sister gets real upset when he dies, and now you find his name on this"—he held up the copy of the list—"hidden away in a safe-deposit box rented by your sister. Odd. Really odd," he concluded.

I nodded in agreement and stood up.

"I'll be at my desk, making some school-board calls," I told him. "I'll take anything you can find."

"It'll take a while, but I'll get you everything I can."

Marlee Evans had left a message on my voice mail, asking me to call her regarding the next day's memorial service for Cara. I groaned to myself, thinking about what kind of ordeal that service was going to be. It was bad enough to have to go through another session of public mourning for my sister, but even worse to have to do it considering the kinds of questions I now had about whether her minister was someone very different from the man he claimed to be. I didn't know what he really was, but the thought of having to listen to him eulogize my sister, however genuinely he might have felt about her, made me uncomfortable, to say the least. Still, I knew there were other people at the church, sincere people, who wanted a chance to show that they had cared about Cara, a chance to say good-bye.

Ambivalent, I returned the call, and Marlee and I reviewed the list of people who would speak. Daniel Brant and myself, of course, Marlee said, and a couple of friends from Cara's Sunday-school class and church social activities had asked to say something. Marlee already had arranged for an organist to play beforehand as people arrived and for a flower arrangement at the front of the chapel, next to the large photo of Cara that Marlee had had printed up from a photo I had couriered over earlier.

With the details agreed upon, we hung up, and I started making a round of phone calls to several school sources while I waited for Cooper to get back to me.

I was in the middle of selling Rob Perry on a Sunday feature idea about the prominent roles that women play on area school boards when Cooper called. I told him I'd stop by his cubicle in a few minutes on my way home, then went back to the conversation with Rob. He finally agreed to the story, then gave me his hard look that says no one is getting anything by him.

"Now, tell me what's really going on, McPhee," he ordered finally. "Are you still trying to find out what happened with your sister?"

"There's something there, Rob. I'm sure of it," I told him. "I don't know what yet, but there was something wrong. I think something frightened Cara, and I've got to find out what. And whether it was connected to her murder. I know the police think otherwise, but I'm becoming convinced that she wasn't just a random victim."

"Have you discussed this with that detective?"

"Peterson? Briefly, but their investigation hasn't turned up anything that says it was more than just bad luck on her part. I'm going to need something concrete to show him before he'll be convinced. I guess they probably deal all the time with distraught family members who want a more meaningful explanation than just bad luck for why someone they cared about died."

Rob gave me another of his long, assessing looks.

"If there's something there, I think you can find it if anybody can," he said finally. "But, McPhee?"

"Yes?"

"I want you to keep me posted on what's happening. And for God's sake, be careful. If you turn out to be right, and someone really did have a reason to kill your sister, they aren't going to appreciate your trying to find out what that reason was."

I nodded agreement. It was good advice, I knew. But good advice that could get me only so far. At some point, I might have to face the person who killed Cara, might have to confront them with an accusation.

Tell the truth, McPhee, my little voice chimed in as Rob went back to his office. *You want to face the person who killed her . . . and then rip his face right off.*

And that's just for starters, I told it grimly as I took my purse out of the desk. To hell with careful. I wanted the truth, whatever it cost me. And I wanted the truth out in the open, for everyone to see. When I could finally point to someone and say, "This is the man who killed my sister," I intended to make sure that he paid a very public price for what he had done.

This time Cooper wasn't smiling. In fact, he looked spooked.

"Well," he said when I sat down at his desk and propped my chin in a hand, "the guys on this list have some things in common that seem pretty innocuous. For example, all three were prominent businessmen in northern Virginia."

"Were?"

"Ah, yeah, that brings up what else they have in common. First, like Nash Marshall, this Pursell and Kelton both went to the Bread of Life Church."

"And second?"

Cooper got an odd pinched look around the eyes that I hadn't seen before.

"Second, they're both dead, too."

I sat back in the chair, my hands falling to my lap. I looked at Cooper, wondering if he now saw the same pinched look on my face. I was almost afraid to pose the next question.

"How did they die?" I asked finally.

"One bought it when his private plane crashed. The

other fried his brain in his garage with a hose hooked up to his car exhaust.''

Immediately, I could hear Phoebe Marshall again, telling me through her hurt and anger that she thought her husband might have killed himself after practically bankrupting his family.

Cooper handed me copies of the articles that had run when each of the other two men died.

According to several brief news items that had appeared in the area papers, Neal Pursell, forty-eight, the owner of a small but up-and-coming computer software company, had died a year ago in the crash of his small plane, which he piloted himself. He had been on his way to a conference in Chicago, and his plane had gone down in the Shenandoahs. The obituary included the information, which Cooper had highlighted, that Pursell had belonged to Daniel Brant's church, and that his only survivor was an aunt who lived in Fort Lauderdale.

James Kelton was the fifty-six-year-old president and CEO of a local chain of day-care centers. Six months ago Kelton's housekeeper had shown up at his Vienna home for her weekly cleaning visit. After a couple of hours she went into the garage to take out a bag of trash and found Kelton dead in his car, one end of a hose hooked up to the car's exhaust and the other stuck through the window on the driver's side. The medical examiner said that Kelton probably had been dead since sometime the previous evening. The car eventually had run out of gas sometime during the night, which was why the housekeeper hadn't heard the engine running and found the body sooner.

As with the Pursell obituary, Kelton's also listed his membership at the Bread of Life Church. His survivors included a son, a daughter-in-law, and one grandchild living in Charlotte, North Carolina, and a daughter, a son-in-law, and two grandchildren in Massachusetts.

Unlike Pursell, however, there was a follow-up article to Kelton's death. A reporter at the Fairfax *Journal* explained that police had learned that Kelton was in big financial trouble. In the months prior to his suicide he had liquidated most of his assets, unknown to anyone around him. A special audit of the day-care chain's books after he died turned up the fact that he also had embezzled at least half a million dollars from the business as well—leaving the other three investors in the privately held company to file for reorganization under the Chapter 11 bankruptcy statutes. An unidentified police investigator in the case was quoted as saying that neither the police nor Kelton's family or business associates had been able to track down what Kelton had done with all the money.

"It all just vanished," I heard Phoebe Marshall saying again. I looked up from the Kelton article.

"Jesus," I said, my chest feeling tight. "What the hell is all this? What did Cara get mixed up in?"

"You really think this is all related to her being killed?" Cooper asked.

"She thought this list was important enough to put it in a bank vault," I told him. "The men whose names are on it all went to Cara's church. She probably either knew them or knew they were members there. But all three are dead. And now their names show up on some list that Cara apparently was afraid for anyone to know she had, a list she hid in a bank vault. And now Cara's dead, too. Maybe it's all a coincidence."

"And maybe not," Cooper finished for me.

By the time I got back to my apartment, where I could sit and think without interruption, I was becoming pretty sure that "maybe not" should be "probably not."

I was sitting at the dining table, all the articles Cooper had copied spread out before me and a second glass of Chianti in my hand when I saw it, when I saw the first outline of a picture beginning to come into focus. It was then that I realized where Cara had gotten the list of names. I was mentally going over what I had learned in the last few days and was thinking back to Marlee and her story of the falling-out between Cara and John Brant. How Marlee and the younger Brant had come back into the main office to find Cara walking out of John Brant's office and how he had gone ballistic at the idea that Cara might have been doing something with his computer.

In fact, I realized, she had. She had printed out this list of names. She had lied to John Brant about what she was doing in his office. And telling such a lie really would have been unlike Cara—unless she had some extremely compelling motive for doing so. I didn't know what, exactly, the list had meant to Cara. And I didn't know whether she really had gone in to look for a dictionary and had seen the list up on the screen or whether she had gone in to look specifically for information about Nash Marshall. But whichever it was, she had found the list and made a copy, a copy that she wanted to protect—or hide—enough to rent a safe deposit box for it. I remembered Marlee saying the run-in with John Brant had happened on the Thursday before Cara was killed the following Monday. The day before Cara had rented the safe-deposit box at her bank.

And, I realized something else. John Brant believed Cara had tampered with his computer. Had he known what she found? He was good with computers, Marlee had said. Did he have a way to identify the file Cara had seen and what she had printed? And if he had carelessly left the file open when he stepped out of the office, then he knew exactly which file Cara had looked at.

Detective Peterson had ruled out John Brant as a suspect. He had questioned other people at the church and had found nothing. Yet everything I was finding kept coming back to the Bread of Life Church: Cara's job there. Her fight with John Brant. The argument between Brant and Nash Marshall. Three dead men who belonged to the church, at least two of whom had mysteriously lost all their money, and all of whom had died as suicides or in unexplained accidents. The questions about Daniel Brant, about his phony résumé and name, and who he really was. The company in the Caymans. I didn't have the connections yet, but I knew the answer was in there somewhere. Somewhere in a jumbled picture that was painting itself in increasingly ugly colors. My stomach suddenly decided that it didn't want any more Chianti. I got up and dumped the rest of it down the kitchen sink and stood there seeing Cara's face again through the viewing window at the medical examiner's office.

Was I prepared to take the next step to find out what I needed to know, even it meant doing something questionable?

We're talking about murder here. Your sister's murder. Isn't that worth a few risks?

I got out the northern Virginia White Pages and looked up Cooper Diggs's home phone number.

"Cooper, it's Sutton," I said when he answered. "I'm sorry to bother you at home, but I need to ask you a question."

"Shoot," he said.

"Is there a way you can use your computer to get into one at another location, someone else's computer?"

"Only if the other computer has a modem. If it does and if you can tell me the phone number for the modem, I can get into it. Do you have the number?"

"Not yet," I told him, "but I think I can get it. Thanks. I'll let you know."

"No trouble," he answered. "I eagerly await your next challenge."

The next challenge facing me, however, was one with which Cooper couldn't help. I had to go to Cara's memorial service at the Bread of Life Church tomorrow morning and pretend that nothing was wrong. Other than the fact that Cara was dead.

Saturday

Fifteen

Promptly at nine A.M., I pulled into the parking lot at the Bread of Life Church. Marlee and Daniel Brant were standing in the foyer, engrossed in a conversation, when I walked in, but they stopped to greet me. Brant gave me another of his phobic handshakes, and I wondered again how on earth he endured his profession when he disliked touching people—or having people touch him.

Brant excused himself and went back into the office, while Marlee walked with me down to the chapel.

"I was just on my way down to set up the guest book," she told me as we reached the chapel's double oak doors. She placed the black, imitation leather-bound book she had been holding onto a wooden stand next to the chapel doors and turned on a small brass lamp over the book's blank pages. From the pocket of her gray skirt, she took a black ballpoint pen and laid it vertically in the crease between the book's pages. "Families always like to have a record of the people who came to the service," she explained, clearly proud of the fact that she was aware of such small but important details.

"Thank you," I told her, even though I never expected to look at the book again after today. Everyone who would be at this morning's service would be a complete stranger to me.

"Oh, we're happy to do it for you," Marlee said, stepping around me to unlock the door to a small sitting room next to the chapel. "If you want to sit down while people are arriving, feel free to greet them in here. I'll stick my head back in to let you know when Reverend Brant is ready to start and it's time to go in."

I thanked her again.

"And would you like to see the chapel before people get here?" she asked. I realized that I would. Regardless of my doubts about Brant, it was my sister's memorial service, and I wanted it to be done in a way Cara would have approved.

Marlee opened both of the chapel doors and dropped the doorstop at the bottom of each to keep them open. We walked inside, where the perfume from the multicolored profusion of roses that stood at the front of the chapel, next to Cara's picture, mingled with the morning sunlight pouring through the east-facing stained-glass window. I inhaled the scent of Cara's favorite flowers and looked again at the now glowing Jesus beckoning to the children around him, and I almost lost it. I clamped my teeth together so hard to keep from sobbing that I was afraid Marlee could hear the sound from where she stood behind me.

Marlee was watching for my reaction to what she had done with the chapel. I swallowed hard a couple of times and finally relaxed my facial muscles enough to speak. I turned my head to look back at her.

"It's beautiful, Marlee," I told her sincerely. "Cara would have loved it like this."

Marlee smiled happily. "I thought a lot of Cara," she said. "I'm glad you approve."

We stood together for a moment longer in silence, and then Marlee touched my arm gently.

"I'm going to leave you here and go back up to the front door so I can direct people this way," she said. "I expect they'll start arriving at any time."

She was right. About five minutes after I claimed an upholstered chair in the sitting room in order to close my eyes and calm my emotions, I heard a hello from the doorway. The first guests, an elderly couple and a middle-aged woman who turned out to be the church organist, had arrived.

The final notes of the organ's melodic drone fell away into the open spaces under the chapel's high ceiling as the Reverend Daniel Brant stepped up to the pulpit.

"Thank you all for joining us here this morning," he said into the microphone, to the sixty or so people who sat around the chapel, "as we gather to honor the memory of Cara McPhee, the sister of Sutton McPhee and a loved and valued member of our church staff and family. Please join me in prayer."

The room was filled with the rustle of heads bowing and bodies shifting for a few seconds before Brant's "Heavenly Father . . ." rang out. As I listened to his voice reflected around the chapel, I began to understand what it was he had, what had affected Cara and, apparently, many hundreds of others who had chosen Brant's church. The voice was full and deep, its resonant timbre at its best in a space such as the chapel provided, where the shape and textures of the room combined in an ideal acoustical chamber. Remembering my own small-town church upbringing, I could imagine Brant's voice ardently proclaiming God's love, passionately exhorting sinners to heed the call to salvation, even instilling the fear of hellfire if necessary. Whether there was a sincere bone in his body or not, I thought, the man's voice was a real gift, one that I suspected could reassure people who were searching for answers in a confusing and frightening world, one that could stir them to an emotional fervor in which they would readily respond to his directives.

"In Jesus' name, amen," he said, and the Christian audience echoed the ancient closing affirmation of its Hebrew roots.

"And now," Brant went on, "Cara's sister, Sutton, would like to say a few words."

I had hoped the passage of several days since Cara's funeral had lessened the immediacy of the pain of losing her. But as I stood and walked to the pulpit, where Brant nodded at me and then stepped back to take a seat in the farther of the two handsomely carved wooden chairs that sat behind it, the loss swept over me again, its pain full-blown and raw, as if Peterson had only just given me the bad news. I stepped behind the pulpit and wondered if I would be able to utter a single word. I had no remarks planned, no speech written. My mind simply had refused in the preceding days to wrap itself around any words for this moment. Now my emotions threatened to paralyze my vocal cords, cutting off whatever comments might form in my mind. I looked out at the rows of expectant faces, the people who had shared a large part of Cara's life that had held no meaning for me. I closed my eyes for a long second and consciously relaxed the muscles of my throat and face. I had no idea what I would say, but I opened my mouth and words came out.

"My sister is dead," I remember telling the other mourners. "And I'm alone. Cara was the last of my immediate family. Now there is just me, left here with my grief and my anger at how she died.

"I know that if Cara were here, she would tell me to forgive, that the only answer to the evil in the world is love. But Cara was an angel, even before her death, and I'm only human. Right now I hurt too much to forgive. The person who killed her has taken too much from me. Taken the Cara I loved. Taken the Cara who would be in all the years to come. Taken away my pleasure in the memories of the Cara who was. At the moment those memories bring only pain.

"My hope is that tomorrow or the day after or some day soon after that, the person who killed my sister will be found and named and brought forward to answer for what they did. Perhaps that will ease some of the pain, dissipate some of the anger. Maybe then I can find room in my heart to be more like Cara was. Maybe then I can find something of her somewhere in me, as I look out and see something of her in all of you.

"I know she must have touched each of your hearts in

some way, or you would not be here today. And so, because she isn't here to ask you for herself, I will ask you for her. Ask you to remember her and who she was. Ask you to keep her alive by touching another in the way she touched you. Whether it was a smile, or a kind word, or a helping hand, or an understanding heart, take what she gave you and give it to someone else. Then something of her still lives here with us, and that thought makes my pain a little easier to bear.''

The words stopped, as unexpectedly as they had begun. I drew a deep, ragged breath, which the microphone amplified, and looked again at the faces before me, some of which now shed tears.

"Thank you for coming," I said abruptly, not knowing how else to end it, and I moved quickly to the front pew and sat back down, feeling drained of every ounce of energy.

Two of Cara's friends from the church spoke after I did. Although their names sounded familiar, I didn't know either of them, and even now I don't remember what they said. My concentration was shot. I just wanted it to be over. And once it was, once Brant had added his brief closing remarks, I still had to stay through all the condolences and good-byes. I couldn't leave until I had the other thing for which I had come here: the phone number of John Brant's computer modem.

"Would you like some coffee?" Marlee asked as we walked back into the church office. We had the place to ourselves. Brant had left as soon as the service was over, saying he had to visit a couple of church members who were hospitalized. There was no sign of either John Brant or Barlow on a Saturday morning.

"No thanks," I told her. "I'm shaky enough as it is."

"Cara would have liked what you said at the service," Marlee told me, sitting down at her desk.

"It was just what came out when I opened my mouth," I said.

"Oh," Marlee went on, turning to look at her computer

screen, "speaking of Cara, I have something I want to give you. It's a poem she wrote for next month's church newsletter. I thought you might like to have your own copy."

"Yes, I would like that," I answered, surprised again by one more thing about Cara that I hadn't known. A poetess, no less.

Marlee turned to the computer and typed several keystrokes, and in seconds a page of type rolled out of the printer and into the tray. Marlee handed the sheet of paper to me.

"If you don't mind, I don't think I can read it right now," I told Marlee, folding the poem and putting it in my purse. "I think I'd better wait until later."

"I understand," Marlee answered, nodding sympathetically. "I just wanted to get you a copy before I forgot."

I saw a segue to getting on with my other pressing piece of business.

"Isn't it great having computers around so you can just print things out in seconds?" I asked her.

"Boy, I can't imagine what office work must have been like when you had to completely retype things if you needed error-free copy," she agreed. "And now I'm learning how to do desktop publishing so I can take over laying out the church newsletter. Our volunteer who has been doing it is moving to Florida in a couple of months and is teaching me how to use the software."

"Good for you," I told her. Steering the conversation in the direction I needed it to take, I said, "Yes, I can see how John Brant could get so interested in computers. Does he have all the bells and whistles like modems and stuff on his computer here?"

"Oh yes," Marlee said. "Everything you can think of. We don't have nearly as much on mine and Cara's computers, but John insisted on getting it all for his."

"So, if I wanted to send you a message or a fax from my office, I could just send it over his modem?"

"That's right."

"That's great," I said enthusiastically, as if realizing the possibilities for the first time. "You know, I was thinking

I should send the church a thank-you letter for everything you folks have done, and you could put it in your newsletter for everyone to read. If you could give me the modem number, I could just modem it over when I've got it written.''

''That is a good idea,'' Marlee agreed. She picked up a photocopied list of what looked like names and telephone numbers and copied a number from it onto a sheet of notepaper.

''Well, thanks for everything, Marlee,'' I said when she handed me the number. ''I can't tell you how much I appreciate all your help. I know Cara liked you, and she would be very grateful, too.''

Marlee told me again how much she had thought of Cara. I took my leave, fled the Bread of Life Church out to my car, and pointed it east on Old Keene Mill Road toward I-95, which would take me back into D.C.

I wanted to spend some time over the weekend outlining the feature on women school-board members, but I had walked out of the paper on Friday afternoon and absent-mindedly left the folder containing the printouts of my interview notes on my desk. So I had decided to swing into the District after the memorial service and get it. It was lunchtime on a Saturday when I walked in, and the only person in sight in the newsroom was Mike Dalton, a summer intern who was working on a journalism degree at the University of Missouri.

We exchanged brief greetings, and I went over to my desk to get the folder. Lying on top of it was a manila envelope with my name printed in block letters. I tore open the sealed top and pulled out a pale green folder with several sheets of paper inside. There was a small yellow Post-it note stuck on top.

Hope these are helpful, it said in an angular, sprawling handwriting. *Although I can't say much for the company you're keeping these days. Let me know if you need anything else.* There was no signature. It wasn't necessary. I knew it must be the background checks for which I had asked David Edwards.

I put the folder back in the envelope without going through it. I really wanted to go home, where I didn't have to see or talk to anyone else for a while. I got the copies of my interview notes as well and called a "see you" to Dalton on my way out of the newsroom.

If I had had any notion of being able to shut my brain down once I got home, the information in the envelope from David Edwards quickly disabused me of that idea. I got a glass of iced tea from my kitchen and sat down at the dining-room table with the envelope. It was an education.

On top was a sheet for David Daniel Brantley. His adult criminal career stretched all the way back to 1969, to an arrest for receiving stolen property that I guessed was the incident that had short-circuited his attempt at being a divinity student. He had received a sentence of three years in prison, which was reduced to one year plus parole. With credit for time already served while awaiting trial, he actually spent only another nine months in the Washtenaw County jail. In 1976, he was arrested again and served three years in the Michigan State Prison in Jackson for fraud and extortion. There were no further entries for Brantley, and the second sheet showed the search under the Daniel Brant name had turned up no arrests. In part, I suspected, because Daniel Brant had come into existence only shortly before or after his appearance in Virginia, sometime in the last few years, as a man of God.

Sort of an immaculate deception? my voice asked.

I sent it to stand in a corner of my brain. I didn't need the distraction right now.

Next was the sheet for Alfred Reuss Barlow. He had a string of arrests and convictions going back at least as far as age eighteen. Assault. Petty theft. Burglary. Receiving stolen property.

Interesting, I thought, as I read further and compared the sheets on Brantley and Barlow. In 1975, the year before Brantley had been sent to Jackson, Barlow arrived there on an armed-robbery charge. The two men were released within three months of each other in 1979. Eight months later Barlow was back in prison for the Ypsilanti bank robbery, in which he had worked with a never-identified accomplice, and this time he stayed until 1986. His record appeared clean after that.

The next two pages showed nothing more sinister than a string of speeding tickets for John Brant, and nothing at all for Nash Marshall. Fortunately, David Edwards hadn't stopped there. He apparently had contacted the police in Michigan and had had them fax down copies of the mug shots for both Brantley and Barlow. I already knew, from the photo in the *Ann Arbor News*, taken during his trial, that Alfred Reuss Barlow, the Michigan criminal, was now Al Barlow, assistant and business partner to the Reverend Daniel Brant. Now David Daniel Brantley's mug shot left no question that, with the exception of some additional facial creases and graying hair brought on by middle age, he and Daniel Brant were also one and the same.

I pondered the information in front of me, while a puddle of cold water formed under my glass of iced tea from the condensation drops that collected on the glass. I got up and went to the kitchen for a paper towel and a coaster. I didn't know how or when they had met, but it was clear to me that Brant and Barlow had known each other in Jackson, I thought as I sat back down and wiped up the growing pool of water. They also had been released at about the same time. Within months Barlow was right back inside for the bank robbery. Could his partner in that robbery, who was never caught, have been Brant? I wondered. If it had been Brant, no wonder he had given Barlow a job when Barlow finished his sentence.

And what about Brant? What were the chances that his getting religion was real? True, he had gone briefly to a Bible college, ostensibly with the goal of training as a minister. But he had blown that in the very first year with his arrest. And then he'd been caught again and done time in Jackson. I'm certain there are people who experience genuine religious epiphanies while gazing out from behind prison bars. But the more I thought about it, the more the cynic in me believed that the much more likely scenario involved either Brant being forced into the divinity college by a family hoping to straighten him out or his having gone on his own, already planning to use the trappings of religion as a disguise for what he was. Either way, years after his expulsion, he had taken the Bible lessons he had learned in his brief time at the school and had parlayed them into a successful alias as a minister.

All of which was pretty interesting and certainly set the reporter wheels turning in my brain. But the real question was how did any of it connect to Cara—and to the three dead executives who belonged to the Bread of Life Church? If it connected. Right now the picture in front of me was still chaotic, disjointed, bits and pieces of information that made no sense. I thought of a book I recently had read, on all the research under way into theories about chaos and complexity and about the hidden order that often lurks within apparent chaos. This hidden order appears, according to the experts, only after something they call a phase transition, in which increasing chaos suddenly condenses into a new level of order. I hoped that, if there was something that could bring about such a phase transition in my thinking, it showed up soon. Right now all I could see was the disorder. Of course, I didn't expect a catalyst to present itself out of the blue. I would have to keep looking for it.

I went to the phone in the kitchen and called David Edwards's office. I knew he wouldn't be in, but I left a voice-mail message thanking him for the "favor" and telling him it had been helpful.

I hung up, and after a minute or so of pawing through my purse, which I had tossed on the kitchen counter, I came up with the piece of paper containing John Brant's computer modem number. With it in front of me, I dialed Cooper Diggs's home phone number.

"Hello?" he said breathlessly, when he picked the phone up halfway through the fourth ring.

"Cooper, it's Sutton."

"Hey, Sutton. Sorry about the heavy breathing. I was on the stair machine."

"Oh, gee, I didn't mean to interrupt."

"Forget it. I'm done anyway. What can I do for you?"

"Can you write down a phone number?"

"Yeah, I can just about manage that. Just a sec," he said, and I heard noises as he scrambled around for pen and paper. "Okay, go ahead."

I read out the number Marlee had given me.

"This is the modem number to the computer that I'm certain contains the list of names I found in Cara's safe-deposit box," I told him by way of explanation. "It belongs to John Brant, Daniel Brant's son. Do you think you could get into his computer and see what else might be in there about the names on that list?"

"Unless this guy is a whole lot smarter than I am, I can get into it," Cooper assured me. "Any idea what I'm looking for?"

"Anything you can find. I'm still feeling around in the dark at this point. John Brant's paranoia about his computer and my gut keep telling me there's more there, but I have no idea what it might look like."

"Okay," Cooper said, "I'll work on it this weekend. If there's anything to be found, you'll have it by Monday."

And if there wasn't, I wondered, then what do I do? Should I just go to the police with what I did have? Which was what? That Brant was a liar and Barlow a crook? Peterson would show me the door, but not before chewing me out for trying to do the cops' job. Or should I just go on, day after day, grieving over my sister's death and furious at my inability to find out who killed her? How long could I do that before it chewed me up?

I was waiting at a table at Copeland's, a bustling, New Orleans–style restaurant on King Street at the northern edge of Alexandria, when Chris arrived. He slipped into the chair across the table and, smiling at me, said hello.

"Hi yourself," I answered, smiling back and taking in the way his decently muscled arms and shoulders were flattered by the navy knit polo shirt he wore over khaki pants. "This was a good idea."

"It seemed like it at the time," he agreed.

Our waiter appeared to take Chris's drink order. We studied the familiar menu in companionable silence for a few minutes before each of us decided what to have, closed the menus, and put them down on the table. At the waiter's return with Chris's beer, I asked for a house salad and shrimp creole. Chris ordered a crab-stuffed flounder and a bowl of gumbo. The waiter left us alone again and we looked at each other.

"You look good," Chris said finally.

"Thanks," I told him. "So do you. I feel like I haven't seen you in ages, even though it's only been a couple of weeks."

"Well, we've both had a lot going on," he said.

"True," I agreed as the waiter came back with our salad and gumbo. "A lot I would rather not have had to deal with. It has been a very hard two weeks, too."

"But you're okay now?" he asked, putting a spoon into his gumbo.

I teased the pieces of lettuce in my salad with my fork. "Sometimes I am," I said, looking back up at him. "Other times I'm not so sure. I find myself going along, doing what I have to do and thinking about things like work, and then all of a sudden it all comes back and just kicks me in the stomach all over again."

Chris nodded and put another spoonful of gumbo into his mouth. "Mmmm," he said as he chewed. "This is delicious."

And that was pretty much the way the evening went. Throughout dinner, we talked about a lot of things: our jobs, one acquaintance who was getting a divorce, another who had just found out she was having triplets, a third who was taking a vacation in Thailand. We topped off dinner with a round of coffee and then Chris took me up on my invitation to come back to my apartment. At no time had I been able to get any closer to the subject of Cara's murder and how I was struggling with it.

When we got upstairs, I went to the kitchen and put on water for more coffee. Chris suggested watching *Last of the Mohicans,* a film we both liked and that I had purchased on video just before Cara had been killed and had not had a chance to watch. We spent a couple of hours propped against each other and making occasional comments as Daniel Day-Lewis and Madeleine Stowe struggled to survive French and Indian treachery in Colonial America. When the movie was done, Chris changed positions on the sofa and proceeded to convince me that we should conquer some new territory of our own.

Predictably, we ended up in the bedroom, where we didn't spend our time talking. And what we did spend our time doing left both of us relaxed and quickly drifting into sleep. Mine was deep and dreamless for a change, a release from the nightmares about Cara that had been regular visitors since her death—and from the nagging question of what was bothering Chris.

The evening had done nothing to answer that question. On the surface, he had seemed his old self, happy to see me, pleasant to be with, imaginative in bed. But at 4:30 in the morning, I awoke and saw that he uncharacteristically had dressed and left sometime during the night. The note on his pillow said he had to go into the office later to get some extra work done. But I knew it was more than that, that whatever had been wrong before was still there between us. As I lay awake in the predawn gray of my bedroom, I mentally reviewed our conversations from the previous evening, remembering how, each time I had mentioned Cara's murder or the pain it was causing me, Chris had found something else to discuss.

Clearly, the whole topic of Cara's death and my reactions to it made him very uncomfortable. I didn't know why, but I did know that I was equally uncomfortable with his reluctance to discuss it. I hoped that, with the passing of some time, he would open up to letting me talk about it. Cara's murder had turned my world upside down, and I needed someone to help me deal with that, to help me endure the emotional upheaval that her death had triggered.

How could Chris and I spend time together if I couldn't broach a subject that was so close to my heart? I wondered, watching the first touches of pink warm the lightening morning sky. And now, with Cara dead, if Chris wasn't there, then who would I have?

Only me.

Well, that really makes me feel better, I thought caustically.

But the truth of my voice's response forced me to admit to myself the true contours of my life, the actual dimensions of its emptiness, which the demands of my job and time with Cara and Chris had conspired to let me hide from myself. I spent long hours at my job, sometimes more than necessary, I knew. Outside of an occasional after-work bar session with other reporters, Cara and Chris had been my social life. And my confidants. It appalled me to understand how far I had drifted, since my parents' death and my brief and unsuccessful attempt at marriage, from having much in the way of real contact with the other people around me. Even Chris. I knew that I couldn't put all the fault for my current irritation with Chris on his head. In fact, I had always been as wary of closeness as he had, perhaps had found him appealing partly because of the emotional demands I knew I wouldn't have to meet. And although I considered people like Rob Perry and Ken Hale as friends, I still kept them—and most everyone else around me—at arm's length, where, if their feelings for me changed or if they went away, they couldn't cause me pain because I hadn't really let them in.

Only I was in pain, anyway, in spite of all my caution. Cara's death had taken away the person I loved most in the world. And apparently had sent the other person I cared for into a full emotional retreat. As the nighttime gloom drained out of my bedroom, I saw around me the flat topography of my present and the distant horizons of my future, an empty plain on which I stood alone.

Sunday

Sixteen

I spent most of the day Sunday brooding over my predawn insights into my psyche and worrying the bits and pieces I had learned about the Brants and Barlow into various configurations, trying to fit them together into some semblance of a coherent picture. But no matter how I jiggled things around in my brain, I still was left with a large puzzle piece missing, the piece that would show me whether or not it all connected to Cara's murder.

And my questions about what was wrong with Chris were never far from my mind either, especially as the day went by and Chris didn't call. Late in the afternoon, I concluded that, whatever it was, we were going to have to talk about it pretty soon, if I could get him to talk about it at all. I wasn't looking forward to the conversation. But I knew something had changed. He had withdrawn from me in some important way. I don't work well in a vacuum. I had to know what the problem was.

It wasn't until I was getting ready for bed on Sunday night that I remembered Cara's poem that Marlee had given me and that I had forgotten to read. I got my purse off the dresser and sat down on the end of my bed, took out the sheet of paper, and unfolded it. It said:

The Dark

When the world becomes too real,
When trust is shattered, truth deceived,
When doubt and fear replace them,
And we question what we believed,
Then is the time for greatest trust,
Not in the words of man,
But trust in the Lord who put us here,
And confidence in his plan.
We cannot see the road ahead,
Blind to our future, we plod.
There is then but one path to take;
We must take our fears to God.

                                    Cara McPhee

And did He take your fear away? I asked Cara silently, remembering her face on the ATM security camera's tape. Was He there when you were killed, to take you to someplace better as you always believed?

And how ironic, I thought, that her poem should be so appropriate. I had learned that Daniel Brant, whom she had trusted and believed, had deceived her and everyone else at the church about who and what he was. What kind of answer would her God have for that? I wondered. Had Brant's deceit made a mockery of Cara's belief? Had she been forced to ask herself these same questions, to wonder if she had been a fool?

I cried myself to sleep, imagining the terror my sister must have faced at the moment when her faith was put to the ultimate test, at the very time when she might have had the greatest doubts about that faith. All night I went from one bad dream to the next, dreams of Cara dying, of Cara dead, and each ended the same way—with Cara trying to tell me something from wherever she was and then leaving me again, alone here with my grief and my frustration at not being able to understand whatever it was she wanted me to know.

Monday

Seventeen

My first stop at the office on Monday morning was Cooper's cubicle. He wasn't there, but his computer was on, so I decided to wait for a few minutes in case he was around somewhere. I'd been contemplating my fingernails for five or six minutes when he walked in, a cup of coffee in his hand.

"I'm glad you stopped by," Cooper said as he shoved aside a stack of papers to put the coffee cup down on his desk. "I was just about to call upstairs to see if you were in." He handed me a sheet of paper. "This is what I was able to download before your friend's computer decided I was trespassing and kicked me out. It was another file in the same directory as the list your sister found." He sat down in his desk chair to watch my reaction.

On the page were five names, three of which I recognized from the list I had found in Cara's safe-deposit box. They were familiar names by now: Nash Marshall, Neal Pursell, and James Kelton. The other two—Stephen Ulm and Carl Rivers—rang some sort of vague bell, but at the moment I couldn't place them.

Each of the names was followed by a column of numbers and dates. I looked at the figures, first in confusion and then, when I realized they must represent amounts of money, in astonishment. The totals must run into the millions of dollars, I thought. I looked again at the numbers and names, trying to make sense of what I was seeing.

It appeared that the five men—at least three of whom we knew had been members of the Bread of Life Church—had been funneling large amounts of cash, apparently to their minister or his son over a period of time that stretched back for two years. I knew that I was holding the answer to the question of where the missing money from the estates of the three dead men had gone. But what had the money been for? What kind of deal were these people involved in with Brant?

I looked up at Cooper, questions running through my head.

"Could these be donations to the church?" Cooper asked me.

"I don't see how," I told him, shaking my head and looking back at the ledger sheet. "The dates are all wrong, at least for Marshall. The other secretary at the church and Marshall's wife both told me he stopped going about a year ago, but these entries go right up until about three weeks before he died. If he had stopped going to church there, why would he keep donating money to it?"

I studied the sheet some more. And what *was* Brant doing with the money they had been giving him? I wondered. Where was it now?

"The Caymans?" I asked Cooper. In asking the question, I knew the answer. "Brant is sending the money to the Caymans."

"Makes sense to me," Cooper said. "I don't know what these guys are up to, but if you want to hide large amounts of money, that's one place to effectively make it disappear."

So where could I go for the answers? Obviously I wasn't going to find out from anyone at the Caymans' bank that Brant and Barlow had listed as their island mailing address and that probably housed their account. Three of the men on the list were dead. Whatever answers they had known, they weren't telling. But there were two other people involved who were, I hoped, alive and well and who must have at least some of the answers I needed.

"I think," I said to Cooper, "that it's time for me to go talk to Mr. Ulm and Mr. Rivers. You think you can track down who they are for me?"

"I'll run their names through right now," Cooper said, turning to his computer. "Will you be around for a while?"

"Yeah, I've gotta go make some phone calls for a feature I'm working on. Okay if I take this?" I was still holding the printout of payments.

"It's yours," Cooper said. "I'll give you a buzz as soon as I have something."

An hour later he called to say that both Ulm and Rivers were still alive and among us. The names had sounded familiar because Ulm was president of the First City Investors, a local brokerage firm, and Rivers was a high-profile developer who had made a fortune redeveloping run-down properties in prime real-estate spots such as Old Town Alexandria and northwest D.C. Cooper found a feature story on Rivers that mentioned his membership in the Bread of Life Church in Springfield. Ulm's church membership was still a question mark, but I figured it was a pretty good bet that he probably belonged to Brant's church as well.

I considered calling the two men's offices to try to make appointments with them for the next day, but finally rejected that idea. If whatever they were involved in with Brant was in any way questionable, I didn't want to give them a chance to duck me or to have time to make up some cover story about what they were up to. The element of surprise can be a wonderful thing.

I hung up the phone and asked myself the same question I had been asking since the beginning: what did any of this have to do with Cara's murder? Could she possibly have been a participant in whatever these men were doing? No way, I answered myself. Cara would never knowingly have been involved in anything questionable.

Okay, I thought, she wasn't involved in whatever it was. But that didn't mean she didn't know something about it. I knew, because I had seen his arrest and prison records, that Daniel Brant was not what he was pretending to be. Now I was beginning to wonder if perhaps Cara had known it, too. If she had somehow learned about Brant's deception, then her letter to Amy began to make a lot more sense. And if Cara had reason to think that Brant wasn't the minister he was pretending to be, that he had lied about who he was and was involved even now in some sort of dubious scheme, she would have been devastated.

Was it Brant who disappointed you so bitterly? I asked her. Did you find out somehow what kind of man he really was?

But, surely, I thought, if she had learned something like that about someone she admired as much as Brant, wouldn't she have said something to me? It was becoming increasingly apparent to me that the answer was no, that there might have been any number of things Cara had not shared with me, and I didn't understand why not.

Because she didn't want you to say, "I told you so."

"What the hell are you talking about?" I asked aloud.

You've always been the cynic, the suspicious one, the opinionated little shit answered. *Cara didn't want you to know that her judgment could have been so bad and that, when you go looking for the worst in people, in this case you might have been right.*

"Well," I responded, "I sure would be in your case."

So if I'm just part of your psyche, what does that say about you?

As usual, there was just no reasoning with him. I gave him a mental finger and picked up the phone receiver to do some more work on my school-board feature. I couldn't let my reporting suffer just because the muck into which I had foundered while trying to solve my sister's murder was getting deeper and deeper.

It was seven o'clock in the evening and just past the first of the three deadlines that rolled around at the *News* on a daily basis. The editors at the copy desk were in the final throes of clearing pages for the paper's first edition. Those who already were off deadline were relaxing, stretching, wandering out to the cafeteria for coffee before the next deadline at nine P.M. I was working on a first draft of the school-board story when my computer blinked a message that I had E-mail. I saved my story, went into the mail system, and called up the message. It was from Rob Perry.

I didn't want to add one more thing to your list of stuff to deal with before your sister's memorial service, but now that it's over, I think we need to talk about some things with your beat. You want to set up some time in the next couple of days to do that?

I looked up and saw he was watching me from his second "office" at the copy desk, where he was sitting because we were coming up on deadline. We eyed each other for a few seconds, and he raised one eyebrow in question. I faced the screen again and sent a response.

Sure. Is there a problem I should know about?

Let's just say, his answer came back almost immediately, *that I think you probably need a change of pace from the school beat.*

I looked at the response for long seconds, then slowly closed my eyes. I should have known better, I thought, than to believe I was hiding my waning enthusiasm from Rob. He watches us like a hawk, not in an effort to catch us in screwups, although those don't get past him either. Rather, it's like his early-warning system. He constantly monitors the temperature and tenor of the city room and its staff, alert to the nuances of body language and voice and to the vitality of the stories we write in an effort to deal with problems before they reach the full-blown stage. Christ, I thought, all I need is to have to deal with this on top of Cara's murder. And I hated with everything in me the idea that Rob might see me as a developing problem.

I opened my eyes. Rob had walked over to my desk. He winked at me and said, "Don't sweat it. We'll work it out." I gave him an apologetic smile and nodded. He walked on past and out the newsroom's back door toward the cafeteria, apparently unperturbed by whatever deficiencies in my work had tripped his monitors.

But I was mortified. The word *failure* is not allowed in

my dictionary. I had never learned how to quit. Not in school. Not at my job. Not in pushing myself to be the best at whatever I was doing. In high school, that had made me "brainy" and a sometimes object of derision. As a reporter, it made me "tenacious," a good thing as far as an editor is concerned. In my own estimation, it just made me reliable and good at what I do. Sutton McPhee always comes back with the story. Sutton McPhee gets to the bottom of what's going on. Sutton McPhee doesn't panic or get intimidated. Sutton McPhee doesn't fall down on the job. At least not until now. Even if the situation wasn't as drastic as that, I was bored with the schools, and I knew it. And Rob knew it. And I didn't like that worth a damn.

Tuesday

Eighteen

I struck out with Stephen Ulm the next morning anyway, even without calling ahead and tipping him off. When I showed up at his Tyson's Corner office, his secretary, an officious woman of about my own age who clearly had an exaggerated opinion of her boss's (and thus her own) importance, told me he was out of the country for two weeks and pointedly suggested that next time I save myself a trip by making an appointment in advance.

I took in her black hair, pinned into a perfect chignon, her navy-blue dress with matching shoes and a strand of pearls, and the taut line of her thin lips and decided that women, too, could qualify as pricks. I fought down about six different cutting responses that surfaced in my brain but that would be extremely counterproductive if I had to make a return trip, and thanked her politely for her help. The number one rule from *Sutton's Book of Practical Reporting* is: "Try not to piss off the secretaries; they control the access to the people and information you need."

At Carl Rivers's Old Town Alexandria office, I had better luck—after a fashion.

"He's in a meeting, I'm afraid," said his secretary, a woman in her mid-fifties, with gunmetal-gray eyes and hair to match. "And unfortunately, he has a very full schedule today. If you'll tell me what this is regarding, I can check his calendar to see if he might have some time next week.'' She unconsciously reached up to pat her short, fluffed hair and then tugged at the hem of her charcoal-gray suit jacket, taking no chances of a chink in any of her armor.

"I'm afraid that would be too late," I told her, still trying to keep my voice neutral and unoffended. I was determined to see him one way or the other, but there was no point in being nasty unless I had to. "Actually," I went on, "I really think Mr. Rivers will want to see me when he knows why I'm here."

I took my reporter's notebook out and wrote a brief note to Rivers, then folded it twice and gave it to the secretary. "If you'll take this in to him, I think you'll be surprised at just how quickly he'll find time to talk to me."

She took the note and began to unfold it.

"I wouldn't read it if I were you," I told her warningly, but with a friendly smile still in place. "It's very personal, and I think Mr. Rivers would be rather put out if he knew anyone else had seen it. Even you."

That earned me a hard glare, but she refolded the note, turned away, and walked to Rivers's office door, where she knocked and then went in. About ninety seconds later she came back out and held the door open. "Please come in," she said unhappily. "Mr. Rivers has a few minutes free."

If Rivers had been in a meeting, it apparently was with himself. As I walked into his spacious office, furnished in lustrous mahogany and black leather above sand-colored carpeting, I saw him standing alone and looking out the bank of windows behind his desk, his back to me, apparently watching the scene below him on King Street. His hands were at his sides, my note grasped in the right one. He turned from the window and took three steps to the large, ergonomically correct executive's chair behind his desk, in which he sat down as if he were twenty years older than the fifty-two-year-old man I knew he was. His hair was completely silvered, but that alone wouldn't have aged him so much. Instead it was the downward turn of the lines of his face, the gun-shy look in his washed-out blue eyes, and the beaten-down angle of his shoulders that added the extra years to his appearance. I had to wonder if he had looked younger before his secretary took my note in for him to read.

Considering the note's message, I decided it was pointless to stand on the formality of waiting to be offered a seat, which Rivers seemed in no hurry to do. I seated myself in one of the two guest chairs facing his desk.

"Thank you for seeing me," I said.

Rivers leaned forward and put the note on the desktop, using both hands to smooth out the wrinkles he had inflicted on it, but touching it gingerly, as if he were afraid it might explode in his hands. He looked up at me.

"What does this mean?" he asked. On the sheet of paper, I had written: *I know about your special financial arrangement with Daniel Brant. We need to talk about it.* I had signed with my name and the fact that I was a reporter with the *News*.

"It means," I said, deciding to try to shake him up more by being blunt, "that I know about the money you've been giving Daniel Brant, the minister at your church. According to my information, it comes to about—no make that exactly—seven hundred and twenty thousand dollars so far. I know that it's going into a bank account in the Cayman Islands. I want to know what happens to it after that, what it's for."

Rivers's face had taken on a gray tinge, as if he weren't getting enough oxygen. God, I thought, I hope this guy isn't getting ready to have a heart attack right here.

If he does, you could withhold CPR until he tells you what he knows.

I'm not ruling out anything, I thought.

"I don't have the slightest idea what you're talking about," Rivers said finally, sounding as if he was going to strangle on the words. "I don't know anything about any such money. I haven't been to that church in months now, so why would I be giving Brant money?"

"So you're saying you haven't given Brant almost three quarters of a million dollars, that you aren't involved in some sort of deal with him?"

"That's what I'm saying."

I didn't believe a word of it. "And you don't know why four other members of your church were giving him money either?"

Rivers had looked back down at my note, which he still held against the desktop with his fingertips. At this last question, however, his head came up sharply and he looked at me in what I was convinced was genuine surprise.

"No," he said finally, convulsively picking up the note and tearing it into small pieces. "I don't." His shoulders had squared as well, and I understood that something about my question had angered him, although I didn't think his anger was with me.

This time I believed his denial. He really had not known about Marshall and the others. I suspected his anger was at Daniel Brant for deceiving him so thoroughly and at himself for the disastrous position in which he had placed himself by trusting Brant in the first place.

"I don't know where you came up with such wild accusations," Rivers said abruptly, standing up, "but I want you to leave now. I don't know anything about this, and we have nothing else to talk about." He emerged from behind the desk, walked heavily over to open the door to the outer office, and spoke through it.

"Mrs. Singletary," he called to his secretary, "this reporter is leaving now."

I could see there was nothing else to be gained here at the moment, so I went without putting up a fuss. But when I reached Rivers where he stood at his office door, I handed him one of my cards.

"If you decide, after thinking about this, that you have some things you want to talk about, please call me." He wouldn't meet my eyes, but he took the card.

I nodded silently at Mrs. Singletary as I passed her on my way out. She looked somewhat triumphant, but I let it wash right over me, thinking that I probably knew more about her future at the moment than she did.

Nineteen

I spent the rest of the day at the office, finishing my draft of the school-board feature. Later that evening I stood at my living-room windows, watching the car lights go north and south on I-395 two blocks west of my apartment. In my hand was the cordless phone from my kitchen, and I was dialing the number for Peter Kelton, James Kelton's son, that I had gotten from the operator in the Charlotte area code. The phone rang three times and was answered by a small voice young enough to obscure the child's gender.

"Is your father home?" I asked.

"Just a minute," the child said, and put the receiver down with a clank, which was followed by calls of "Daddy" and muted adult voices in the background.

"Hello?" Peter Kelton said a few seconds later.

"Mr. Kelton?"

"Yes, speaking." His voice sounded frazzled, the syllables clipped, as if I had intruded in the middle of something he was busy doing.

"Mr. Kelton, my name is Sutton McPhee. I apologize for calling you at home at night, but it was the only way I knew to reach you. I'm an education reporter for the Washington, D.C., *News.*"

"Oh?" he said, clearly mystified by why I would be calling him.

"But I'm not calling you as part of my job as a reporter," I explained. "I'm calling because I think you might be able to help me with a personal matter. My sister, Cara McPhee, was shot to death at a bank ATM here a few days ago. She went to the same church as your father, Mr. Kelton, and although this probably sounds odd, I was hoping that you might be able to help shed some light on any possible connection she might have had with your father."

I could tell that my brief explanation for my call had left Kelton even more confused.

After a few seconds' silence he said, "Ms. . . . uh, McPhee, was it?"

"Right. Sutton McPhee."

"Well, Ms. McPhee, I don't see what possible connection there could be. My father committed suicide several months ago. I'm sorry about your sister, but I've never even heard of her. I don't understand what her murder could have to do with my father."

"It's a little complicated," I told him, "but I think the connection may have been through the Bread of Life Church. My sister also was a secretary in the church office."

"I'm sorry," Kelton said, beginning to sound irritated. "I really don't know how I can help you. Now, if you'll ex—"

I interrupted him.

"Mr. Kelton, please don't hang up," I pleaded. "I know I'm imposing on you and that this probably makes no sense to you. But I really think you may be able to help me piece together what happened to my sister. If I could just ask you a couple of questions."

He thought some more, but at least he stayed on the line.

"All right," he said finally. "I can't see what good it will do, but I'll answer your questions if I can."

I turned from the windows and sat down in one of the two club chairs opposite my sofa.

"Thank you," I said in relief. "Why do you think your father killed himself, Mr. Kelton?"

"If you're a newspaper reporter, I'm sure you've read the stories that were done when he died. We'll never know for sure, I suppose, since he didn't say anything to anyone beforehand and didn't leave a note, but he apparently was having some . . . ah . . . some financial problems."

"I saw one story that said the police learned your father had liquidated everything he had and that there was no trace of what he did with the money."

"Yes," Kelton said somewhat hesitantly. "That's right."

"Could he have gambled the money away or lost it in bad investments?"

"My father didn't believe in gambling," the son replied. "And his stockbroker had no record of any sort of bad investments. In fact, my father had pulled out everything he had invested as well, and his stockbroker wasn't happy about it."

"I know that he was very active for a while in the Bread of Life Church and that it completed a large expansion program just over a year ago. Could your father have donated the money to the church?"

"That was one of the things the police checked," Kelton said. "Dad did make regular donations for a while, but according to the church records, they were nowhere near the amount of money that was missing. And the dates when he sold off his assets were all later than any of his donations to the church."

"How could you be sure the church records were accurate?"

"I asked the same question at the time. The police said that all donations were logged in by a rotating subgroup of the church's deacons. There was no reason to think their records were anything other than accurate."

Of course, I thought to myself, it wouldn't be the first time the leader of a church had found a way to take his followers for a financial ride without their knowing it.

"Did your father ever mention any sort of personal business arrangement with Daniel Brant, the minister at the church? Anything they might have been involved in together that your father was putting money into?''

"Never. Not that he would have necessarily, but why wouldn't the minister have told us about it when my father died? He never mentioned any sort of business either.''

"So where do you think your father's money went?''

"I have absolutely no idea,'' Kelton said emphatically. "I wish I did. I'm a high-school history teacher. I could use the money. But it's as if it just disappeared.''

I thought again of Phoebe Marshall. Her comments to me had sounded disturbingly similar.

"Mr. Kelton, I really appreciate your patience, and I know this must still be difficult for you to talk about, but did you or the police have any reason to think your father's death might have been anything other than a suicide?''

"Well, it clearly wasn't an accident, since the hose couldn't have gotten from the exhaust to the car window by itself. So what you're asking,'' Kelton concluded, "is whether someone else killed him. Is that right?''

"Yes.''

"I take it you didn't know my father,'' Kelton answered, sounding offended. "People loved him. The police looked into all the possibilities, but they never came up with any hint of anyone having a reason to kill him. And there was no evidence in the house or garage, or on his body, that there was anyone there at the time but him.''

"I'm sorry,'' I said quickly. "I know this brings back painful memories for you. But clearly there was something going on in your father's life that you didn't know about, something big enough to drive him to kill himself. I'm just trying to find out who killed my sister, and I was hoping that the answers to your father's death might help me.''

"Well, as I said, I've never heard of your sister, never heard my father mention her, or any business with Reverend Brant. So I just don't see what possible connection there could be.'' Kelton now sounded exasperated and out of patience. I figured there was nothing to be gained by pushing him any further. If he knew anything that might help me, he didn't know he knew it.

"You're probably right," I answered. "Again, I apologize for imposing on you. But my sister was murdered, and I have to do everything I can to find out why."

"I know how you feel, and I really wish I could help you," Peter Kelton said, clearly getting ready to end the conversation, "but I just don't know what I could tell you that would have anything to do with your sister."

I thanked him for his time, apologized again for disturbing him, and hung up.

But I didn't turn my brain off with the click of the phone. Peter Kelton had told me more than he probably realized, I thought, rising to walk over to the windows again. He had confirmed the story about the elder Kelton's money disappearing. He had ruled out the Bread of Life Church as a recipient of the money, so I knew the ledger sheet Cooper had downloaded from John Brant's computer was not an accounting of church donations by the five men. And Peter Kelton's lack of any theory about where the money had gone meant that my suspicions about it were still a possibility. The money, I was convinced, had gone directly to Daniel Brant. But for what?

I couldn't imagine that businessmen of the caliber of Marshall and Rivers were investing their money in Brantlow, Inc., which appeared to be a one-man show in the person of John Brant. Was the Cayman Islands company a front for what they really had been investing in? Was the money going through the account and then being shunted off to someplace or something else?

And I didn't understand Carl Rivers's reaction to my question about the other men. If he was involved, and I knew he was from the ledger page Cooper had downloaded, why wouldn't he have known about Brant's other partners?

It was then that I saw another key piece of the puzzle, or at least a key question, a piece that Rivers had given me without my realizing it at the time.

Why, Rivers had asked, would he be giving money to Daniel Brant when he had not been involved with the church or Brant in months? As I rehashed our brief conversation I realized just how important that question was. Why would he, indeed?

And he wasn't the only one. Both Marlee and Phoebe Marshall had said the same thing about Nash Marshall, that he had stopped attending the Bread of Life Church a year ago. Was this some sort of pattern? If I checked with Marlee, who seemed to keep close tabs on people's comings and goings at the church, would I find out that Kelton, Pursell, and Ulm also had dropped out of church? If the answer was yes, what did that mean? And why would they continue to give Brant such huge sums of money? Or were their breaks with the church simply a way to try to erase any evidence trail to whatever it was they were doing?

I didn't know the answer, but I knew it was an important question. I could feel it in the tingle that went up my spine and neck as I thought about it. If I could find the answer to that, I thought, somewhere in it I might find at least a hint of what had happened to Cara.

Wednesday

Twenty

The next morning I was at my desk working on revisions to the school-board feature, based on suggestions from Rob Perry, when I got a call from Detective Peterson.

"Sutton," he said in a very unhappy voice, "what are you doing?"

"I'm working on a story about—"

"That's not what I meant," Peterson interrupted. "I mean why are you stirring up problems with old investigations that have been solved and closed?"

"What are you talking about?" I asked innocently, not willing to confess to anything without knowing how much he knew.

"I'm talking about the phone call I got first thing this morning from a Peter Kelton down in North Carolina. He called one of the investigators on his father's case to complain, and he was transferred to me. Mr. Kelton says you called him with all sorts of wild ideas about his father's suicide having something to do with your sister's murder."

"Oh really?"

"You mind telling me where you got such an idea?"

Actually, I realized, I did mind. I didn't have it yet, that irrefutable piece of information that would force the police to give credence to everything else I had learned. Would I ever find it? Maybe, maybe not. But I was determined to keep looking until I either had that piece or could satisfy myself that it didn't exist.

"I'm grasping at straws, detective," I told him, which was true at the moment, even if the straws were looking pretty suspicious. "I thought if there was some chance Kelton didn't commit suicide, it might connect somehow to Cara's murder. They did go to the same church." While I realized how flimsy that sounded as a reason to connect their deaths, I wasn't certain if I was ready yet to tell Peterson about the real connection: the lists from John Brant's computer.

"He killed himself," Peterson said shortly, clearly exasperated with me. "Months ago. So how could that have any connection to your sister's murder? I've pulled the files on the investigation. The detectives on the case are good. If there had been any sign of foul play at the scene, they would have found it. He pissed all his money away somewhere—gambling, women, who knows where—and when he went through the last of it, he sat down and sucked on his exhaust pipe."

"You do have a way with words, detective," I said sarcastically.

"I apologize if you think I'm being harsh," Peterson replied somewhat stiffly, "but you don't do yourself any good this way. Kelton and your sister belonged to the same church. Period. So what? At a church that size, people die on a regular basis. From all kinds of causes. That doesn't mean there's a conspiracy."

"I'm sure you're right," I told him blandly.

"I know you're a reporter, and you look for answers for a living," he went on, now in full lecture mode. "But you really ought to just let the police do our job. We haven't given up on finding the guy who killed your sister. I've got people out every day asking questions about it. And if you think you've got some kind of real evidence in the case, I want to be the first one to hear it. But it isn't helpful when you take up our time with stuff like this. You see what I mean?

"Yes," I answered, and I did. He thought I was letting

my imagination run away with me, seeing evidence where none existed, so unnerved by my sister's death that I had lost all perspective. "I'll try not to create any unnecessary work for you."

What I didn't say was that it was because I intended to keep doing the work myself.

Doing the work myself seemed to be the story of my life lately, I thought after I hung up from my conversation with Peterson. Because there was another area where I knew that I was going to have to do the work—finding out what was wrong with Chris Wiley. Here it was Tuesday, and I had not heard a word from him since his unexpected early-morning departure on Sunday. Regardless of our lack of some sort of commitment to each other, this was not like him. And I couldn't let it go any longer. I wanted to know what was going on. I picked up the phone and called his office.

His secretary answered, even though I had dialed his direct line.

"Marsha," I told her, "this is Sutton." I didn't have to say Sutton who. Although I hadn't met her, Marsha had been taking my calls and occasionally calling me with a message from Chris for months now. "Is Chris around?"

"He's in a meeting with a client right now, Sutton. Would you like me to have him call you?"

"Do you know whether he has lunch plans for today?"

"Just a minute. I'll check his calendar." She put me on hold, where I was treated to a sluggish, elevator-music version of "Proud Mary."

"It looks like he's free," Marsha said when she came back on the line.

"Great," I replied. "There's no need for him to call me. I'll be out of reach anyway. Just tell him to meet me at noon at the Blue Point Grill at Sutton Place Gourmet. If he hasn't been there, it's down on South Washington Street at Franklin. Tell him it's important."

"I'll give him the message," Marsha assured me. "Oh, and Sutton?"

"Yes?"

"I just wanted to say I was sorry to read about your sister. It must be very hard for you."

"Thanks, Marsha," I told her. "It's nice of you to think about me."

Christ, I thought as I hung up, even Chris's secretary is more concerned about how I'm handling my sister's murder than he is. It just reinforced my decision to bring things to a head. I went back to my story, determined not to answer my phone if it rang because I didn't want to give Chris an out. We were going to meet for lunch. And one way or the other, I was going to find out what was on his mind.

I was waiting at an outdoor table in front of the Blue Point Grill when I saw Chris's red Miata turn off Washington Street and drive down Franklin past the restaurant, on his way around the corner to the entrance for the underground parking garage. A couple of minutes later he came up the stairs that opened into the foyer between the popular Alexandria restaurant and its even more popular gourmet-foods shop and joined me at the table. He didn't look pleased to see me.

"So what's so urgent, Sutton?" he asked, sitting down in the other chair and leaning back as if distancing himself from me. "I wish you had checked with me instead of just leaving a message. I had to put off a client who wanted to go out to lunch with me today." He was making no effort to hide the irritation in his voice. It was clear he felt I had overstepped my bounds in my assumption that he would make himself available. I didn't like his tone of voice one bit, but I decided that it would defeat my purpose in getting him here if I started out by getting angry, too.

The waitress came by to fill our water glasses and to get our drink orders. We both asked for iced tea.

"I apologize," I told Chris when she left. "But there's something we have to talk about, and it just seemed very important that we do it today."

Chris gave me a long look, then turned at an angle in his chair and crossed one leg over the other, out to the side of the small table. He put his right arm down on the table-top and picked up a fork, which he proceeded to tap lightly against the hard white surface. He looked up at me, the fork still tapping. It was an offensively irritating gesture that said I was on trial here and that my reason for pulling him away from the office had better be worth his while.

"Okay," he said, "I'm here."

In body, anyway, my little friend opined.

The waitress reappeared with the glasses of tea and wanted to take our order. Flustered, I quickly grabbed the menu and order the grilled salmon salad.

"I'll have the same," Chris told her, without looking at his own menu. The waitress left again, and Chris and I looked at each other for a few seconds in silence. In those seconds I was overcome with the feeling that this was a pivotal moment, one of those times when you intuitively understand that you aren't going to like what you're about to hear and that it's going to send your life off in a whole new direction. The damned fork kept up its drumming on the table. Chris looked back down at the fork when the meeting of our eyes became too intense. My stomach felt hollow, but I plunged ahead, unable to back away from the cliff edge I felt I was suddenly facing.

"I need to know where you've gone," I told him, deciding that I owed him no more apologies and might as well get straight to the point.

"I don't understand what you mean," Chris answered, finally looking up for a few seconds. The fork paused.

"Yes, I think you do," I responded, unwilling now to let him escape by pleading ignorance. I was determined to make him say what had to be said. "Come on, Chris, this is me. I haven't spent the last eight months getting to know you without being able to tell when something is wrong."

"What makes you think something is wrong?" he asked, apparently equally determined to avoid confronting it if he could. He knew the answer, of course, as evidenced by his shifting gaze, which kept moving to look anywhere else—at the lanes of passing traffic on Washington Street, at the sky, at the other diners—anywhere except directly at me.

"You've withdrawn," I told him flatly. "It's as if only part of you is there. I need to know where the other part is and why."

"This is crazy, Sutton," Chris responded, his voice carrying the message that he was really put out with me. He laid the fork down next to his glass, uncrossed his legs, and swiveled back to face the table, where he leaned forward to talk, his voice now lowered as the conversation took such an intimate turn. "There's nothing wrong with me. I've just been really busy."

"Don't do this, Chris. I deserve better. I know we've both been satisfied with where our relationship has been, and I'm not looking for anything beyond that at the moment. But ever since my sister was killed, it's as if we're no longer even at that point anymore. As if you've disengaged for some reason and I'm not reaching you."

I paused to give him a chance to respond. Instead, he looked down and picked up the fork again to resume the tapping. It was the wrong thing to do. I reached over and took the fork away, then took the hand that had been holding it. That got his attention. He looked back up at me with very annoyed green eyes.

"I've had a rough couple of weeks," I went on. "The worst in my whole life. I really, really need a friend. Someone to care about me and how much I hurt right now. I thought that was you, but every time I try to talk about it, you change the subject. You don't call. You don't seem interested in how I'm doing. You got up in the middle of the night and left my apartment, as if you didn't want to be there when I woke up. This is not my imagination. Now, what's wrong?"

One possibility occurred to me even as the words left my mouth.

"Are you seeing someone else?" I asked, uncertain of how I would react if he said yes, but knowing that I wanted the truth.

"No," Chris answered, apparently offended enough to pull his hand away. "I'm not."

"Then what?" I could see in his eyes that he was trying

to decide exactly how to phrase words he was very uncomfortable saying in any form.

"I guess I'm not ready to move to the next step," he said finally. "I just don't want to have to deal with any new demands on my emotions. I've always been up front with you about that. If you were looking for something more, I'm sorry. I've tried not to mislead you about what this was."

"Chris, I'm not asking for anything more than what we have. But you've withdrawn even that. You might as well not be there at all. So what is it really?"

He looked at me some more, saying nothing. Finally, I thought I understood.

"You want out of this altogether, don't you?" I asked.

He took a deep breath.

"I think so," he said. "It was fine before . . . before your sister was killed. I always thought you were strong and independent, like me. I liked things the way they were. But I can't deal with this . . . neediness I've seen in you since she died."

I wanted to throw my iced tea in his face. I was absolutely furious.

"I *am* strong and independent," I told him hotly, trying to keep my voice at something below a shout, "but I'm also human. Somebody killed my sister. Do you have a clue what that means? I'm not asking you for a wedding ring or any other kind of commitment. I'm not trying to trap you or make demands on you. I'm not asking you for a goddamned thing you don't want to give! But are you so afraid of emotions, of caring about somebody, that you can't even be there for me when my sister is murdered? Christ Almighty, Chris, I've gotten more support from people at my office and strangers from Cara's church than I have from you. Are you really this afraid of someone needing you?"

"Stop it, Sutton," Chris said, now angry, too. "You're making a scene. This is emotional blackmail, and it won't work!"

"Here are your grilled salmon salads," the waitress said

from above our heads. We both looked up at her in surprise, as if we had forgotten all about lunch. She put a huge and delicious-looking salad down in front of each of us.

"Is there anything else I can get you right now?" she asked innocently, unaware of the quarrel that had developed so quickly between two of her customers, who probably had looked like rational people when they had sat down at her table.

"Not a thing," I said, standing up abruptly and almost overturning my chair. "There's absolutely nothing here I need! Or want!" I reached into my purse and pulled out a twenty-dollar bill. "This is for the cold fish," I said, looking down at Chris, whose eyes were wide in surprise. I threw the money down in front of him and walked away, leaving him, the waitress, and several other diners staring after me.

Feel better now?

Jesus, don't you ever shut up? No, I don't feel better now. I'm mad as hell, and my feelings are hurt. And I wish the rest of these drivers would stop poking around!

I was several blocks from the restaurant by now, driving north through the center of Old Town on Washington Street to go back to the office. My anger had carried me out of the restaurant, to where my Bug was parked on the street, its convertible top down in the May sunshine, and away from the man I had foolishly trusted and depended on. Now that anger was directed at the other drivers who moved through Old Town with me, making right turns without giving turn signals, trying to make left turns where signs clearly said not to, and just generally getting in my way.

Shit, I said to myself, you would think I'd know better. Didn't I learn anything from Jack?

Well, at least this guy was better in bed than Jack was.

Yeah, and that's just one more thing to be pissed off about, I responded. Now I'm celibate again!

I could almost swear I heard laughing.

Twenty-one

I mentally hashed and rehashed my argument with Chris, as brief as it had been, all the way back to the office and up to my desk. Although there were any number of other reporters who were in the newsroom working on stories or sitting around talking, they all took one look at my face, which must have been thunderous, waved, and went back to whatever they had been doing.

I threw my purse in the bottom desk drawer and sat down to start going back through all the information that Cooper and I had collected. But Chris's words still reverberated in my head.

"Emotional blackmail," I could hear him saying accusingly, again and again.

"Hah," I muttered to myself, picking up the copy of the ledger sheet that broke down the payments given to Daniel Brant by five of his congregants. "Just where does he get off? Emotional blackmail, my ass!"

That's when things finally fell into place in my thick head, and the sound was deafening.

Blackmail. That was what had been staring me in the face all this time and that I had been missing completely.

Daniel Brant was blackmailing members of his own church, and they had been making him a rich man. They had not been giving him their money willingly for him to launder or invest. They had been paying him to keep his mouth shut.

Frantically, I shuffled the pieces of paper around, realizing that I already had the puzzle pieces that I needed, until I had them in an order that made sense, at last, out of what I had learned.

Both Daniel Brant, in his previous life as David Daniel Brantley, and Al Barlow had police records that showed they certainly were capable of blackmail. Whatever Brant's reasons for starting a church, he eventually had found a much more lucrative scam than any earlier plans he might have had for skimming money off the top of the church donations or padding expense accounts. Whether or not he had started out to steal money from the church, he eventually had tumbled to an idea that made anything else look like petty thievery.

Somehow, he had learned damaging information about at least five of the wealthier men in his congregation, something so damaging that he had been able to use it to extract millions of dollars from them, something that they would give up everything they had and bankrupt their families and businesses over rather than risk its revelation by Brant.

Was their secret something in which they were all involved? I wondered. But I still thought Carl Rivers's apparent surprise when I mentioned the other men had been real. So Brant must know something different about each of them, which would explain why they hadn't felt enough safety in numbers to threaten Brant with exposure of his own treachery. Each man thought he was alone. And so he paid. And paid.

The money was going to the Caymans, all right, as I had said to Rivers, but it wasn't going in the victims' names. It was going right into the numbered accounts, no doubt, of the Brants and Barlow. And, I suspected, John Brant's frequent "business" trips that Marlee had mentioned were actually runs to the Caymans, cash in hand. His computer company simply gave him a way to pass himself off as legitimate and to make airport officials less likely to be suspicious of all his comings and goings.

But what would happen when the men who were being blackmailed ran out of money? I felt certain that Brant was busy lining up some new victims to take their places. Still, he couldn't afford to have men with nothing left to lose telling what he had done, in some misguided effort to explain to their families or business partners why all the money was gone.

Granted, if Brant were lucky, his victims might commit suicide, as the police believed Kelton had. Even Pursell's plane crash and Marshall's car wreck could have been suicides disguised as accidents. But I didn't think that Nash Marshall's fury, which even Marlee Evans had witnessed the day he confronted Brant at the church, sounded like a man who wanted to kill himself. He would have been far more likely to have threatened to kill Brant, I suspected, if Marshall had been as angry as Marlee had described.

And that was the argument Cara had heard. Had she heard Marshall refer bluntly to the fact that Brant was blackmailing him? Did she hear him threaten Brant because Brant had taken everything Marshall had? Was that why Marshall's death had been so distressing for her—because she had understood what Brant really was and suspected that he might even have taken steps to keep Marshall quiet? The reality of Daniel Brant's Jekyll-and-Hyde life must have appalled Cara. Did Marshall's subsequent death make her fear for her own safety as well? Feeling sick, I knew that it must have.

There was no question in my mind now, as I looked at the pages spread out in front of me, that Cara had seen the list of names on John Brant's computer and had understood immediately at least something of its significance. She had stood there for the few extra seconds needed to print it out, and the delay had kept her in his office just long enough for him to see her as she came back out. And when John realized what Cara would have seen on his computer screen, he also must have understood immediately the problem she presented. No doubt, his father had already apprised him and Al Barlow of the fact that Cara had overheard the argument with Marshall. If there was any chance she had seen the list, or worse yet, the ledger sheet that tracked the blackmail payments, they couldn't run the risk of having her make the connections or tell someone else what she knew. Cara suddenly had become a liability that couldn't be tolerated. They would have had to do something about her.

And one of them had. In spite of their alibis, one of them had murdered Cara.

I sat back in my chair, numb with shock at the cold-bloodedness of what I knew they had done. It made me want to run home, to lock my doors and crawl under layers of covers, where I would be safe and warm and hidden away, and where I could cry hysterically for days, in pain at my sister's fear and disillusionment and in outrage at what these venal sons-of-bitches had done to her. Except that I had no time to fall apart now. They had killed my sister, and now I had to prove it.

It was, I decided, time to put in a call to Carl Rivers.

I could tell by the tone of her voice when I identified myself that Mrs. Singletary, Rivers's secretary, had yet to forgive me for finding a way to get around her earlier. But the impact of whatever I had said to her boss must have been clear enough on his face for even her to see, so this time she put me through to him without argument.

"I thought I should call," I said to Rivers when he got on the line, "to see if you might have changed your mind about talking to me about the money you've paid Daniel Brant."

"I told you before," Rivers said, his voice firmer now, as if he had had time to convince himself that I was guessing or that he could bluff his way out, "I have nothing to say to you. I don't know what you're talking about."

"Let's not play these games, Mr. Rivers," I said back to him, even more firmly and not put off by the change in his voice. "You know exactly what I'm talking about. I'll admit that I've been a tad slow in putting it all together, but I finally have."

"What do you mean?" he asked reluctantly, as if he really didn't want to know.

"I mean that I now know the money you've been giving Daniel Brant is to keep him quiet. He's blackmailing you, Mr. Rivers. I haven't figured out yet with what, what it is he has on you, but I'll find it out eventually. What I do know is that he'll keep on blackmailing you if you don't help me stop him, until he's squeezed you for every cent you have."

"Why does any of this concern you?" Rivers asked, somewhat faintly now. His bluster had died quickly in the face of my newest accusation.

"Because my sister is dead, Mr. Rivers. She was killed two weeks ago by someone who tried to make it look like an ATM robbery. But I think she was killed because she accidentally learned what a sleazebag Daniel Brant really is, what he has been doing. To you and to at least four other men who used to attend the Bread of Life Church.

"Let me lay out your future for you as clearly as I can," I went on. "Brant already has extorted more than six million dollars from the five of you. There's just one problem. Three of his victims ran out of money, and those three are now dead. I'm talking about people you knew, Mr. Rivers. About Nash Marshall. And James Kelton. And Neal Pursell. So you know I'm not making this up. The police think their deaths were accidents or suicides. But I know better, and now you do, too. You not only are going to lose everything you have before Brant is finished with you, but it's possible your life is even in danger."

Rivers was silent.

"I think we can help each other, Mr. Rivers," I concluded. "If you can confirm that what I believe is correct, you may be able to help me solve my sister's murder. And I may be able to help you extricate yourself from Daniel Brant's grip."

It went without saying that it would require him to come forward and tell the police about the blackmail, to risk public exposure of the secret—whatever it was—that Brant knew about him, the very thing he had been paying through the nose to keep hidden. I wouldn't have wanted to be faced with the decision I'd just put in front of him.

"I'm afraid I can't help you," he answered finally, sounding thoroughly defeated. "I'm sorry about your sister, but there's nothing I can do."

Whatever he was hiding, whatever Brant had learned about him, Rivers's fear of having that secret exposed apparently was greater than his fear of Brant.

"All right," I told him. "I can understand what a difficult decision this must be for you. If you change your mind, you have my card. Call me anytime, day or night. But, Mr. Rivers?"

"Yes?"

"Just remember. I followed a trail of bodies, including my sister's, to find out what Brant is doing and to get to you. For your sake, I hope you have plenty of money left."

I heard him hang up the phone and break the connection. I had meant what I said. I hoped he didn't come up empty-handed before I could do something to stop Brant. I put my own telephone receiver down in frustration.

Carl Rivers was frightened. I could hear it clearly in his voice, even over the telephone line. I didn't like thinking I had added to his fear, had put him between the Scylla of public exposure and the Charybdis of wondering if his life was in danger if his money ran out.

Can't you just say between a rock and a hard place like everybody else?

"Piss off," I muttered, and went back to my calculations.

I couldn't see that I had had any choice but to upset Rivers. I wasn't going to unravel the mystery of Cara's death by being nice. I needed to find a chink in Brant's defenses. I had hoped Rivers would be it. I didn't know if I could convince Detective Peterson otherwise that I wasn't imagining things.

What could Brant be holding over Rivers and Ulm? I wondered. What had he held over the three dead men? Whatever it was, it was so serious that each was willing to bankrupt himself and his family to keep Brant quiet. So serious that Rivers even could entertain the possibility of being killed once his money ran out rather than risk having anyone else know his secret.

And how could Brant have learned whatever it was he knew about his victims? But I suspected I knew the answer to that, too. He was a minister. People liked and trusted him; that was part of the reason they came to his church, part of the reason it was so successful. That also explained why the men themselves probably told Brant whatever it was he had turned against each of them. Although most Protestants don't use a formal ceremony of confession as Catholics do, I knew that many Protestant churchgoers rely on their ministers as secular as well as spiritual counselors. Ministers often find themselves in the role of marriage, career, or behavioral therapist, whether they are qualified or not. It was entirely possible that each of the men had been the unwitting author of his own downfall by unburdening a guilty secret to Daniel Brant.

Brant must have congratulated himself regularly on the genius of his scheme. He was in the perfect position to learn from their own mouths the worst secrets people in his church carried around in their hearts. And when he preyed on that, when he turned their weaknesses and their secrets against them, their only recourse was to leave his church and pay up—for as long as they had the money to pay. Brant needn't worry about word getting out to the rest of his congregation. Whatever the men had told him about themselves was so damning that they wouldn't risk revealing it by trying to warn others away from the Bread of Life Church. It all apparently had worked well for almost two years, according to the payments sheet. Even the three deaths, which I was convinced were Brant and Barlow's doing, had been passed off successfully as accidents and a suicide. Other than his victims and his partners, no one, absolutely no one, had had the slightest clue about what Daniel Brant was doing. Until Cara.

Detective Peterson had been right in a way. Cara had been in the wrong place at the wrong time. But it wasn't when she was abducted and taken to the ATM. There was absolutely nothing random about that. It was when she had sat at her own desk, in the office of the church she loved, and overheard the words that would end up putting a bullet in her head.

I knew, without any doubt whatsoever, that I finally had pieced most of it together. But what I believed and what I could prove were still two different things, at least by the standards Peterson required. So now what do I do? I wondered.

Give up?

Of course I'm not giving up, I told my voice. Try not to be any more stupid than necessary.

Maybe, I thought, it was time to call Detective Peterson anyway and tell him the specifics of what I had learned. I knew much of my theory still was just that—theory. But maybe it would be enough to get his attention at least, to get him to listen to me with an open mind. It was clear that Daniel Brant was not who or what he had been pretending to be. I had managed to find the records of Brant's criminal career that had eluded Peterson. I could only hope that Brant's change of identity and his prison record would be enough to convince Peterson to dig deeper at least. If they weren't, I knew I still wouldn't let it go, even though I might end up hanging out there on a limb all by myself. My sister had been murdered, and I was convinced that I knew who had killed her and why. But I had to find proof of that reason and put a name to her killer, and in such a way that Peterson would have no choice but to take action against the men responsible for Cara's death.

I opened a file in my computer and typed up brief summaries of Brant and Barlow's criminal histories and the points where their paths had crossed. There was no need to expose David Edwards's hand in what I had learned, after all. I sent a copy to the printer that I shared with several other reporters. I gathered up the pages of Daniel Brant's story, walked to the printer for the summaries, and then crossed the newsroom to the photocopier, where I made copies of everything I had. I would, I decided, give it all to Peterson. I would find out just how determined a cop he really was.

Twenty-two

With my photocopies in hand, I had gone back to my desk and paged Detective Peterson. When he returned the call, I told him that I needed to see him, that I had more information, concrete information this time, that I was certain related to Cara's murder. He told me he was up to his ears in paperwork but that if I could come out to Fairfax, he would make the necessary time to look at what I had. So here I was, pulling into the parking lot at the Massey Building where the Fairfax County Police Department's Major Crimes Division was housed on the upper floors.

The Massey Building, which is now occupied by much of the administrative hierarchies of the county's fire and rescue and police departments, formerly was the main office for the Fairfax County government. It sits just south of the intersection of Chain Bridge Road and Main Street in the center of the city of Fairfax. In the boom years of the early 1980s, the Fairfax County supervisors determined that the answer to the county government's rapid expansion, which had outstripped the available space, was to build an all-new governmental center at a site just west of the city, next to I-66 and the Fair Oaks Mall. In those days, real-estate values throughout the county were skyrocketing, and developers, both commercial and residential, couldn't put up buildings fast enough to meet the demand. County tax coffers, filled by real estate and business taxes, over-flowed. Very few quibbled when plans for the center were drawn up.

By the end of the decade, however, fiscal reality had set in, as it had for local and state governments throughout the United States—just in time for the huge, posh complex to be completed and the bills to come due. Home owners and businesses who were at the limits of their ability to pay their county tax bills raised all manner of hell when the real costs of the new facility were unveiled, and there were even demands for recalls of supervisors and calls for the county government to sell the structure, cut a lot of bureaucratic fat, and stay where it was. All of which the county supervisors, already comparing their allocations of office space and outrageously expensive furnishings, ignored. They moved anyway, into what has come to be called a variety of less than fond but surprisingly accurate epithets, the most popular of which was the Taj Mahal.

At Peterson's serviceable but no-great-shakes Massey Building office, I stopped at the open door. He was sitting at his desk, his feet up on a corner and his back to me, engrossed in a thick file folder of information. From behind, I noticed that his black hair was thinning rapidly over his crown. His job would be enough to make my hair fall out, too, I thought as I rapped on the door frame to get his attention.

Peterson's feet came down, the folder went on his desktop, and he swiveled around to face me in one smooth motion.

"Come on in," he said, serious as always, at least around me. "Have a seat." He motioned to the two industrial-gray, metal-armed chairs opposite his desk. I followed his direction and plopped myself down on the black vinyl, imitation-leather seat of the one nearest the door.

"Thanks for taking a look at this stuff," I told him, pulling a folder of pages out of the brown accordion portfolio I was carrying. I handed the folder to Peterson. He took it and pushed aside a couple of stacks of paper on his desk to clear a space on which to open it.

"Okay," he said, sliding out the folder's contents, "let's see what you've got."

As Peterson looked at each sheet on the stack, I took him through the scenario I had developed, piece by piece. I explained what I had learned about the real identity of David Daniel Brantley, aka Daniel Brant, and his assistant, Al Barlow. I showed him the newspaper clippings, their mug shots, and the summaries I had written of their criminal records, which got me a hard look beneath raised eyebrows. Peterson looked at the articles and obituaries on Marshall, Pursell, and Kelton, and I pointed out their connection through the Bread of Life Church. I explained the fax from the state corporations office, which showed the Caymans address and the officers of Brantlow, Inc.

"Just looking at all this separately, there wouldn't seem to be any connection among these things, much less any connection to what happened to Cara," I told Peterson, who looked up at me again and continued to listen patiently and without comment to my recital. "But I found out that Cara herself actually told me how it all connects. Look at the next page." He turned to the copy of the sheet from Cara's safe-deposit box and looked it over carefully.

"I recognize Marshall and Kelton's names on this," Peterson said. "So what is it?" I hoped that what I was seeing in his face was interest, genuine curiosity.

"A couple of days ago I found out Cara had rented a safe-deposit box just before she was killed. This was the only thing in it, which makes me think she rented it solely for this sheet of paper."

"Okay." Peterson nodded. "Why was it that impor-tant?"

I told him about my conversations with Marlee, in which she described how Cara overheard the argument between Brant and Marshall and how upset Cara got when Marshall died. And about Cara's run-in with John Brant over his computer. For all Marlee's talkativeness, it was, I suspected, the first Peterson had heard of either incident.

"I went out to talk to Marshall's wife," I went on. "She told me that she doesn't believe her husband wrecked his car trying to keep from hitting a deer. She thinks he killed himself because he had gone through every dime they had and left her and their kids with almost nothing.''

"Since when?" Peterson asked, frowning. "There was nothing like that in the investigation files.''

"The only thing she has left is one insurance policy that he couldn't sell,'' I explained. "But it had an exclusion clause for suicide. The investigation already had been closed, and she was desperate to keep the money for her and her kids. So she kept her mouth shut. But neither she nor the family attorney has any idea what Marshall did with the money.''

"Let me just take a wild guess here,'' Peterson said drolly. "You do know what he did with it.''

"I'm convinced,'' I told him, "that Marshall was fighting with Brant, maybe threatened him, because Brant had been blackmailing Marshall and Marshall had no money left. Whatever Marshall said to Brant, it was enough for Cara to realize that Brant wasn't on the up-and-up. When Marshall died, I think Cara had her suspicions about whether it really was an accident, and Brant probably already was worried about what she had overheard. That list,'' I said, pointing to the paper in Peterson's hand, "is what she saw on John Brant's computer screen. She printed out a copy when she realized that one of the names on it was Nash Marshall's and that all three men on it were dead.''

"I suppose you can prove this blackmail you think was going on?''

"Take a look at the last sheet.'' I reached over and tapped the copy of the ledger sheet that Cooper had purloined for me. Peterson studied the page while I went on with my explanation.

"These five men have given Brant millions of dollars in payoffs,'' I said as he looked at the numbers. "The church deacons apparently kept careful records of donations to the church, and I think you'll find that those records don't match what's on this ledger sheet in any way. No doubt this money is stashed away in some account in the Cayman

Islands, to which I suspect John Brant travels on a regular basis under his guise of computer-system consultant. And when three of the men on that list ran out of money, they died.''

"Where did you get this?" Peterson asked, now looking more intent as he glanced up at me from the ledger sheet.

"It came from John Brant's computer as well, although I don't think Cara ever saw it. Never mind how I got it. But it's for real.''

Peterson put the page down on top of the others I had given him and swiveled around in his chair to look out the window. After a minute or so of watching him think, I couldn't stand it any longer.

"So what are you planning to do about all this?" I asked.

He slowly turned back to face me.

"I think you're right that there's something here," he said directly. "Whether it led to your sister's death is another question, but I don't like what I'm seeing.''

I sighed heavily in tremendous relief. With his next words, however, I saw that my relief was premature.

"But I have to be frank with you," Peterson was saying. "You haven't brought me anything I can take to the commonwealth attorney's office. It's all completely circumstantial and supposition. I can't make an arrest based on what's here.''

"But the pieces are all there," I told him, my voice rising embarrassingly in my frustration. "You see it as well as I do.''

"Maybe," he said, "but it's not evidence, at least not the kind of hard evidence I'd have to have to make an arrest, either for blackmail or murder. You have to understand, Sutton, that what common sense and logic require for proof and what the law requires are very different things. I could sit here and agree with you all day that what you've brought me makes me think these guys are guilty of exactly what you say. But that's not good enough for a court.''

"Can't you at least bring them all in for questioning?"

I wanted to know, not believing that all my work was going to be for nothing.

"I could, but I couldn't hold them, and if you're right, the minute they walked out the door, they probably would disappear off the face of the earth."

"Jesus!" I exploded, standing up suddenly. The portfolio fell out of my lap, and I let it lie on the floor where it landed. "How much more does it take before somebody does something about Cara's murder? What else do I have to do?" In my impatience, I was pacing back and forth in front of Peterson's desk. "Tell me," I said, stopping to bend down and rap both fists sharply on the desktop. "What?"

"Listen to me," Peterson said sternly and leaning forward across the top of his desk. Clearly he wanted to calm me down.

Fat chance of that, my own little voice said.

"You've done well here," Peterson went on. "I have to give you credit. You've put together enough evidence to at least give us a direction to look. But there's a lot more to be done. I'll need to go back to the investigation files on all three men's deaths, and talk to the detectives who handled them. It's still very possible that they all might have killed themselves. And we'll have to check out the backgrounds of the Brants and Barlow ourselves. Daniel Brant and Barlow swore they were together at Brant's house when your sister was killed, which means I have to have physical evidence or someone's eyewitness testimony linking at least one of them to her death, and I don't have either."

"What about the gun she was killed with?" I asked. "Couldn't you test the bullet for—"

"Show me the gun," Peterson interrupted. "I don't have a gun to match the bullet to. Even if we could come up with grounds for search warrants to try to find the gun, that's still more delays.

"And," he went on, "I'll need to talk to this Ulm and Rivers, although I can just about guarantee you they'll clam up to the nth degree. And we can't touch the company in the Caymans or get any sort of access to records or bank accounts, at least not based on what's here.''

''So what can you do?'' I asked, my heart sinking at my failure to move his investigation off what looked to me like dead center.

''I promise you that we'll take it just as far as we can. We'll go through everything you've brought me with a fine-tooth comb. If there's anything there to prove what happened, we'll find it. If there's anything that connects these guys to your sister's murder, eventually we'll nail them for it. Maybe not tomorrow. But sooner or later.''

''Well, I'm grateful for that anyway,'' I said. I sat back down in the chair, but my fists were still clenched to keep from doing worse than pounding the desk.

Peterson wasn't finished, however. ''But there's something I want you to do, too,'' he went on.

''What's that?''

He gave me the stern look again. Jeez, I thought, he's as bad as Rob Perry.

''I want you to stop trying to conduct your own investigation. You've done okay so far, but if there's a case to be made here, I can't run the risk of you screwing up evidence inadvertently or having you tip my hand to the Brants or to these other two guys you think they're blackmailing.''

My fingernails dug into my palms.

''Sorry,'' I said, ''but I can't promise that. It's already too late where Rivers is concerned. I tried to talk to him earlier today. And if it weren't for me, you wouldn't even have this much. There's no way I'm going to just sit back and let the people who killed Cara get away with it because someone hasn't dotted every *i* and crossed every *t*.''

''I mean what I say, Sutton,'' Peterson reiterated, sounding as if his patience with me was growing pretty thin. ''You could screw up the whole investigation because you don't know what you're doing. And besides that, if what you suspect is true, if Brant and Barlow really did kill your sister or any of these guys, they don't hesitate to play hardball with anyone they see as a threat. You could end up like your sister.''

He really did sound disturbingly like Rob, and I felt fear nudging at my mind again. I suppose that in my thinking (all right, fantasizing), I had seen myself as putting the information together that would identify Cara's killer and then handing it to the police to make an arrest. Things weren't working out so neatly, however. Was I willing to risk my own safety, possibly my life, to try to expose the murderer? But there was only one possible answer. I knew I couldn't rest until Cara's murder was solved. I wanted some peace, a good night's sleep again. And I wanted Cara to know that, though she hadn't confided in me for whatever reason, in the end she could rely on me to do what needed doing.

I bent down to pick up the pages that had slid out of the portfolio, straightened them, put them back inside, and then stood up to face Peterson's wrath—which I was about to provoke.

"No," I told him. "I can't stop. I appreciate your concern for my safety, and I know you'll follow up on what I've given you. But if that evidence isn't enough to convince you, if it isn't enough to put a stop to what these people are doing, then I'll have to find something else." I turned and walked out before he had time to say more. By the stormy look on his face, I knew he had plenty more to say.

So what now, Sherlock? my voice asked as I walked through the Massey Building lobby and back out to my car.

Time for desperate measures, I suppose, I answered in my mind. I've run the paper trail about as far as I can. Ulm is out of the country, and Rivers is scared shitless to talk.

Daniel Brant had woven an intricate web for himself, one that had hidden from his followers what he truly was until, one at a time, several inadvertently had put themselves at his mercy—a quality he apparently lacked completely. It was a clever web, one that hamstrung the police because the witnesses, who were also the victims, either were dead or too frightened to talk, and the money was hidden in an offshore account. Perhaps, I thought, my only option now was to shake the web itself to see if I couldn't bring the head spider out into the open.

There also was one thing I hadn't pointed out to Detective Peterson. While my evidence might not yet be good enough for the police to make an arrest, it was good enough for a news story about the two things I could prove: that Daniel Brant, respected minister of the Bread of Life Church, was not a minister at all, but a reject from his divinity school and an ex-con named David Daniel Brantley, and that he was a principal in a mysterious Cayman Islands company that had a lot more assets than a minister had any right to accumulate. I wondered what his apparently unsuspecting congregation would make of those pieces of information. It just might, I thought, be enough of a tug on the web to send some shock waves right to Brant's doorstep.

Satisfied that at least it gave me one more thing to try, I drove home to a frozen dinner, an empty bed, and my hopes for a less restless night.

Thursday

Twenty-three

At 8:30 the next morning, I called the office at the Bread of Life Church and told Marlee I'd like some time with the Reverend Brant as soon as possible.

"I have a personal situation I think I'd like to discuss with him," I said. Which was true. I thought killing my sister was pretty personal. "I assume that he does counseling for people who attend the church, and I thought that he might be willing to talk with me about my own problem."

"Oh, I'm sure he would," Marlee responded. I felt like a hypocrite for deceiving her about my motives, but I knew it would be folly—and perhaps even dangerous for her—to take her into my confidence this time.

"It's rather important," I told her, "so if there's any chance he could make some time for me this morning, I really would appreciate it." I was worried that if I didn't move quickly, Carl Rivers might lose his nerve and warn Brant that I was onto what he was doing. More importantly, I was worried I might lose my own nerve.

"If I can put you on hold for just a minute, Sutton, I'll check with Reverend Brant to see what his morning is like," Marlee said helpfully.

I thanked her and then listened to the silence of the phone line that followed the click of the hold button. True to her word, however, Marlee returned in just about a minute.

"Good news, Sutton," she said cheerily when she retrieved me from the limbo land of those on hold. "Reverend Brant had a meeting scheduled with one of the church committees, but they called him last night to postpone it, so he can see you at ten if that's good for you."

"That's perfect," I told her, and thanked her again.

I spent the next half hour in a Lotus position, facing the morning light coming in my bedroom window and calming my mind in order to steel myself for the confrontation I shortly was going to instigate.

David Daniel Brantley, ex-con, was firmly in his Daniel Brant, Man of God, identity as he came around his desk to greet me when Marlee ushered me into his office.

"Sutton," he said, holding out his right hand for a handshake I knew he loathed. Of course, this time I was at least as revolted by his touch as he was by mine. He gave me his smile, the one that I now knew was as phony as everything else about him. "It's good to see you again," he said. "Please, have a seat."

Marlee quietly slipped back out, closing the door behind her, and I took the proffered chair as Brant went back to his own. I looked at him here in his comfortable lair—with its leather chairs, its expensive oak desk, credenza, and bookcases, the signed and numbered lithographs on the wall, next to an obviously forged diploma for a "Bachelor of Divinity Science" degree from the Holy Word Divinity College—and I hated him. I didn't think Cara would have been proud of me.

"We all miss Cara a great deal," Brant said solicitously, almost as if he had read my thought. "She was such a help here in the office."

"Yes," I agreed, "she was a first-rate secretary."

"So now tell me what it is I can do for you," Brant went on. I could swear he looked almost hungry, as if he got off on hearing the details of other people's problems. A more detailed portrait of the kind of personality I was dealing with was beginning to paint itself in my mind. This was a man, I suspected, who disliked other people, who thought himself a breed apart. One of the things on which he fed was their foibles, their weaknesses, which reinforced his belief in his own superiority. The fact that he also had managed to make a small fortune off a few of them probably just added to his disdain.

"I know that you haven't been to our church with your sister, although she always hoped that you would. So I'm very pleased that the trust Cara placed in us has led you to come to us with your own problems," he was saying. I wanted to gag.

"Let me be honest with you," I answered, unable to listen to any more of his sanctimonious bullshit. "While I did come to discuss with you something that's troubling me, I'm afraid that I'm here under somewhat false pretenses. I'm actually here in my role as a reporter, not to tell you about my personal problems."

"I don't understand what you mean," Brant said, his smile fading just a bit. His eyes took on a slightly harder look, one that hinted at an underlying wariness and suspicion. This, I suspected, was an inkling of David Daniel Brantley, the real man who hid behind the fake name and a cleric's words.

"Then let me unconfuse you," I said. "I've come here to get your side of a story I'm writing for my paper."

"And what story is that?" he asked, still trying to maintain the last vestiges of a smile, just in case I turned out not to be threatening after all. He was good, I thought. He should have chosen honest work in acting. It was no wonder he could take in those who were looking for someone in whom to believe.

"It's a really fascinating story, one that I suspect few of the people in your congregation know anything about. One that I doubt they're going to be very happy to read about. It starts with the fact that your real name is David Daniel Brantley and that you have a prison record that ought to send your deacons into quite a tizzy."

"I'm afraid I don't know what you're talking about," Brant said, his smile having dropped off into the void.

At least you wiped that grotesque smile off his face fi-

nally, my friend piped up. I pushed him back into a mental closet and firmly closed the door.

"Don't bother pretending ignorance, Mr. Brantley," I said, shaking my head from side to side. "I have the mug shots from your arrests to prove it. Anyone with eyes in their head will be able to see that it's you. And your felon friend, Al Barlow, too. I expect people will wonder what it was exactly that qualified him to be your assistant. Was it his experience with bank robbery, maybe? Did that help keep the church coffers filled? Or your pockets?"

"So what is it you really want?" Brant asked, looking at me with anger and calculation in his now completely cold eyes. "What would it take for you not to run such a story?" At last, I knew, I was dealing with the real man, the criminal, not some ministerial facade.

"I'm afraid that there's nothing you could offer me that would be enough," I told him, now smiling a little myself. "This is far too good a story for the reporter in me to pass up. And my editor is especially interested in it." Well, he would be once I told him about it, anyway.

"I see," Brant said, and I watched as he calculated his next move. Finally, he leaned forward and put his arms on the desk, his hands clasped together. A shadow of the counterfeit smile was back. "Well, frankly, Sutton, I don't know that it's much of a story. I've lived a spotless life since those days. There have been other ministers who committed serious transgressions, and theirs were not all in the distant past as mine are. And they still enjoy the support of their followers." He paused, waiting for me to respond.

He still was trying to bluff his way out, I thought in amazement. Given that there were millions of dollars and his very successful racket at stake, I couldn't say I blamed him. And he wanted to find out just how gullible I might be. I looked at him unblinkingly.

"That's not going to wash, Brant, not with your congregation and not with me," I told him.

His whole face tightened.

"Then you go ahead and run your story about my record," he said, still bluffing to see what cards I really held.

"And then I'll go before my congregation to make a heartfelt and tearful confession of my previous life as a sinner and ask for their forgiveness. Who's to say those good Christian people won't find it in their hearts to understand how any young man could have made a mistake? Especially with all the good things I've done for them. It's happened before. Look at Jimmy Swaggart. Look at Jim Bakker. They still have supporters." Brant gave me his genuine smile this time, one that narrowed his eyes in a cynical sneer and sent little tendrils of fear wrapping around my heart.

In spite of my fear and distaste, however, I laughed. Brant hadn't gotten where he was through lack of balls, I thought. He clearly intended to brazen this thing out as long as possible—and so did I.

"Even when I tell them about your secret bank account in the Cayman Islands and the millions of dollars that are sitting in it?" I asked. "At least six and a half million, if I'm not mistaken. Don't you think they're going to wonder how much of that came directly out of their pockets? And don't you think they'll wonder just exactly what kind of business Brantlow, Inc. is involved in?"

Brant hissed. Honest to God, he actually hissed at me. The sound was so filled with malice that I physically recoiled from it.

"You little bitch," he said, standing up and leaning toward me over the desk, his voice low and menacing. "You nosy, meddling little bitch!" I thought the Brant facade probably was gone for good this time, at least where I was concerned. I looked into his ominous eyes and wondered if this was what Cara had seen, that day at her desk when Brant realized she had overheard the things Nash Marshall had said to him. If it was, no wonder she had left the office early and refused to discuss what had happened with Marlee.

"You have no idea what you're messing with!" Brant went on, his voice still threatening but low. Obviously he wasn't taking a chance on repeating the mistake he had made the day Nash Marshall stormed into his office. He didn't want Marlee to hear what we were saying to each other. "I want you out of here now. And I want you to keep your mouth shut as if your life depends on it!"

I held up my reporter's notebook, pen poised to write. "Should I take that as a 'no comment'?" I asked smartly.

"You take it any way you want," Brant answered. "But if I see one word of this in your paper or anyplace else, ever, if I hear one bit of talk about it anywhere, you'll find you've bought yourself such a world of trouble that you can't believe it!"

I stood up, but he still was taller than I was. My heart was beating rapidly. My hands were sweating. This David Daniel Brantley meant business. I knew he wasn't making idle threats. Fuck you, I thought venomously. I played my final card.

"You mean like the trouble my sister bought? The kind that got her killed? But then, I suppose you don't know anything about that, either, do you?"

With a growl, Brant came around the desk and grabbed me roughly by the arm, jerking me toward him. He put his face right down into mine. "You watch your ass!" he said. The hiss was back.

The next thing I knew, he had opened his office door, all concerns about Marlee's presence pushed aside, and basically flung me out it into the reception area. At my unexpected and ungainly entrance, Marlee looked up from her computer and then sat with her mouth hanging open as I stumbled over my feet, trying not to fall, while dropping my notebook and purse in the process.

"You watch your own ass!" I said loudly back to him as I bent down to pick up my things and his office door slammed behind me.

"Sutton?" Marlee asked, standing up and putting her hands on the top of her computer monitor to look over at where I crouched on the floor, gathering up my belongings. "What in the world?"

"PMS?" I asked her, standing up and giving her a shrug

and a tepid smile. Then I left quickly—fled actually—before she could see the smile was all bravado and that inside I was already feeling sick from adrenaline and fear. I hoped I'd be able to drive to the office without wrecking my car.

Twenty-four

I almost had gotten my anger and fear and their physical effects back under control and was getting out of my car in the parking garage in D.C. when my pager went off and flashed Rob Perry's extension at me. I hurried down the block to the *News* building, said hello to George, the daytime security guard, and instead of waiting for the notoriously slow elevators, took the three flights of stairs up to the floor that housed the metro section. Which, I realized halfway up, didn't do my breathing any good. Apparently, I had been neglecting my sessions on the NordicTrack, too.

As I came into the newsroom I saw Rob sitting out at the city desk and watching me walk toward him with that look in his eyes. You know the look. The one you get from the principal when he raises his eyes from his work to find you standing in his office with a glowering teacher hovering behind you.

"Hi, Rob," I said, pretending I hadn't noticed the look. "I got your page on my way upstairs. What's up?"

"Let's step into my office, shall we?" he asked politely, standing up and leading the way. A couple of heads raised around the copy desk and gave me questioning looks and raised eyebrows. They had heard the principal in Rob's voice, too. I followed him into his office, busy racking my brain for what I could have done that had pissed him off.

"Have a seat," Rob said, closing the door, and walked over to sit down at his desk.

"Not ten minutes ago," he said, holding my eyes with his in a sort of visual death grip that no reporter alive dared break, "I got off the phone with Detective Peterson. We had an interesting conversation about you." Rob always was a master of understatement.

"Oh," I said, in my best meek voice.

" 'Oh' is right," Rob replied. "From that response, I think you must know why he called me."

"About my checking into Cara's murder?" I asked, trying to imbue my question with as much innocence as possible.

"Yeah, about that."

"What did Peterson say?"

"I take it," Rob said, "that you had an argument with him. Apparently, he wasn't finished yelling when you left. So he finished with me. He told me, more than once, that you're a loose cannon and that he thinks you're going to screw up any chance the police may have of getting the person who killed your sister. Of course he went on about it at much greater length than I'm going into here. But he wants me to order you to cease and desist."

"And are you ordering me?" My throat suddenly felt very tight at the idea of being forced to give up, and my words came out with an unflattering squeak.

Jesus, you're not gonna cry like a girl, are you?

I swallowed hard and got myself in hand.

"No, I'm not," Rob said, surprising me, "at least not yet. At least not before I get a full accounting from you of what you've been up to." He settled back in his chair, prepared to wait for however long it took me to tell it.

So I told him, the whole thing, all the details I had glossed over with him until now. Including my morning visit with the Reverend Daniel Brant and my promise to run a story about his background in the paper.

"I didn't specify what day it would run," I finished, "but tomorrow wouldn't be too soon for me."

Rob raised his hands, whose fingers had been interlaced

in his lap, and touched both index fingers to his upper lip, a classic Rob thinking pose.

"All right," he said finally, after mulling it all over for several long seconds. "Get some quotes from some of the church deacons. We'll say that Brant denied the allegations, in spite of the evidence the paper has obtained, and that he wouldn't make any other comment, except to threaten the reporter who questioned him. We'll put it on the metro front, maybe even page one if I can swing it. I want the first draft on my desk in the next two hours, if possible. I'll want to run it past one of the legal guys just to be on the safe side."

I was breathing again. It was one of the things I loved about Rob. No amount of pique ever got in the way of his recognizing a good story.

"Thanks, Rob," I told him gratefully, thinking I was free to go and standing up.

"Not so fast," he said, disabusing me of that idea. "Sit back down. There are a few more things I want to say."

I sat. "I'm listening," I said, trying to sound properly chastened.

"I hope so," Rob replied, but the tone of his voice said he doubted it. "First, the next time you spend days chasing a story like this without giving me some real idea of what you're doing, I'll have your job. I don't have to know all the details, but I don't like being blindsided by some police detective who's having a meltdown and threatening to go over my head."

"Okay," I promised. "I promise."

"Second, tomorrow's story is strictly about Brant's shady background and the existence of the Cayman company. There's no way you have enough yet to get into questions about dead CEOs or any possible connection to your sister's murder. This first story may help shake some of that loose, but we can't go with it yet."

I nodded in agreement. Well, why wouldn't I agree? Rob's instructions followed my own thinking on the matter.

"Third, you call Peterson and tell him what you've done. He's going to be pissed as all hell, but them's the breaks, and at least he won't read about it in tomorrow's paper first.''

"Okay," I said, sinking a little in my chair at the thought of just what reaction I could expect from Peterson.

"And finally," Rob said, smiling for the first time since I had walked into the newsroom, "go back to your desk and give yourself a pat on the back. You done good, even if you have been a little ham-fisted with it."

Relieved, I returned his smile and escaped from his office. I had some unpleasant calls to make and a story to write. It wasn't yet the story I wanted to write. But, as Rob said, it might help shake some things loose so that I could write that story eventually, too.

My first call, and the one I dreaded most, clearly had to be to Detective Peterson. He was the lead investigator on my sister's murder, after all. I didn't want to push him completely over the edge.

He was livid.

"I thought Perry was going to talk some sense into you!" he shouted when I explained about the story I was working on and that he could expect to read in tomorrow's paper.

"He talked a lot of sense into me," I replied, "but he told me to go ahead with this story about Brant's background and his company in the Caymans. That much, at least, we can document, and it's a story in its own right, even if I can't prove yet that he's killed four people."

"Tell me you didn't say that to Brant?" Peterson asked furiously. "Did you accuse him right out of murdering your sister and those guys?"

"Well," I said, equivocating, "I might have alluded to it somewhere in the conversation."

"Goddammit!" Peterson yelled. "You're going to bust this thing wide open. How the hell will we ever make a case against him if you do this?"

"Maybe he'll panic, do something stupid," I said, hoping to show him a possible bright side to the situation.

He wasn't buying it.

"Oh, he'll panic all right," he answered acidly. "And probably skip town, if he hasn't already. He'll disappear without a trace, and then your sister's murder will never be solved. And he'll be free to surface someplace else under another name and do it all again!"

He had a point, I supposed. Maybe I had acted a little precipitously, but it was too late for apologies now.

"I'm going ahead with the story," I told him. "I have to."

"I tell you what, Ms. McPhee," Peterson said (no more Sutton, I noticed), "you had better hope for your sake that you haven't blown the case we might have been able to make against these guys, because if you have, before I'm done I'm gonna have your job and maybe Perry's, too!"

Peterson slammed down the phone. I heard an explosive "Jesus!" just before the receiver clanked and the line went dead.

I took a few deep breaths, letting them out long and slowly to drain off the adrenaline and tension that had built up during the abortive conversation with Peterson. Then I dialed the Bread of Life Church. I needed to get the deacons' names and phone numbers, and Marlee was the only source I had for them.

"What on earth did you do to Reverend Brant?" Marlee asked in a dismayed voice when I told her it was me. She sounded as if her jaw was still hanging.

"What happened after I left?" I asked, my imagination relishing the picture of Brant in an apoplectic fury.

"Well, Sutton, he came back out of his office looking just awful, and when I asked if I could help, he just about took my head off." Marlee sounded as if she was going to cry just remembering it. "And then he told me to get John and Mr. Barlow on the phone, and he went back into his office and slammed the door again."

"Did you reach them?"

"Yes."

"And what happened after he talked to them?"

"He went into John's office and came back out with the hard drive to John's computer. And he left without saying another word! I haven't seen or heard from him since. Sutton, what is going on?''

I took pity on Marlee and briefly told her the gist of tomorrow's story.

"Oh no! Oh no!" she kept saying in a shocked and mournful voice. By the end, she was weeping in earnest. I felt badly for her, just as I would have for anyone whose idol had turned out to have feet of sewage. And then I realized that that was what Cara had gone through, too. Her letter to Amy Reed, perhaps even her poem, *had* been talking about the Reverend Daniel Brant, the man she had admired and respected, and who preyed on the people who trusted him most. When she wrote Amy, she had been dealing with the twin burdens of her disillusionment and the fear invoked by the awful secret she had learned.

"Marlee, listen," I said firmly, needing her to collect herself enough to understand what I wanted from her. "I need to get hold of at least a couple of the church's deacons for comments before I can write this thing. I want to be fair to the other people at the church, because I think Brant had everyone fooled. I need you to give me their names and telephone numbers. Can you do that?''

"Oh. Yes. Just a second," she said, sniffling. "Let me get my list."

She read me off the names of the seven deacons and their home and office telephone numbers, stopping once to blow her nose.

"Thanks for your help, Marlee," I said when she was done. "I'm really sorry you had to find out about him like this, but take my word for it. Daniel Brant is a very bad man, even more than I can tell you right now. And if I were you, I think I'd call it a day and go home and unplug your phone."

"Oh, dear Lord," she said, and started crying again. She hung up, and I figured it was just as well. I had more calls to make and a story to write. I just didn't have time right then to provide Marlee with a more sympathetic shoulder. I had too many other things to worry about. Like getting quotes from the church deacons. And those conversations didn't promise to be any more pleasant than the one I had just had with Marlee.

I was right. I managed to reach four of the seven deacons, each of whom was disbelieving of the devastating news that I delivered. All four declined to comment until they saw the proof for themselves. Two had angry kill-the-messenger reactions, one of them chewing me out for trying to drag a ''man of God like Daniel Brant'' through the ''liberal, left-wing media's mud.'' It would make great copy, I thought as I opened a file in my computer to start writing.

Twenty-five

The tack I took with the Brant story was that the leader of a very successful local church, which had raised megabucks from its members for programs such as its elaborate sanctuary, was really an ex-con who was using a phony name, who had been tossed out of his divinity college because of his criminal habits, and who was a partner with his prison buddy in a Cayman Islands company that was reported to have several million dollars in assets, based on confidential documents the *News* had obtained. It was a start anyway.

I stood over Rob's city-desk chair while he read the draft. He asked me a couple of questions, fiddled with several sentences, and then gave me a thumbs-up.

"I'll fax it over to one of the attorneys right now," he said, "but I don't anticipate any problems with it. It looks solid to me."

"If there is a problem, just page me," I told him. "I'm gonna go home." I was suddenly very tired. Part of my fatigue, I knew, was because the adrenaline of the day finally was wearing off. But I also thought part of it might simply be that taking the first real step toward doing something about Cara's murder had drained away some of the tension my body had carried since her death. I might, I thought, actually get a good night's sleep. And once my

story hit tomorrow's papers, I suspected it might be the last
good night's sleep I got for several days.

"Will do," Rob said. "Go home. You did a good job,
Sutton. Get some rest."

I went to my desk for my purse and then headed out of
the building and down the block to the parking garage. As
I walked I reviewed the mental checklist I kept in my head
of things I needed to do and decided I should stop at the
dry cleaners on the way home. A few minutes later I backed
the Beetle out of its space and headed south out of the
District and toward I-395.

Traffic was moving moderately well for four o'clock on
a weekday afternoon. In the Washington area, four o'clock
means the "evening" rush hour already has been under
way for half an hour or more. I-395 South is the major
commuter route that leads from all the government buildings that line the Mall, then crosses the Potomac next to
the Pentagon, and finally feeds directly into I-95 for all
points south. As such, it often is a parking lot by four P.M.
But today, either I had managed to catch it before the heav-
iest traffic or the first of several daily accidents that usually
created instant gridlock hadn't happened yet.

At Duke Street, I exited onto the westbound ramp and
stayed there as it became a right-turn lane from which I
could pull into the Plaza at Landmark, the shopping center
where I frequented Kim's Beltway Drycleaners. As much
of the through traffic from Little River Turnpike merged
into my lane to turn right onto Beauregard Street, I barely
managed to brake in time to avoid rear-ending a young
gentleman with D.C. license plates and subwoofers that
could set off earthquakes, and who apparently thought turn
signals were meant for everyone but him. I didn't even
bother to blow my horn at him. Horn blowing in traffic has
become a killing offense in D.C. and its suburbs these days.

I pulled safely into the shopping-center parking lot, however, and managed to find a space halfway down the row
that was directly in front of the dry cleaners. Double-
checking that my car doors were locked, I went in to get
the two dresses that Kim—I wasn't sure whether that was

the Korean owner's first name or last—was holding for me.

I stood in the late-afternoon heat and steam of the dry cleaners while Kim found my two dresses in the rows of cleaned and pressed garments that ran along the huge conveyor gizmo. He rang up my bill, and we chatted briefly, as well as we could anyway, since his English was broken and my Korean was nonexistent. I paid for the dresses, which were arranged on white metal hangers and covered by a full-length plastic bag. Kim and I smiled and nodded our good-byes, and I walked back out the door, grateful to leave the steam bath inside and trying to decide whether or not to drop the dresses off at my car and run into the discount store for the new toaster I had needed for weeks.

The decision was made for me, however, by the advent of Al Barlow, who suddenly appeared next to me and rudely poked a gun into my ribs.

"Don't say a word," he told me, jabbing the gun even harder into my side with his right hand and grabbing my upper arm with his left hand in a hold that I knew would leave bruises. "You just do what I tell you if you don't want to end up like your sister."

It's true what they say about time slowing down in a crisis. In real time, it must have taken all of two or three seconds, but in my mind, my thoughts seemed to go on for at least a minute. I remember thinking that it must have been Barlow who had killed Cara, dispatched by Brant after Cara went into his son's computer, to keep her from telling anyone what she knew. I could even see how it might have happened: Barlow abducting Cara outside the church that night after she had worked late, forcing her to drive to an out-of-the-way bank and withdraw money as a cover for the real reason for her death. A Cara too paralyzed with terror to do anything other than exactly what he had told her to do, sitting in the car as Barlow raised the gun and shot her in the head.

The rapid movie in my own head ended as Barlow pushed me forward to get me moving toward wherever his car was parked. I looked around the parking lot, where any number of people were coming and going on foot or in cars, but none of them paid us any attention, all of them intent on their own errands.

Do I go as easily as Cara did? I asked myself. Do I let them win without any resistance from me? I knew that if I went with Barlow, there was no question he would kill me. I realized I had left him and Brant no choice, at least by their calculation. They had too much at stake to let me go so I could tell what I knew. I was terrified, as I knew Cara had been. But beyond that, I was angry, overcome by one of those black furies that my mother used to refer to in almost reverential tones, anger that she said sometimes turned me into someone she didn't know.

So what do you have to lose? my voice asked.

Nothing, I told it. Absolutely nothing.

I guessed that the dresses I was carrying draped across my body, the neck of the hangers in my right hand and the skirts hanging over my left arm to keep them from brushing the ground, helped hide from the people around us the fact that Barlow had a gun jammed in my side. I tightened my grip on the hangers, and as Barlow pushed me again I took a step forward onto my right foot. He thought I was following his orders to keep walking. Instead, I used the momentum to turn to my right just enough to reach up and back with the hangers and rake the sharp ends of the curved wires down across his face, managing to strike one of his eyes in the process.

Barlow, I suppose, had made the mistake of assuming that I would be as biddable and as intimidated by him and his gun as Cara had been. Clearly he had not expected me to resist, much less try to attack him. He shouted in surprise and pain and let go my arm to grab his face with his left hand, while still trying to keep the gun in my side with his right. But his instinctive flinching away from the hangers had pulled the gun away momentarily. In the second that I felt the pressure from the gun ease, I turned even more in Barlow's direction and pushed at him with all my strength.

He was fast; I'll give him that. He saw my movement coming, and even as I pushed him away he already was reaching to grab me again. I turned back away from him to run, only to have him lunge into me and send me flying into the side of a parked car and then sprawling on the ground, where I got entangled in the dresses and the dry-cleaning bags.

Barlow was pretty mad. I'd done quite a job on him with the coat hangers, and a small river of blood was running down all along the twin furrows the metal had made across his face. It must have hurt like hell. If killing me had been an impersonal act of self-preservation before I wrecked his face, it was clear that it suddenly had become extremely personal. Now he wanted to kill me for the pleasure of killing me.

I had done something to my left hip and leg in the fall, and they didn't seem to be working or to have any feeling in them at the moment. I couldn't stand up. All I could do was cower there beside the car, desperately trying to get the plastic bags and dresses off me, and watch as Barlow bellowed at me in fury and raised his gun to kill me. This is the last thing Cara saw, I thought as I looked at the rising gun barrel. I heard a shout from somewhere behind me. My brain, still in slow-time mode, had sufficient time to think that it was nice that someone had figured out what was going on but also to observe that it was a little late.

What surprised me most was that I was able to hear the shots when Barlow killed me. I had thought I'd already be dead by the time the sound could reach me. And then I realized that it was Barlow who suddenly was bleeding from his chest and falling to the ground near my feet, his gun cartwheeling away from his hand and skittering across the asphalt to end up under the car against which I had fallen and into the side of which I was vainly trying to disappear.

My brain clicked once more into real time as another man, who was holding a gun of his own in a double-handed grip, stepped around the back of the car. He put the gun to Barlow's head as my would-be murderer lay on the pavement. When the man was satisfied that Barlow was unconscious and would offer no resistance, he brought out a pair of handcuffs from somewhere in his clothing, and in one smooth motion, pulled Barlow's arms behind him and put the cuffs around his wrists, where the cuffs locked with reassuring clicks. As the man reached forward to check Barlow's neck for a pulse, he raised his head in my direction and said, "I'm a police officer. Are you hurt?"

"No," I said. "I just banged my leg when I fell. I guess he didn't have time to shoot me before you got him."

"Then what's that?" he asked, pointing just to my left. I turned my head to look at the side of the car against which I was sitting and saw the nice round hole that had been punctured in the rear quarter panel, about six inches from my head.

"Oh," I said, feeling faint.

"Yeah," he agreed.

He straightened up and took out a small radio, on which I heard him call for two ambulances. In the distance, I could hear sirens; he must have called for police backup already, as soon as he had seen I was in trouble. Somewhere in his radio conversation, I heard him say "Peterson," and I groaned at the thought that I might have to confront the detective yet again, especially now that his direst predictions seemed to be coming true.

If you ask him nicely, maybe this cop will do you a favor and shoot you.

It was worth considering.

Peterson surprised me completely. He was sitting across from me in the back of one of the two Fairfax County Fire and Rescue Department ambulances that had responded, where he was listening carefully to my account of what had happened. I had not yet heard a single "I told you so" from him. Mentally, I gave him credit for being much more professional than I wanted to admit, especially since I knew how much he would have preferred to have locked me up along with Barlow.

Barlow had been transported in the other ambulance— along with two uniformed officers as guards—to Fairfax Hospital, which housed northern Virginia's trauma center. Although he had been alive when the ambulance left the scene, his chest wound looked pretty vile, and he had been losing significant amounts of blood, some of which still was congealing on the surface of the parking lot. If he survived the gunshot, I fervently hoped that the wounds I had managed to inflict on his face with the coat hangers would leave some permanent and nasty-looking scars of their own.

Gawkers in the parking lot were in their element. As soon as the people around us had realized the sounds they heard were gunshots, the smart ones had fled screaming; the others had come running to see what all the excitement was about—and probably hoping for some dead bodies. My plainclothes savior, whose name I eventually learned was Officer Rich Healy, had his hands full, retrieving Barlow's gun and keeping people back until the first of four marked police cars arrived on the scene to help.

I had continued to sit where I was on the pavement. I tried to get up, of course, but my leg still wouldn't cooperate, and Healy, after satisfying himself that I really hadn't been shot or seriously injured, had told me in the firmest of voices to stay still until the ambulances arrived. Within another minute or so, both ambulances had wheeled in together, right on the rear bumper of the third police car, and all of them had lights flashing and sirens tearing the air to bits. Not being particularly prone to obedience, I had been rubbing my leg and hip, trying to work the feeling back into them, with some limited but painful success, when my very own EMS crew—a blond and a redhead (males)—came my way with a stretcher. I had put up a fuss about wanting to walk to the ambulance under my own steam, which they immediately refused to allow. So I had ridden the thirty feet to the ambulance's rear door in style and had been hoisted inside, stretcher and all, and told to stay on the stretcher. The paramedics' examination revealed that my left hip and the whole outside of my thigh were pretty scraped up from my fall and already were discoloring.

"I don't think there's anything serious going on here," the blond-haired one had said as he pulled my skirt back down.

I hope it was good for you, my voice said. *That's the*

closest thing you may have to a date for the foreseeable future.

"But," Blondie had continued, "we're going to transport you anyway so the ER can X-ray things and make sure you didn't sustain any hairline fractures. At the very least, you're gonna be sore as hell tomorrow, and they can give you something for the pain."

I had agreed, albeit reluctantly, to go to the hospital.

"Before we go, if you feel up to it, the cops want a few minutes with you," said the red-haired one.

"I guess I'd better," I told him, tugging my skirt down all around. As soon as the paramedics climbed out, I sat up on the stretcher in spite of their instructions. I had heard a voice outside that sounded ominously like Peterson's. Facing him would be difficult enough without having to do it flat on my back.

At the look in Peterson's eyes when he had climbed into the ambulance ahead of Healy, I briefly considered having a serious relapse, but decided Peterson probably didn't have the patience for it at the moment. And frankly, neither did I.

So I had given Peterson my version of events, including Healy's timely appearance from thin air. I assumed that Healy coincidentally had been in the parking lot on some errand of his own and had, luckily for me, witnessed my attempt to escape from Barlow. I thanked Healy for being so observant and for saving my life, and then listened in astonishment as he proceeded to tell me what really had happened—that he had been following me, at Peterson's instructions, from the time I had left the paper in D.C.

"You had me followed?" I asked Peterson, offended by his doubt that I could take care of myself—the recent proof of the validity of that doubt notwithstanding.

"Lucky for you, yeah," he replied tersely.

Peterson told me that as soon he had hung up the phone from yelling at me, he had requested that an unmarked car be dispatched to follow me. He was, he said, concerned that Brant might attack me to prevent me from printing my story. I suspected it was as much out of wanting to see where I went next as to protect me, but I wisely kept that thought to myself.

Healy picked up the story again and explained that he soon had figured out that a second car, which was between us, was following me as well, a car his computer showed was registered to the Bread of Life Church. Healy had driven into the shopping center right behind my Beetle and the car driven by Barlow. His seemingly miraculous appearance in the parking lot when Barlow tried to kill me had been anything but coincidence.

It didn't say much for my powers of observation, I mused to myself, that I had been followed by not one, but two cars all the way from D.C., and never noticed a thing.

"But how did you know what I looked like and when I left the paper?" I asked Healy, trying to ignore Peterson's satisfied expression at having been several steps ahead of me for a change.

"I showed your lobby guard my badge and then slipped him ten bucks to point you out to me when you came downstairs," Healy explained, looking as if he wanted to grin but not sure Peterson would appreciate it. "I was sitting in my car right outside the door, and he signaled to me as you went out. I watched you go into the parking garage down the street and just waited until you drove back out. I'd already checked the computer for your car make, so I knew to look for the white VW Beetle convertible and your license plate."

Clearly, I was going to have to have a little talk with George, the security guard, once I got back to the paper. He'd be lucky if I didn't take the coat hangers to him.

You idiot, just be glad you're alive to be mad at him, my voice piped up. *If Peterson had left it up to you, you'd be dead by now!* I had to concede that it had a point and tried to get over my vexation.

"What about the Brants?" I asked when I finally ratcheted my anger down a notch or two. "Where are they?"

"Nobody knows," Peterson said, giving me a rather baleful look. "As I predicted, they've disappeared."

I had to give Peterson still more credit. He must have

been pretty pissed at me, too. Probably the only reason he hadn't yet shot me himself, I thought, was that he figured I wasn't worth wasting a bullet on.

"Don't they always say follow the money?" I asked, trying to be helpful and to take his mind off shooting me— or worse. "If I were wanted for murder and had several million dollars stashed away in the Caymans, I'd be headed that way as fast as I could go."

"We're working on that now," Peterson said. "Let's just hope they don't manage to get through a hole in the net we're throwing out."

I summoned up my courage. "I apologize for making your job harder," I told Peterson. "All I wanted to do was find out who killed my sister."

Peterson eyed me for a moment, probably trying to decide whether the pleasure of throttling me would be worth the prison term. Apparently the answer was no. He looked down to jot several lines in his notebook. I didn't expect to get off this easily, however. I knew he eventually would have some more to say to me, but he evidently had decided this wasn't the time or the place.

Through the open doors of the ambulance, I saw a mobile satellite truck for one of the local television stations pull up. A slim blond woman clutching a notebook climbed out of the passenger's side and headed toward a couple of the uniformed officers.

"Here comes the press," Healy said, watching her approach the other cops.

"Oh shit," I said suddenly, and reached for my purse, which Healy had rescued in the parking lot and which now was on the stretcher beside me.

"What's the matter?" both Peterson and Healy asked.

I had fished out my cellular phone and was punching in numbers.

"I'd better call Rob Perry and tell him I've got to completely rewrite tomorrow's story!" I told them.

Peterson slapped his notebook closed in a gesture of disgust and climbed out of the ambulance shaking his head. Healy followed him, nodding an acknowledgment as I silently mouthed a "thank you" at him while Rob's extension rang in my ear. I heard Peterson tell the paramedics, "She's all yours." He said it with obvious relish.

"Metro desk! Perry!" Rob barked abruptly in my ear as Blondie climbed into the back of the ambulance with me while Red went up front to drive. Rob's surliness was an indicator of how quickly the evening's first deadline was approaching.

"Rob, it's Sutton," I told him. "We've got to make some changes to my story."

"We're on deadline here, McPhee," he pointed out. "This had better be worth the interruption."

"Oh, I think it's worth bothering you with," I answered coyly, smiling at Blondie. "Al Barlow just tried to kill me in a shopping-center parking lot, and the Brants have disappeared. I'm okay, but a cop shot Barlow and he's been taken to the hospital."

"Fuuuck me!" Rob said, his Alabama accent adding several more syllables than that serviceable Anglo-Saxon obscenity had ever contained. "Are you sure you're okay?"

"I'm fine," I assured him. "Just a bruised hip that they want to X-ray, and I'm still a little shaky." He really didn't need to know just how shaky I was beginning to feel now that the reality of what had happened, particularly that bullet hole in the car beside me, was sinking in.

"Are you up to dictating a story?" Rob asked. "I'll take it down myself." I heard the rapid clicking of computer keys.

"Yeah, if you'll smooth out the edges."

"Okay, I've got a file open here and hard copy of your other piece. Give me a quick run-through of what happened and then I'll help you put it together."

Blondie hung on to every word I said to Rob as I spent the ride to the hospital taking Rob through Barlow's unsuccessful effort to kill me. We made the first deadline with five minutes to spare.

Eight Days Later

Twenty-six

I was right. Peterson did have some more things to say, which he said at length to me and Rob and Mack Thompson, the managing editor, in a less-than-pleasant little get-together in Rob's office. Basically, Peterson explained to us that my ego was surpassed only by my stupidity and recklessness. The list of my egregious transgressions was long, including interfering with a police investigation, reckless endangerment of innocent bystanders, and putting the life of a police officer at unnecessary risk in order for him to save mine.

"And those," Peterson said angrily to Mack Thompson, "are just the things I personally witnessed. I don't even want to think about what else she did, beginning with computer theft."

About the only reason he wasn't going to recommend that I get the death penalty, apparently, was that my irresponsible behavior had not prevented the police from wrapping up the case against the Brants and Barlow.

"The ingrate!" Cooper Diggs responded later that same day when he returned from the vacation he had begun the day before my little run-in with Al Barlow and I filled him in on what had happened in his absence. He had been enthralled by my account of my near-miss in the parking lot and the fact that I had almost made the trip to my eternal reward prematurely. Now, he was laughing his ass off at my rendition of the scene with Peterson in Rob's office.

"I don't think Peterson saw it quite that way," I told Cooper dryly.

"So they caught the other two?" Cooper asked. It was fun to watch him hanging on my every word, as happy as a kid with a new toy.

"Yeah," I said, "a week after Barlow grabbed me in the parking lot. They found the Brants at a small airfield outside Tampa, where they were trying to charter a private plane to the Caymans. The two of them never had a chance. I mean, it's not like any idiot couldn't figure out where they would try to go. The FBI not only put out an alert to police agencies, airlines, airfields, and marinas up and down the eastern seaboard and around the Gulf, but there was even an alert on *America's Most Wanted.*"

"Hey," Cooper said, "John Walsh always gets his man!"

"He did this time," I agreed. "It turned out that the pilot the Brants approached used to be a cop himself once, and he had no hesitation about turning them in when he recognized them. He sneaked a call to the local police and then stalled the Brants by going through some elaborate preflight check of the airplane that went on long enough for the police to arrive."

"So where are they all now?" Cooper asked, relishing the idea of just desserts.

"Well, at the moment, the Brants are in jail in Hillsborough County, fighting extradition to Virginia, which should be forthcoming shortly anyway."

"And Barlow?"

It was my turn to smile.

"He's going to live, according to his doctors, although he probably will want to bundle up in his prison cell in the winter to avoid catching cold in the lung that Officer Healy's bullet shredded. The trauma surgeons at Fairfax Hospital saved his life. I guess they don't get a choice of asking whether it was worth saving."

"It's a tough job, et cetera, et cetera," Cooper commented.

"They couldn't save the sight in his right eye, though," I continued. "Apparently I did quite a number on it and the rest of his face with those coat hangers. According to the cops, that's probably why he missed me when he shot at me. With only one eye working, he lost his depth perception."

In fact, what Rich Healy, who had been ordered by Peterson to keep me informed so Peterson didn't have to talk to me himself, had said was that Barlow's face looked like a wildcat had been at him. Then Healy had started laughing. "Actually," he had told me, "I guess one had." I took it as a compliment.

"Are any of them talking?" Cooper wanted to know.

"Barlow is spilling his guts, metaphorically speaking," I explained. "The cops made sure he understood that as soon as the Brants got together after I confronted Daniel Brant, they immediately lit out for Florida. They had told Barlow that they would wait for him at their house while he went to dispose of me. He was pretty mad when he figured out that his partners tried to screw him, too."

"What is honor among thieves coming to?" Cooper asked, shaking his head.

"Well, Barlow was even madder when he heard that the Brants are denying any knowledge of anything and that they told Peterson, when he flew down to Tampa to question them, that they had been going to the Caymans on vacation and that if Barlow killed Cara, he had acted on his own."

"That's a dirty trick," Cooper observed.

"Barlow thought so, too. At first he offered to tell the police and commonwealth attorneys what he knew and to testify against the Brants if he could be sure he wouldn't get the death penalty. Everybody involved said no deal because the cops have reopened the investigations into the deaths of Marshall, Kelton, and Pursell, which means Barlow might be looking at four murder charges."

Cooper turned serious for a minute. "Have they found

anything good enough to pin your sister's murder on him?"
he asked.

"No question," I told him. "They searched Barlow's
apartment in Annandale and found my mother's jewelry.
He wasn't even going to try to sell it until he was out of
the country. He had stolen the jewelry to keep up the pre-
tense that Cara's death was all about a robbery. Of course,
his real reason for going through the apartment was to make
sure Cara hadn't left anything incriminating there, if she
had put things together. The police also matched the bullet
that killed Cara to the gun Barlow used to shoot at me. And
they think they'll be able to match some hair and fiber
samples they took from Cara's car to Barlow. The evidence
against him is a lot more than circumstantial now."

"So at the very least, they're all going away for pretty
much the rest of their lives," Cooper said.

"And there's always the possibility that Barlow, and
even Daniel Brant, might get the death penalty," I added.
"When Barlow heard the Brants were trying to pin everything on him, he told the cops that if he was going to be
put to death, he fully intended to take Brant to hell with
him. I guess some of those sermons must have sunk in after
all. He has agreed to testify in both the Brants' trials, with
no immunity and no deals."

"And so what did Brant have on these guys he was
blackmailing?" Cooper asked. "You were right about the
blackmail, weren't you?"

"That's another interesting story," I said, and explained
that my guess about the source of Brant's blackmail material had, in fact, been correct. Each of the five victims
unwittingly had confided a secret to Brant, in an effort to
ease a nagging conscience.

For Nash Marshall, it was his approval to use a substan-
dard component in a surgical machine that his company
produced, a component that made an extra half million
bucks for the company. The machine was in use in more
than thirty hospitals around the country, and failure of the
part already had killed a patient, at which point Marshall's
conscience apparently had woken up.

Caught between admitting what his company had done, with the attendant lawsuits and possible criminal charges, and waiting for the next patient to die if he kept quiet, Marshall had confided in his minister, Daniel Brant, in hopes of receiving guidance about what to do. Instead, he had found himself with a whole new set of problems. When Marshall finally was bled dry, he had gone to the church and shouted dire threats at Brant. A week later he was killed when, Al Barlow told police, he forced Marshall's car off the parkway and down a steep embankment, where it had caught on fire with Marshall trapped inside.

In the case of Kelton, the blackmail was over his predilection for young boys, with whom he had sex on twice-yearly vacations to Thailand. He apparently confined his abuse to children overseas, but he had become afraid someone would find out about him and that it would destroy his business, which was built on caring for other people's children. When Kelton's money was all gone, Barlow said, he went to Kelton's house one night and forced him, at gunpoint, to asphyxiate himself in his car while Barlow watched through a garage window to make certain Kelton went through with it.

Pursell had killed a woman, five years before, in a hit-and-run accident for which he had never been caught. His conscience bothered him more and more as time passed, but he feared being sent to prison even more than he feared his conscience. He had gone to Brant for advice and absolution. Once Brant and his partners had bankrupted Pursell, Barlow had done a clever tampering job on the engine of Pursell's plane, which Pursell frequently flew on business trips.

The police were still being closemouthed about whatever secrets Brant had on Ulm and Rivers, who presented possible slander and libel liabilities that the dead men did not, but I fully expected their stories to come out during the trials. No doubt they were as ugly and pathetic as those of the other three.

Barlow also gave a full accounting to police of how Brant's blackmail scheme had worked. Once Brant had something to hold over a victim's head, he required them to buy his silence in large and regular cash payments. That way, he didn't have to fool with converting assets such as property into cash, thus avoiding any paper trail to link him to the disappearance of the men's wealth. John Brant was the courier, using his phony job with their phony company to provide him with a reason for frequent flights to the Caymans, where he deposited the cash into numbered accounts. As the group's computer guru, the younger Brant also kept track of the money, letting the church pay for the computer he used and to which, ordinarily, no one had access but himself.

Except that he got careless one day, and in a hurry, he had left up on the screen the file that Cara saw and printed. Clearly, she already had been suspicious of Daniel Brant after hearing the argument with Marshall, and Marshall's death probably had made her even more suspicious. So when she saw Marshall's name on the list in the computer, along with the names of other well-to-do church members who recently had died, it got her attention in a way it might not have at an earlier time.

Daniel Brant already had been worried about Cara, Barlow said. During Brant's argument with Marshall, Marshall had been pretty explicit about the fact that Brant was blackmailing him and that he had no money left to give. When John later went to his father with his suspicion that Cara had tampered with the incriminating file in the computer, Brant decided she had to be eliminated and ordered Barlow to do just that. And so Cara had died in a phony ATM robbery, and the three men smugly went on with their blackmail. When Barlow found nothing at Cara's apartment, he came away confident that they were out of the woods. Except that Cara had left a trail after all, a single sheet of paper that Barlow and the Brants had not known about, that she had put into a bank vault and that had led me back to the Bread of Life Church.

"So the bad guys got what was coming to them," Cooper said when I finished my story.

"Thanks to Cara," I said.

"And now you're back to your nice, calm education beat?" Cooper wanted to know.

"Not exactly."

In fact, when Peterson had run out of steam and shown himself out of Rob's office, Mack Thompson had left as well, saying he and Rob would discuss it all later. I got up to leave, too. Rob called me back.

"Hang on here for a few more minutes, McPhee," he said. "There's another matter we still need to discuss while I have you here."

Oh Lord, I thought, it must finally be time to pay the piper over my growing boredom with the school beat.

Rob closed his office door again behind the departing Thompson and deposited himself in front of me, leaning against his desk, one ankle crossed over the other, both hands in his pockets. He looked down at me over the rims of his reading glasses, a contemplative expression on his face.

"Look," I said, deciding to bite the bullet, "I know you're concerned about my coverage of the schools and that I haven't been—"

"Your stories have been fine," he cut me off.

"They have?" I asked, my mood improving at the thought that maybe things hadn't been as bad as I thought.

"I wouldn't have let them in the paper if they weren't," he said, and when I thought about it, I knew that was true.

"But I also know that you're bored with the schools."

At that, my spirits sank again.

"So now I want you to help cover cops," he said.

"What?" I asked, gaping at him. I thought he had lost his mind, or I was losing my hearing.

"We've got an opening to cover the Fairfax County Police," he said. "I'm putting you in it."

"But, Rob," I said, still trying to absorb what he had just said, "don't you want somebody with a track record on the police beat?"

"As far as I'm concerned, you've got one," he answered, his face still serious but the beginnings of a smile reaching his eyes. "The work you did on solving your sister's murder ought to be track record enough for anybody.''

"But that was one case," I pointed out. "And the Fairfax police will probably shoot us both if I show up to cover them.''

Rob started to laugh. "You're probably right about that,'' he said. "Detective Peterson will have to be sedated.'' He took his hands out of his pockets and crossed them loosely in front of him.

"Listen to me, McPhee,'' he went on, switching to serious again. "You can do this. You'll do it well. I think you'll even enjoy it. I've been watching you. You have the right instincts for it. You ask the right questions. You've got the same cynicism and suspicion that makes a good cop. Whatever Peterson thinks about your methods, you did one hell of a job on this story. And you don't give up.'' He paused for a second.

"In fact,'' he said, the smile reappearing, "you may be one of the most goddamned stubborn people I have ever known in my entire life.''

"Why, thank you," I responded, finding myself smiling back. But then I had to get serious again, too. "You're sure about this?'' I asked, because I wasn't so certain myself.

"I am," Rob said confidently. "But let's do it on a trial basis. We'll give it three months. I'll keep an eye on your copy, and you just be your usual pain-in-the-ass self.'' He smiled broadly. "Whaddaya say?''

What was I going to say? The thought of covering schools one more day suddenly was suffocating. I had not given the possibility of covering the police as my regular job a single minute's thought. But maybe, I thought, Rob knows me better in some ways than I know myself. The more I thought about it, the better I liked the idea. I knew I had been more focused, more determined, and more interested in tracking down my sister's killers than in anything I had written about the schools in a year. Of course, I had had a personal interest in the outcome this time. But as I thought about it I wondered if I might not find myself responding the same way to other police stories, to the idea of seeing to it that the other Brants and Barlows out there had to face their consequences as well. I looked back up at Rob. I always had trusted his judgment before. I decided to trust it now.

"Okay," I told him. "I'll do it. But Rob?"

"Yeah?"

"Who's going to tell Peterson?"

Rob laughed again. A lot.

There was one final and even more surprising result from my exposure of the Brants and Barlow and my own near brush with death. I got an unexpected call from Chris Wiley, who asked me to meet him for drinks one Friday night after work.

Reluctantly, I agreed, as much out of curiosity as anything, since I had not heard a peep out of him since the day I had walked out on our lunch.

He was waiting for me for a change, in a bar booth at Houlihan's, a Springfield restaurant that successfully manages to cater to singles and families at the same time. When I walked up, Chris gave me one of his gorgeous smiles, apparently genuine, and told me he really appreciated my meeting him.

I asked the waitress who had followed me to the booth for a Guinness, that wonderful Irish stout that can stand up without a glass and that tastes as if it were squeezed from the bark of a burned tree. It never fails to raise eyebrows when I order it, apparently not being considered a woman's drink. Chris had seen me order it before, so he didn't bat an eye, but he ordered a scotch rocks for himself. From the empty glass in front of him, it would be at least his second one. It made me wonder just what he was fortifying himself to say.

While we waited for the waitress to return with the drinks, Chris asked me about my run-in with Barlow and about Barlow's and the Brants' subsequent arrests. I gave him the short version, wondering if he really was interested or was just making conversation until he gathered up his nerve to present me with his real agenda.

"And you're really okay?" he asked, looking genuinely concerned.

"I'm fine. I was just banged up a little from falling when I was trying to get away. But they didn't even keep me at the hospital. It was just scrapes and bruises."

"That must have been pretty scary," he observed, just as the waitress put our glasses down in front of us.

"It was," I agreed. "I thought I was dead. If it hadn't been for the cop who was also following me, unknown to me, I would have been. Barlow missed me with the first shot, but I have no doubt he wouldn't have missed a second time."

Chris picked up his glass and took a large swallow. When he put it back down, I could see his facial muscles tighten as he steeled himself to say whatever had brought us here.

"Sutton," he started, looking at me with those always arresting eyes, "I'm sorry. I'd like to have another chance."

I was surprised into silence for a moment. I don't know what I had expected, but it certainly wasn't this.

"What?" I asked, sounding stupid but trying to buy time to collect my own thoughts.

"I want us to try again," Chris explained. He glanced down at his drink and then back up at me, as if trying to make himself look me in the eye. "I've spent a lot of time thinking about this. I've missed you, and I hadn't expected to. When I saw in the paper that that guy tried to shoot you, it made me realize just how much I have missed you and what a jerk I've been." He paused again.

I waited silently for him to continue, wanting to hear every word of this.

"I was really angry at first over what you said at lunch that day," he admitted ruefully, "but I figured out that it got under my skin so much because it was mostly true. I have been afraid of getting too close to anybody. But after you told me off, and especially after I read what almost happened to you, I had to ask myself a lot of hard questions. The answers I came up with made me see some things about myself that I didn't like very much. I'd like to try again with you; I promise things will be different this time."

He was sincere. And hopeful. And I was going to dash that hope, I realized. In the weeks since our argument, I had faced a lunatic with a gun. Even scarier, I had faced some tough truths about myself and my own fears of getting close. I was realizing that I had made some decisions about what I wanted from life. Things like the satisfaction and renewed interest I was finding in my job on the police beat. Like a real, adult relationship with a man, one built on trust so that we didn't have to be afraid of each other. But I also had realized that Chris wasn't that man.

"I'm sorry, Chris," I said simply. "I can't go back."

He looked crestfallen as he comprehended what it was I was saying, that I was turning him down. Finally, after searching my face carefully, he nodded his head but continued to hold on to my hand.

"Are you sure?" he asked.

"Pretty sure," I told him, reaching out to put my hand over his.

He looked at me. "Yes," he said finally, "I think you are."

He gave me a sad smile at that, took back his hand, and raised his glass to drain the last of the scotch.

"Well," he told me, "it was worth a shot. You were worth a shot."

"Exactly what Al Barlow said," I replied.

Chris laughed and got up from the booth. He took a money clip out of his pants pocket and peeled off several bills, which he folded once and put down by his glass.

"Take your time and finish your drink," he said. "You paid for the salmon salads. This is my treat." Now I laughed, glad to see that he wasn't devastated by my rejection of his offer of another chance.

He put the money clip away and picked up his suit jacket, which was folded on the seat beside where he had been sitting. And then he took a step to my side of the booth, put his hand against the seatback behind my head, and leaned toward me.

"Thanks, Sutton," he said, smiling again. "For everything." He kissed me, and I knew I would miss that, at least. We had been good together in the physical department.

And then he was gone, and I sat for another half an hour, long after I had finished the Guinness, my head against the seatback and my thoughts wandering a long way away.

Epilogue

Another few weeks later I stood at my living-room window, looking out into the night and watching the string of car headlights on I-395 sparkling in the dark like the stones that lay in the blue velvet jewel case that was open in my hands. My mother's jewelry finally had been returned to me by the police, who had been holding it as evidence until the Brants and Barlow were convicted and sentenced.

As I studied the necklace and earrings, relieved to have them back in my possession, it was as if I could see my parents again, on the evening of their last anniversary together, my mother glowing happily in the soft light of the living-room lamps as my father stepped behind her to fasten the necklace around her neck. She had leaned against him and reached up to clasp one of his hands. He had bent his head down to kiss the top of hers. Cara and I had watched them from the sofa, the intimacy and intensity of that moment between our parents raising goose bumps on our arms.

Now they were gone, all of them. My mother, my father, my sister. I was alone here, with my memories and my mother's jewelry.

The diamonds collected the light of the lamps in my own living room and threw it onto the dark blue of the sapphires, which reminded me of some recent but now almost forgotten dream about a man with blue eyes. Gently, I closed the jewelry box's piano-hinged lid and held the plush velvet softness against my cheek as I looked back to the world outside. I wondered if, somewhere among those rushing cars and the busy lives of the people they carried, there was a real someone to take the loneliness away, someone to fasten my mother's necklace around my neck and kiss my hair in the lamplight.

Guess you'd better go get your own safe-deposit box to keep those in, my ever-practical little voice said.

No, I told it, holding the box tightly, trying to recall the details of the dream, I think I'll keep them here.